Teddy Brewster's Hold On Me

PACIFICA ACADEMY DRAMA SERIES
BOOK THREE

CHRISTINE MILES

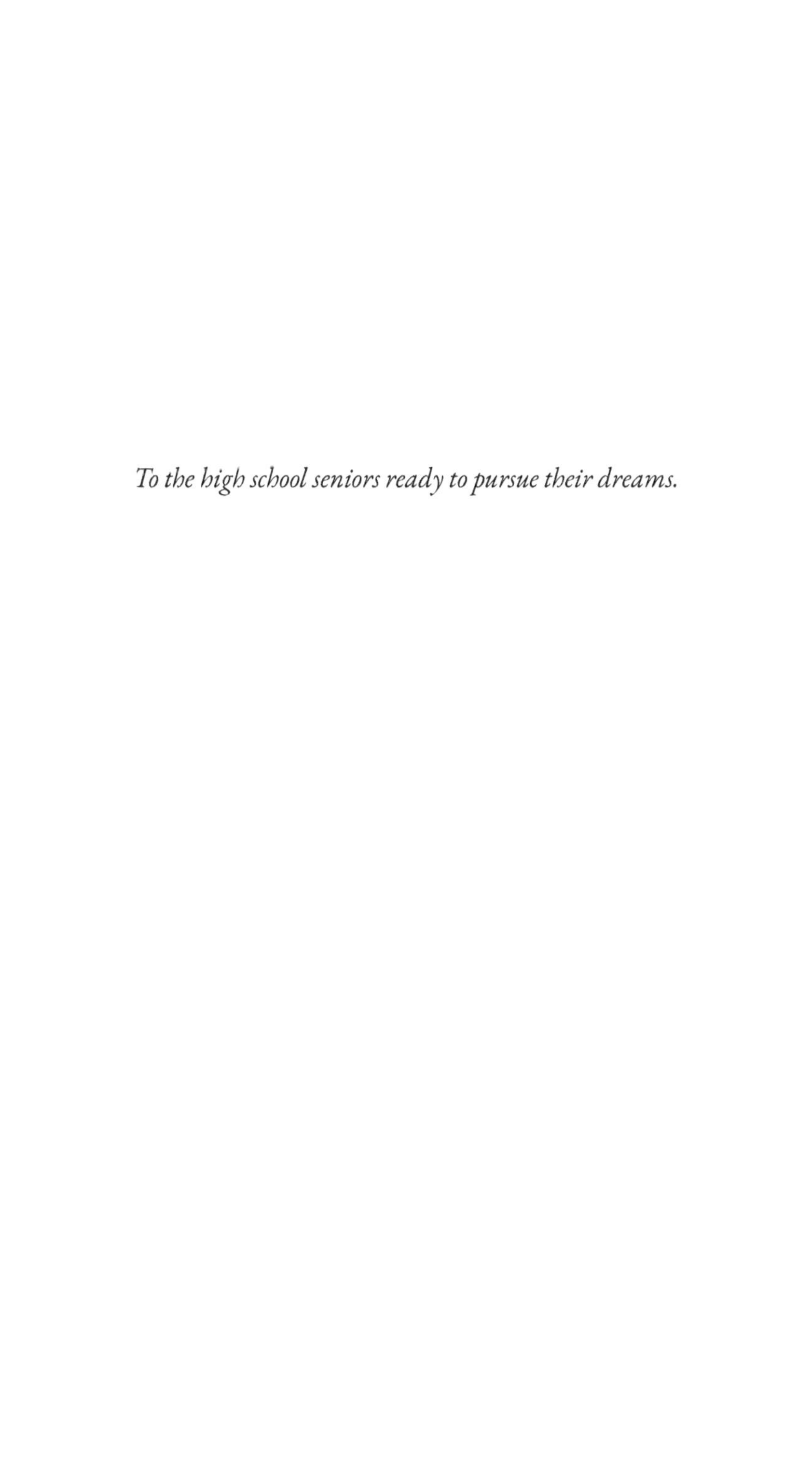

To the high school seniors ready to pursue their dreams.

Books by Christine Miles

Adult Contemporary Romance

Timing is Everything Series

Last Time We Loved (Book One)

First Time We Laughed (Book Two)

The Time We Met (Book Three)

This Time It's Forever (Book Four)

Smart is Seriously Sexy Series

Off-the-Charts Chemistry (Book One)

Passion Under the Microscope (Coming Winter 2024)

Young Adult

Pacifica Academy Drama Series

Me, Shakespeare and the Anti-Love Club (Book One)

The '68 Camaro Between Kenickie and Me (Book Two)

Teddy Brewster's Hold On Me (Book Three)

Silver Bells for Me and (Saint) Nicolas (Book Four)

You and Me Dancing to Gershwin (Book Five)

Summer in Winter Wonderland (A Cozy Mystery)

Chapter One

"No. I can't." I stopped in the doorway of the Theater Department's surprisingly quiet office, considering the day. But then, *Arsenic and Old Lace* had a small cast and not as many kids had tried out for this year's fall play. A possibly good thing for me. "I just can't look."

Noah Sanchez faced me. "Maddie, your neurotic is showing."

"I don't care right now." I folded my hands under my chin and batted my big brown eyes. "Please, please, please look for me?"

He rolled his equally dark eyes. "You're really using that brown-eyed girl thing on me?"

I'd learned long ago my eyes could, more often than not, help me get what I wanted. Especially with boys. But I guess they didn't work on boys who were only friends.

"I'm sure you got the part," he added.

At least one of us thought that. Past year's plays had always proven the opposite.

"Noah, please. And it's not like you don't need to look at the cast list."

"Fine." He walked toward Mr. Peters's closed office door.

As Noah looked at the list, I squeezed my eyes shut and crossed my fingers.

I'd spent hours perfecting my kind, patient, yet oblivious to insanity, old lady voice. And I'd walked away from the auditorium yesterday feeling I'd nailed my audition. Unfortunately, I'd felt that way a few times before and walked out of this office with bitter disappointment.

I slowly inhaled as *Oh please, please, please* filled my head.

"Maddie, relax. You got the part."

I stopped my slow exhale and opened my eyes.

Noah gave me a triumphant smile. "I got Dr. Einstein. This play is gonna be so cool."

I released the air in a burst of, "What did you just say?"

He grabbed my hand and led me toward the door. He then pointed at the first line.

Abby Brewster............Maddie Harrington/Understudy, Taryn Marshall

My eyes widened as I stared at the most awesome thing I'd ever seen. Because, for the first time in my high school theater life, I'd gotten the lead *and* the part I wanted. "Oh, my God, oh, my God. I got it. I got Aunt Abby." I raised my fisted hands into the air. "I finally got the part I wanted and it's the lead!" I lowered my arms, took a bouncy step to the left, to the right, and ended my little dance with a Dab. "This is going to be the best school year." Giggles rippled out of me, and I bounced in place.

I'd finally proven in an audition that I, Madeline Renée Harrington, could be the leading lady. Even an old leading lady.

"Great. Fantastic. But don't ever do that in front of me

again." Noah stared at me. "The Dab is the Worst. Dance move. Ever. And you're a better dancer than that."

I laughed my thanks at the same time two fellow senior boys I'd been in plays with since our freshman year walked into the office.

They stopped when they saw us, and I locked eyes with the tallest of the two boys. But even seeing my ex-boyfriend, Shane *effing* Easton, right now wouldn't burst my Abby Brewster high. So I kept my smile in place, even though an uncomfortable silence fell.

I'd hoped to avoid the ex since Noah and I ducked out of our last class before lunch. Another reason for it being quiet in here. But it had to be lunchtime, which meant other kids who'd auditioned would be making their way to where we stood.

I tore my eyes from the ex's that had dimmed at seeing me and caught Liam Langley's puppy-dog brown eyes full of warmth.

Liam's mouth curved into his dimpled smile. "So what'd Mr. Peters give you?"

My smile took on a plastic, Barbie feel as I answered, "Aunt Abby."

His smile grew. "You got the lead. That's great. Congrats."

"Yeah." The ex tried a friendly smile. "You deserve it. You'll be freakin' awesome."

I did deserve it after *never* getting the lead or the part I wanted. And I would make sure I was "freakin' awesome." But I couldn't very well agree with the ex doing a perfect job of playing nice, considering this was the first time we'd spoken since he'd crushed me in the spring. So I said, "Thanks!" Which came out sounding like I'd turned into a bird and chirped.

"Liam, you got Teddy," Noah interjected.

Thank God he was here.

Liam released a quick laugh and headed for where I stood. "I'm going to kill it as your nephew, Aunt Abby," he said in a convincing Teddy Roosevelt voice before focusing on the list.

Noah pointed at the ex. "And you got Mortimer."

The ex's eyes brightened and he went straight for Mr. Peters's office door.

It didn't surprise me he'd gotten Mortimer. He was a boy who could do funny with no effort and fear.

I pushed that thought aside and said, "Well, it looks like we're going to be a big, eccentric *nutty* family. It's going to be so much fun!"

Shoot. I'd sounded just like Barbie from the *Toy Story* movies.

The boys looked at me. But Liam was fighting a smile.

My face burned as if I'd set it on fire. "Okay, then. See you two later." I glanced at Noah, adjusted my heavy backpack, and inched my way toward the doorway. "Ready?" I fled the office without waiting for him.

I sprinted down the corridor that led to the school's hallway, then turned left and joined the sea of khaki skorts, pants and navy-blue cardigans worn over white polo shirts. Fellow Pacifica Academy students talking and laughing as they made their way to the cafeteria.

I stopped and leaned against a locker. I also tried to block out the noise around me while I took another slow, deep breath. But flowery perfume or lotion coming from nearby giggling girls who looked like freshmen filled my nose and made me cough.

Noah appeared beside me. "I think that went well." He pushed a lock of almost black hair away from his eyes. "Sure, you sounded and looked like a cheerleader on crack there at the end. But I'd give you an Oscar for your performance."

Before I could respond, Liam walked up to us. The ex, on the other hand, carefully avoided us and kept walking.

I straightened.

I had to stop acting like this. Now. For myself and the play. Especially the play. I absolutely couldn't blow my first chance at being a leading lady because of a *stupid* boy.

Liam flashed his smile, and I noticed for the first time he'd let his dark hair grow out a bit over the summer break. Still shorter on the sides, but the top was thick and styled as if he'd rolled out of bed and ran a hair product for boys through the strands.

"Maddie, you were awesome just now," Liam said. "In there. With Shane?"

I gave him a tiny smile. Because of everything that happened between his best friend and me, Liam's friendliness and support warmed my insides.

I couldn't stand the thought of losing another friend.

"I told her the same thing," Noah volunteered.

"Thanks, guys," I murmured. "I needed to hear that. And it's going to be great. *Right*?"

They nodded, and a breath of relief escaped me in a soft puff.

"This play will be phenomenal," Liam added. "I know it's our last play with Mr. Peters, but everyone will be phenomenal because of that."

Noah nodded again, though he was a junior.

The thought of this being our last play with my favorite teacher and director caused sadness to creep through me. Being a senior would be fantastic, but in a bittersweet way.

"And, yeah, Shane's my best friend, but it's a new year, and you're not clingy like he said—" Liam's eyes became round and he paled.

I froze, and my Abby Brewster high evaporated.

His words hung between us as kids loudly walked by.

No. He didn't just say what I thought I heard.

But as Liam's face went from pale to crimson, I narrowed my eyes.

Noah lowered and turned his head away from me.

I inhaled and remembered the reason I'd started meditating during summer break. As a way to better control my emotions in every kind of situation. But as I reached count four, the word "clingy" landed in my brain. Then exploded and formed a mushroom cloud. "He said *what* about me?" I screeched, catching the attention of those girls still at their lockers.

"Maddie, I'm such a dick." Liam stepped toward me. "I didn't mean to say that out loud—" He cringed.

Oh. Perfect. Even better.

I started trembling. With complete, girl-scorned fury.

"Not helping," Noah mumbled.

"Why? How?" I said through my teeth. "He crushed me for another girl." I shook my head, the ends of my light-brown hair slapping my chin. "How could he say that about me? Because I—wanted us to get back together?" I'd stopped myself from saying *stupidly*.

"He was pissed and frustrated when he said it. You weren't acting like yourself—"

"Dude, seriously?" Noah faced him. "Stop. Talking."

Liam ran a hand through his hair, messing it up even more, and nodded.

Okay. I hadn't been myself and my behavior at the end of last year hadn't exactly been that of a sane, seventeen-year-old girl. But I'd been heartbroken. For many reasons. And clingy?

That was a word no girl *ever* wanted to be called.

Forgetting all about meditative breathing, I said, "That rat bastard won't be able to show his face again after I'm done with him."

I took a shaky step. Then Noah grasped my right arm,

Liam grasped my left, and they all but dragged me back and toward the auditorium's huge, deserted lobby.

I tried to shake them off as I said, "Hey! You're supposed to be my friends. Well, Noah, you're supposed to be my friend. It's obvious where *Liam's* loyalties are."

He ignored me and my trying to tug my arm free from his grasp.

"We are your friends," Noah replied, despite my struggles. "And as your friends, we're saving you. From yourself."

They stopped once we'd reached the first set of auditorium doors and released me.

I crossed my arms and glared at them. Mostly Liam.

Noah concentrated on me. "Maddie, the stuff with Shane happened back in April. And it's September. I'm one of your best friends and telling you to Let. It. Go."

I'd worked hard during the summer to let him go, and so many other things that had happened in the spring. But hearing what he'd said about me had brought it all back with the force of an ocean wave. And a memory from April broke through my anger and humiliation.

I focused on Liam. "Is *that* the real reason you asked me to prom?" I'd turned down his friendly invite, and on the bitchy side. Another reason his friendliness and support had warmed me. But the warmth had turned into a glacier. "Because you felt sorry for me?" My mind zeroed in on something else. "And, come to think of it, aren't there rules against asking out your best friend's ex?"

Noah turned toward him, and frustration and hurt filled Liam's eyes. But I didn't give a crap if I'd hurt his feelings.

"Tell me the truth, Liam."

"No," he muttered. "That isn't why I asked you to prom as friends."

I searched his face for deceit, but all I saw were the same

two emotions. Still, it didn't stop me from doubting him, and I lifted my chin. "Well, I'm not clingy."

"I never said you were." He sighed. "Maddie, I'm so sorry I said that."

"You should be." I leaned forward. "I'll prove I'm not clingy, too." Proving that might prove I was more insane than neurotic, but I'd work on that adjective later.

Liam raised his eyebrows, and I turned and marched back the way they'd dragged me.

Now I had to figure out a way to follow up my vow with the best actions. And somehow stop myself from confronting the rat bastard as he sat in the cafeteria with his friends and the girlfriend. Who he so clearly loved.

Chapter Two

I leaned slightly left to see past my open locker door.

The ex still hadn't made it to his locker.

All around me kids were chatting with their friends or neighbors while replacing books with the ones they'd need for homework. I'd already done that so I could leave right after I, as calmly as possible, confronted the ex. Hopefully the girlfriend wouldn't be with him.

For almost three years, she'd walked around here with a scary, razor-sharp personality. But I had to grudgingly admit, like other kids, she'd changed after getting together with the rat bastard. And dropping Quinn Abbott and that *CruElla* Walker as friends. Girls I had thought were my friends. Until that stupid lip sync competition in April.

"Hey there, my fave, sweetly insane Brewster sister. You ready?"

I dragged my eyes away to look over my shoulder at Heather Mayfield. "Not yet. I have some very important business with *him.*"

Heather's green eyes, shielded by red, square-framed glasses, rolled upward. She had her long brown hair styled in two French braids. "Madeline, you're about to cross over into acting mad. Abby Brewster mad." She gripped my shoulders and gave me a hard shake. "You should be bouncing around here like Tigger because you got Abby." She released me. "And you're going to have to figure out a way to get along with him since he's Mortimer. As stage manager for this show, I will *not* tolerate any backstage drama." Her eyes softened. "You're also better than this."

I tried to smile at her words, but at this moment I wanted the ex to know what I thought of him, and his unkind and unfair description of me. But in an extremely less dramatic way than my stunning performance in front of the girlfriend back in April.

"Heather, this is exactly what I need to move forward. Before rehearsals start tomorrow afternoon." I gave her a stronger smile. "Think of it as a cleansing of the heart, mind, and soul. And you and Noah are also going to help me figure out a way to prove I'm so *not* clingy."

I still couldn't believe he'd said that about me. And to Liam. Okay. So they were best friends. But Liam was my friend, too. I'd known him for the same amount of time.

Heather groaned. "Maddie, it doesn't matter what he thinks or thought. It was months ago. And I thought your meditation stuff was supposed to be helping you with all of this."

"It has. It'll be fine." I turned forward. "I swear I won't make a scene." I caught him sauntering toward his locker and, thank God, minus the girlfriend. I shut my locker door, squared my shoulders and said, "I'll text you later."

I avoided students hurrying toward the stairs that led down to the school's main entrance and exit, and headed straight for him. I knew exactly how this would start, too. I'd been seeing it in my head all afternoon to the point I couldn't quite remember what my teachers had covered in my classes. But I'd been aware enough to write down all my homework.

I kept my eyes on the target while he put books into his backpack. A target who looked, in the spirit of Barbie, like a human Ken doll, with his height, sandy-blond hair, and bluest eyes ever. Between his looks, easygoing personality, and the fact he made me laugh, I'd developed a massive crush on him; the reason I'd asked him to Snowflake Formal last December. I'd known the risks of us crossing the friendship line, too, and hadn't cared one bit.

Which would *never* happen again.

I stopped when I reached him, his back facing me, then said only loud enough for him to hear, "You have everyone in this school fooled but me, you rat bastard."

His shoulders slumped at my snarled words, and it took him a few seconds to face me.

His eyes and face were full of apology, but I held my vicious, totally justified glare.

"Liam told me what happened at lunch, and I can't believe he did that." He sighed. "Maddie, I was pissed at you when I said it, because I didn't understand why you wanted—"

"Are you kidding me?" I snapped without being too loud. But his confusion was beyond irritating. Shane *effing* Easton wasn't stupid. "I know I screwed up telling Sloane about everything going on with us." I crossed my arms at the memory of that mess. "But you know I had a lot going on then and...needed you." I stepped closer. "And you lied to me. Because the real reason you didn't want to get back together was because of that crazy—"

"Don't." His eyes hardened.

I gritted my teeth.

"You don't know anything about Natalie. And I'm really sorry Liam told you what I said. But you know we didn't work as a couple, and I helped you as much as I could. If you'd stop being *this* Maddie Harrington" —he used both hands to gesture toward me— "long enough to be the *real* Maddie Harrington, you'd realize all this. And that I never lied to you."

I tightened my crossed arms.

He made it sound like we'd never been happy. Okay, so not the kind of happy he seemed to have with *her*. But still. It couldn't have been that awful being my boyfriend. Right?

I looked at the floor and rapidly blinked my eyes. I would never shed another tear over him. Over them. Those days were over.

The hallway traffic had thinned and become quieter, and I needed to get out of here, too. I'd said what I wanted. Called him a rat bastard to his...back. Had even gotten an apology from him that seemed genuine. So why didn't my heart, mind, and soul feel cleansed?

"Maddie," he said in a softer tone, "we have to figure something out. I mean, we have lead parts for the first time. And I know you're going to be awesome as Aunt Abby. But we have a lot of scenes together. We can't screw this up." He zipped up his backpack. "This play is too important. Mr. Peters gave the biggest roles to seniors this year."

I remembered what Heather said about not tolerating any backstage drama. And he was absolutely right about us getting our first lead roles, about the other casting, and the play's importance. Especially to the seniors.

Inhale to count four...exhale to count eight...

I glanced up at him. "I agree. And I swear everything will be fine when we get on the stage tomorrow."

He nodded, looking like he wanted to sigh again, but with relief.

I started to turn, but stopped and said over my shoulder, "This doesn't make us friends again. And it never will." I finished my turn and walked away from him. But my walk didn't ease the renewed sting of his rejection. Or from him calling me "clingy." A despicable word no boy would ever call me again.

* * *

I finished reading the last line of chapter three in *To Kill a Mockingbird*. Keeping an eye on my grandpa, now softly snoring in his bed, I bookmarked the page. I then put the book in its place beside his meds and glass of water on the nightstand.

He appeared so peaceful right now, but also fragile. He had almost no hair left and had lost so much weight since moving in with us six months ago. Because his appetite had nearly vanished. If he ate three small meals a day, we considered that a good eating day.

Ruth, his caregiver when we couldn't be with him, said she'd taken him out for some fresh air with it being a nice, San Francisco day. But she'd added the trip had "tuckered him out."

I reached out and gave his cool hand a gentle squeeze before I stood.

I glanced at his window open enough to let in the salty, sixty-five degree breeze, courtesy of the bay blocks from our condo's building. His hand had been cool, but having the window open kept the air in here from getting stuffy with that yucky, musty smell.

I usually talked to my grandpa about my day while he slept; the only time I could without adding to his confusion. But there was something else I needed to do right now, so I turned and tip-toed from his room to keep the hardwood floors from creaking. I hung a right and headed for my bedroom at the end of the hallway. My mom's room was in between mine and my grandpa's room. For quick access to her dad.

I quickly changed into yoga pants and a tank top. I had to make up for the steps backward I'd taken today since I started meditating in June.

I lit my green "Healing" meditation candle, and its citrusy scent filled my nose. I then went to my backpack to dig out my phone so I could play one of my New Age ambient, mediation songs. The music helped me focus on my deep breathing.

I sat cross-legged on my floor, went into meditation pose, and took deep breaths in time with the hypnotic music. But after a few breaths, I replayed what the ex said about being the *real* Maddie Harrington. Then the word clingy appeared.

I squashed both by using empowering images of me on stage in my first leading role as a sweetly crazy old lady.

Crazy. Clingy.

I shook my head, stretched my neck, shook out my hands, and tried to refocus.

I inhaled *I'm stronger than this.* I exhaled—clingy? Really?

How could I prove the ex had been wrong about me? Not that I'd be doing any of it for him because I still wanted him back. After seeing him and the girlfriend looking at each other with so much love, I knew I'd lost—focus, focus, focus.

I took another deep breath while I chanted *I'm stronger than this* in my head. But moisture burned behind my closed eyes. Because Shane had never looked at me that way.

No boy had ever looked at me with so much love.

I slouched, opened my eyes, and blinked them clear.

Yep. I'd taken way too many steps backward today.

I frowned at the floor.

Why did Liam have to word vomit in front of me? I'd been ecstatic about getting Abby and almost in control of my emotions before he opened his big mouth.

The front door opened and closed seconds later.

I heard Mom's light steps as she passed my grandpa's room. Then she reached my doorway. She had on nice jeans and a black, professional top that flattered her curvy figure. The black top complemented her dressy, black flats. And, per her usual, she had her brown hair with blonde highlights pulled up in a loose knot. Though she started each day with her hair hanging loose. But her big brown eyes, that we'd inherited from her mom, filled with concern.

"Before we talk about your day," she began as she walked into my room, "how was your grandpa? Did you or Ruth have any troubles?" She slipped the strap of her black laptop bag from her shoulder before sitting on my queen-sized bed's edge, and placed it at her feet.

I paused my music, pulled my legs up to my chest, and hugged my knees. "He thought I was you at first. Then went back to calling me grandma's name." I shrugged.

I'd stopped correcting him months ago, ever since Ruth had said that would be best for him.

Mom sadly nodded.

A part of me didn't mind too much he thought I was my grandma who'd passed away from a stroke several years ago. From really old pictures I'd seen of my grandparents when they were my age, I looked *a lot* like my grandma. In fact, we could almost pass as identical twins. My grandpa loved her so much, and I understood, with his Alzheimer's, why he thought I was his beloved Molly. But sometimes, especially on days like today, I wanted to hear him say *his* name for me—Miss Maddie Renée. So I imagined him saying it. And cracked a smile.

"Ruth didn't mention any problems, though," I added. "And he seems to like me reading *To Kill a Mockingbird* to him." Also known as one of my favorite American Literature books.

She smiled. "That was an excellent choice. As a matter of

fact, I'll be discussing that book with my freshman class later this semester."

Mom was a tenured literature professor at the city college.

She straightened and put on her "serious Mom face" that I also called her "teacher face."

"What do you want to talk about first? The good or the bad?"

"The good." I grinned. "I got Abby Brewster."

"*Yes!*" she hissed before joining me on the floor to wrap me in a tight hug. "I knew your sweet, old lady voice would win over Mr. Peters." She released me and leaned back. "Why aren't you acting like a college student after finishing their final test of the semester? You finally got what you've been wanting." Her expression reverted to serious. "Oh. I see. But Sweetie, you knew he'd be in this play with you. Who did he get?"

"Mortimer." I sighed. "And it's not that. Really." And it wasn't.

The rat bastard part of him aside, he worked hard in the plays and was talented. Still, it's not like I'd tell her what he said about me to Liam.

"Based on all the plays and choir concerts I've been to the last few years," she slowly said, "I have to say there are other, just as cute boys, at that school. Maybe it's time to think about giving someone new a chance? It has been...several months now."

Okay. Fine. *Everyone* was right about it being time to move on from—my eyes widened as a lightbulb illuminated the realization I'd only dated a few boys. Including Shane. My first boyfriend. I'd never truly enjoyed being a single high school girl. And all the fun I could have.

Why did I have to date one boy? Like Mom said, there were other cute *boys* at Pacifica Academy. Why did I even have to go on more than one date with a boy? I certainly didn't have to kiss or do anything else with them. That's what boyfriends were for. And after what happened with the ex, I had zero interest in getting close to someone new. Especially now, when I had way more important things going on in my life. I also had a point to prove and there was nothing wrong with having some fun. I'd have to come up with rules for my mission, like no kissing, but this could be exactly what I needed.

I gave Mom a big hug and said, "You're right. And you're a genius."

She laughed. "If only I could convince my students of that."

Now I had to figure out what boys I wanted to date. But only once. That also needed to be a rule. Along with no dating boys I considered a good friend.

"Are you ready for your audition tomorrow morning?"

That last rule would eliminate most of the boys active in theater. And who were in show choir with me. But not all of them.

"Yeah," I replied, sifting through boys' faces. "I chose an Andrew Lloyd Webber song."

"Very nice. But is it wrong of me to say I think it's ridiculous Mrs. Chaplin makes you guys, who have been in show choir *previously*, audition every year?"

I stopped my face sifting at her comments and swung my eyes in her direction. "No. It's stupid. But that's Mrs. Chaplin."

She shook her head. "Just one more year." She opened the side pocket of her bag and withdrew some mail. Right on top of the small pile, she held a rare, Bradley Harrington postcard. That I glared at while she read whatever he'd written, usually in no more than four scrawled sentences.

"Your brother's still in Vancouver and with that girl,

Autumn, he's been seeing for a while. Says he has some news and will call when he can."

Not effing likely.

"Would you like to read this one?"

Too weird. Hearing from my so-called brother on a day like today. And two questions landed in my mind. What about me made guys—men—leave? And practically forget me?

I shoved my useless, not-empowering questions into the back of my mind, turned from her and stood. "No. I don't." I needed to start learning my crazy important lines, do my homework, and decide who would be boy number one in my big plan I would call...Project Dating Spree.

Chapter Three

Mrs. Chaplin's gentle piano playing filled the choir room as I stood on the mini-stage, which faced the seats occupied by my fellow members of show choir.

I tightened my diaphragm, opened my mouth and continued singing the somber lyrics to "Tell Me On a Sunday."

When I finished, everyone clapped, and I caught Liam's eyes. His half-smile seemed filled with too much sympathy for my comfort level. Because I'd been drawn to the song about deep loss for reasons beyond my messy break-up with his best friend.

I broke our eye contact, and Mrs. Chaplin said, "That was nice, Maddie. Thank you. Welcome back to show choir."

I managed not to roll my eyes while I stepped off the mini-stage.

Two sophomore boys jumped up and went to our choir teacher.

I couldn't roll my eyes because Sloane, a senior and Mrs. Chaplin's daughter, was in show choir, too.

I went for my seat between Sloane, a first soprano, and Taryn, a second soprano like me, but she was a junior. We normally had to sit in our formal stage arrangement—sopranos, tenors, baritones, altos—but since there were a few more students who had to *audition*, Mrs. Chaplin had allowed us to sit where we wanted. Which was why Liam, a tenor, and Barrett, another senior and tenor, were sitting in the soprano section.

I sat, and Liam leaned forward.

"Are we okay?" he mumbled. "I really am sorry about yesterday. My brain and mouth aren't always in sync. Which equals total dumbass."

Between him being a good friend, his pleading, apologetic eyes and funny words, I could only say, "It's fine. Really." But that didn't change the fact I had a project to begin.

Relief replaced his apologetic expression, and he leaned back.

I shot him a friendly grin, which he returned, and I focused on Barrett. "Congrats on getting Officer O'Hara in the play."

Barrett had a 1000-watt smile. It always reached his blue eyes that stood out because of his dark hair he kept military short. "Thanks, Aunt Abby. Should be a fun character to play." He laughed. "But not as much fun as being on stage, half-naked as Tom the Jock in *Grease*. And hearing girls whistle."

Liam laughed with him as I remembered Barrett strutting around shirtless while wearing red basketball shorts. He'd looked good, too. Toned in the important upper-body places on a boy.

I'd gotten Marty, though I'd *really* wanted Rizzo.

I glanced at Taryn. Based on her pink, lightly freckled cheeks, I suspected she was remembering how Barrett looked in the musical, too.

She had the longest, thickest hair the perfect, natural shade of auburn. Her eyes matched the color of her pale-brown freckles. She was so pretty, and I couldn't understand why she was single. And rarely dated. I then looked at Liam, talking with her and Barrett, and it hit me. Liam and Taryn would make a super cute couple. He didn't date much, either. But maybe all they needed was a little push. Why not toward each other?

My eyes drifted to Barrett, and the memory of him shirtless and wearing red basketball shorts became strong—I smiled. He was not only cute and nice, but known as a serial dater.

I still had to share my Project-Dating-Spree plan with Heather and Noah. I also had to come up with the rest of my rules. But I didn't consider Barrett and I close friends.

Which meant he'd be a great choice for boy number one.

"Well, I'm so glad I didn't audition for the play." Sloane dropped her phone in her lap and flipped a fake blonde lock of hair off her shoulder.

I used to be one of the few kids in show choir and theater who would hang out with Sloane. Because she was too much like her snotty mom. I guess I'd always felt kind of sorry for her. But I'd pulled away from Sloane after she'd blabbed to her bestie, Brandy Espinosa, last spring about everything going on between Shane and me. Sloane didn't seem to be sensing my distance, though, since she'd chosen to sit by *me* since school started.

"And why's that, oh great and wonderful Sloane Chaplin?" Liam asked with a smile that matched his sarcasm.

Taryn giggled quietly beside me.

She'd definitely be perfect for Liam.

Maybe I could start dropping hints with them. At rehearsals might work, since all of us were in the play together. Taryn had gotten Mortimer's girlfriend, Elaine.

Sloane glared at Liam. "High school kids playing *really* old people?" She snorted. "So not my thing or worth my time. Just like *The Crucible* two years ago."

Liam looked at me, then Taryn, and rolled his eyes sideways.

I faced Barrett. It was time to get serious about Project Dating Spree.

"Barrett Wagner, come up here, please," Mrs. Chaplin said as she stood. "It's your turn."

Shoot. I'd have to catch him before, or after, our first rehearsal today. Preferably before. It would also give me time to dig out my flirty side and practice the conversation in my head.

* * *

"Project what-the-hell-are-you-talking-about?" Noah said.

I straightened. "You don't have to say it like that."

I sat at the end of our long table in the cafeteria with Noah, Heather, and Liam. I'd quietly mentioned Project Dating Spree since I didn't need everyone knowing about my big plan. Several other theater and choir kids, including Barrett, filled the table's middle and other end.

Noah looked at Liam. "This is all your fault."

Liam responded by staying focused on his enormous, submarine-type sandwich stuffed with meat, cheese, lettuce, and pickles.

I'd hoped he'd be sitting somewhere else today. Some days he sat here with us at the "drama table," and other days he sat at the table toward the middle of the noisy cafeteria. With his best friend, the girlfriend, and other friends.

Discomfort settled around me at Liam knowing about Project Dating Spree. No matter our friendship, his *true* loyalties were with someone else. But I couldn't turn back now.

Heather finished her baby carrot. "No. If you really think about it, this could be a good thing. And just what she needs."

I smiled.

I knew a fellow member of my gender would understand.

"Maddie, this isn't you." Noah glanced again at Liam, staring at a spot on the table as he chewed his bite of sandwich. "Back me up here. You've been friends with her way longer than I have. Maybe she'll listen to you."

I hadn't become good friends with Noah and Heather until those last weeks of working with them on *Grease*. During that rotten time, I'd pulled away from friends the ex and I had shared. Including Liam. Then soon afterward realized who *weren't* my friends.

But right now I wasn't feeling the love from Noah, and said, "*She* is sitting right here. And I don't need permission from my friends to date a few boys." Though it really couldn't be considered a spree if I only dated three or four.

Liam swallowed his bite, looked up, and our eyes met. "She's right." He turned toward Noah. "I said I was sorry. And we're not her keepers."

I gave Noah a triumphant smile.

He groaned. "All of you have Lost. Your. Minds."

"Then sit there, eat your lunch, and be quiet while we figure this out." Heather focused on me. "But he did have a point about this not being you. Have you thought about the whole, how-this-might-make-you-look thing?"

I shook off Noah's grouchiness and answered, "Yes. Which is why I'll have a list of strict rules." I leaned toward her while keeping my eyes on Noah and Liam, who were watching me. "Absolutely *no* kissing will be rule number one, followed by *no* dates with boys I call a good friend, followed by no more than *one* date, per boy."

Heather smiled. "Nice. Excellent start."

"Yeah," Liam said, "that's a super list of rules."

I couldn't be sure, but he'd sounded a little like sarcastic Liam from earlier with Sloane.

Noah swallowed his huge bite of red apple. "So speaking of crazy, I have a crazy thought. What if one of these guys ends up liking you?"

Okay. I hadn't thought of that. Then again…I shrugged. "I'll choose boys who aren't interested in having a girlfriend." Like Barrett, the serial dater. And why was it a-okay for boys to serial date, but if a girl did it she earned the label of crazy? Possibly other, much worse labels if she wasn't careful. Like I would be.

"But how are you going to know that? Are you going to interview these guys first?"

Liam faced Noah. "*Bachelor* number one," he said in a deep, game show host voice, "are you interested in anything beyond one date with our *bachelorette*?" He released a quick, phony laugh. "If so, you'll be shit out of luck on today's episode of—"

"Liam Langley, you're not funny." I glared at him as Noah shook with laughter.

He went back to his sandwich.

"And it's not like dating histories are a big secret around here," I added.

"Very true." Heather laughed. "I think this will be awesome. But just so you know I plan on living vicariously through you until you're done with Project Dating Spree."

Heather was striking in her own, unique way, and had such a bubbly personality I couldn't understand why she didn't put herself out there when it came to boys. I had a feeling if she stopped seeing herself as one of the boys she might notice some of them seeing her, the girl.

"So when do you think this *project* will be over?" Liam asked, using his normal voice.

I frowned. "I'm not sure. I guess when I've proven my

point. And it stops being fun." But I couldn't see that happening soon.

"You don't need to prove anything, so I think this is dumb and not you. At. All."

I wrinkled my nose at Noah. "Tell me how you really feel."

"But since you're determined to do this," he continued, "will you at least be careful? Seriously, Maddie. Call or text if you need me."

"Me, too," Liam strongly echoed, but without looking at me.

So this was what it was like to have best friends. Well, except for Liam. But still. And I smiled at them as my soul heated to cozy at their genuine care for me. For my safety. But it's not like I'd be going out on dates with boys with questionable dating reputations.

"That should be a rule," Heather stated. "You have to text us before going on your dates. Text us at least once during the date. And text us the second you get home. Okay?"

"I promise." I mentally hugged their care to me. But I needed them to make me a promise, too. "This is only between us. Got it?" I almost added *Liam*, but he seemed so lost in thought all of a sudden I didn't think he'd like me calling him out.

Noah and Heather nodded, and though Liam also nodded, his seemed more forced.

Maybe his kind of weird reaction did have to do with Noah's accusation that "this was all his fault." And the fact he was the ex's best friend? Still, I'd accepted his apology. I also deserved to be happy and have some fun. So if he was feeling guilty about my project and really couldn't handle this, we would have to stop hanging out together.

But sadness twisted through me at that thought.

"And you'll probably want to choose your date outfits very carefully," Heather added.

I blinked and forced the sad thought from my mind.

No. If my bad break-up with his best friend hadn't hurt our friendship, then surely Project Dating Spree wouldn't affect us. Everything would be totally fine.

"Right. Good one. No inappropriate outfits." I'd have to write down these rules the first chance I had this afternoon.

"We'll add more rules later if we need to." Heather's eyes turned playful. "Do you have a bachelor number one in mind?"

I eyed Noah and Liam, staring at me. Unfortunately, they *were* good friends with Barrett. But I had no way of keeping this from them since we all fell into the "drama crowd."

"Yes." I casually slid my eyes down the table and they landed on Barrett, laughing at something someone said. "I've chosen my bachelor number one."

Chapter Four

Project Dating Spree Rules
    1. No kissing.
    2. No dates with boys who are good friends.
3. Only date boys who don't want a girlfriend.
4. Only one date per boy.
5. Be safe. Text friends before, during, and after date.
6. No inappropriate outfits. (Refer to Rule 1.)
7. Dates in public places only. (Refer to Rules 1 and 5.)

"So?" I asked Heather as we stopped outside the first set of auditorium doors.

She handed me the list I'd written out during my study hall period. "Very thorough." She nodded. "I think you covered the most important stuff."

I refolded the paper and slid it into my sweater pocket. "Okay. Now I just need to be alone with bachelor number one long enough to work my brown-eyed girl magic."

I wanted to catch him before Mr. Peters started our first

rehearsal. I had to get Project Dating Spree going, but also needed to be at my best, focused self for the next two hours.

Heather reached for the door handle, then stopped. "You ready for this, Abby Brewster?"

I paused.

I'd been so caught up in Project Dating Spree all day, I hadn't spent one second reflecting on the fact this was the first time I'd be walking into the auditorium with a leading-lady role. In fact, this time last year I'd walked into the auditorium with the ridiculously small part of Lady Montague in *Romeo and Juliet*. Though I'd auditioned for Juliet. But I'd tripped over the language from the beginning of my audition, which had amplified my nervousness, and set the tone for the rest of my *disastrous* performance.

I guess I should've been relieved Mr. Peters gave me a part. But that rotten audition had been what fueled me to nail Abby Brewster. And here I was a year later, with a leading role.

Okay. I'd be sharing a lot of stage time with the ex. Still, I had Heather and Noah to lean on for support. If I needed it. And though I wanted to include Liam, I knew he'd be buddied up with his best friend for the next several weeks. But absolutely nothing would affect my first time being one of the main stars of the show.

Excitement and determination sizzled through me, and I squared my shoulders. "Without question."

She smiled. "Excellent."

She opened the door, I walked inside, and she followed me.

And of course the first person I saw was the ex, standing near the front row seats and talking with some of our castmates, including Kassidy and J.R., Romeo and Juliet from a year ago. They were also a super cute couple who were good friends with the ex and the girlfriend. I liked them a lot, too, but had barely spoken to them since the end of last year. So when Kassidy's face lit up with a huge smile when she spotted us walking down the aisle, relief shrouded me.

I sent her an equally enthusiastic smile, followed by a wave.

She darted around her boyfriend, the ex, Barrett—good, he was already here—and Noah, to meet us at the end of the aisle.

She threw her arms around me. "I'm so happy we get to be sisters for the next two months." She gave me a tight squeeze. "And insane sisters at that. Thank goodness Mr. Peters finally chose a comedy."

I squeezed her back. I'd always liked Kassidy. She had no fear, and not just when it came to acting. And though she was crazy talented, it didn't stop her from working hard.

"Yes, Aunt Martha." I pulled away from her. "This play will be so much fun." Every part of me meant that since it was not only my first leading role, but I would also be experimenting with my comedic side for the first time.

Kassidy and Heather hugged for a second, and my eyes connected with J.R.'s. We exchanged smiles, and I released a soft sigh at his friendliness. A good sign he also wasn't holding my embarrassing and questionable behavior from the end of last year against me.

"Was J.R. excited about getting Jonathan?" Also known as the *real* bad guy in the play.

Kassidy giggled. "It was the part he wanted. He's been smiling since yesterday."

I giggled, too, since I couldn't imagine her sweet, cute, soccer star boyfriend wanting to play such an evil character. But the main reason I'd wanted Rizzo so bad was the challenge of playing a character nothing like me.

Heather grinned. "I think Mr. Peters nailed his casting again. And speaking of the cast..." Her eyes flitted to me. "I'm going to say hi to everyone else. Okay?"

Which meant saying hi to the ex, but I nodded and shrugged. The only way I could reply. *Arsenic and Old Lace* had a small cast, and we were in this together for just over two months.

She dashed away from us, and Kassidy concentrated on me. Though her smile had faded.

I strongly suspected what was on her mind and held my smile. But now it felt Barbie-ish.

"How are you doing?" she asked.

My Barbie smile slipped as I remembered Kassidy had been through being on stage with J.R. this time last year. After a bad break-up with him. Our biggest differences were she hadn't expected to be in the play with him *and* Sloane, who he'd briefly dated.

And thank God the ex's girlfriend wasn't active in theater.

"Kassidy, I'm fine." For the most part. "This is a new year. Our last year. And it's all good. But thanks for asking." It would definitely be all good with the help of Project Dating Spree. And it's not like Kassidy hadn't done something fairly rash last year as a way to deal with J.R. and their break-up. She had started that club.

"Maddie, you're my friend." She peered at me. "You know that, right?"

The coziness returned at hearing her say those words.

"And I get what you're going through," she murmured. "I also know you were going through a tough time in the spring for other reasons. If you need to talk, I'm here."

Only my closest theater friends knew about my grandpa's illness, and that he had to move in with us in March. But I said, "Thanks, Kass. Everything's going to be great, though. I promise. We're totally going to nail being the Brewster sisters."

She laughed, and Heather, towing Barrett, walked up to us.

"You needed to talk to him before rehearsal started?" Heather's eyes widened as she fought a smile.

Right. Back to Project Dating Spree.

"So, Kass, how was your summer with your tall, dark, and *hot* Romeo?" Heather asked as she slipped her arm around Kassidy's shoulders and steered her away from us.

Barrett flashed his 1000-watt smile. "What's up?"

I took his left hand and casually led him away. I had to make sure we were as alone as possible to unmask flirtatious Maddie Harrington. When we were halfway up the aisle, I stopped us and stepped toward him. Leaving what I considered a friendly gap between us. But that wouldn't last long. Especially if he resisted. "Barrett," I softly began, gazing at him, "we had fun last year. As Lady and Lord Montague?"

He shrugged. "Yeah. It was cool. I liked that play."

Hmm.

I took another step closer, making us hugging distance. "What I really mean is that we had pretty good chemistry. Don't you think?"

He frowned. "I guess. But it's not like we were Romeo and Juliet."

Okay then.

I opened my mouth. And Liam walked up to us.

"*Greetings*, Aunt Abby and Officer O'Hara," he said with a thick, Irish accent.

Barrett laughed. "Man, I wish I could do the accents. You're really good at that shit."

Liam puffed out his chest. "Well, *Officer O'Hara*, it takes years of practice and—" He shook his head. "Not having a life in middle school," he finished, but in his real voice. He smiled and pointed at his face. "This didn't happen overnight."

Barrett laughed again.

"Liam," I tightly said, "I'm talking to Barrett right now." I gave him a long, hard stare.

He, now barely smiling, held my stare for a few seconds before taking a step back. "Yeah. Got it." He slapped Barrett on the shoulder. "Good luck."

Barrett watched him turn and walk down the aisle, and I straightened.

"So what'd you need? I'm sure Mr. Peters will be here any minute."

I mentally snarled at Liam and his terrible timing. But for Barrett I turned on *my* blinding smile and stepped closer; the closest I could be without being plastered against him.

He leaned slightly away from me. "What are you doing?"

Really? I had to knock serial dater Barrett Wagner upside the head with my words?

"I think we should go on a date. This Saturday night?"

He stared at me, blinking.

Now for the final act.

I demurely pushed my hair behind my ears and batted my eyes twice. More than that and he might think I had a weird eye tick. I also gazed at him while keeping my smile in place.

He swallowed. "I'm flattered. Really. But isn't this kind've...sudden?"

"Not really." I lifted my shoulders in a demure shrug. "It's just *one* date. Could be fun."

At that moment, Mr. Peters, a slight man with dark, curly hair, barreled into the auditorium. "Sorry I'm late! Theater Department business. Please take a seat so we can jump into our first comedy together." Mr. Peters rushed by me and Barrett, and said, "You, too, Aunt Abby and Officer O'Hara."

Shoot. I guess I had no choice but to finish this later.

"Yeah," Barrett said, and again wearing his 1000-watt smile. "It would be fun."

Perfect. I hadn't lost my touch after all.

"Exchange numbers after rehearsal?" I asked.

He nodded. "Definitely."

We turned in unison and headed down the aisle. I then caught Heather's inquisitive look and answered with a sly smile.

She tilted her head back and laughed.

Project Dating Spree was officially on. And it was time to become Aunt Abby.

$$Chapter\ Five$$

"I don't like your hair like that, Molly."

I stayed focused on the open book for a breath before lowering it to my lap.

I looked up to find my grandpa scowling at me, specifically my head. I'd piled my hair up and into a messy knot. "I'm sorry, Grandpa. But it's warm in here today." In truth, it was stifling. His bedroom window had been closed until I came in here to read. He liked his window shut more often than not. Though today had been a warm, sunny, late summer day, he seemed to always have a chill, probably because he'd lost so much weight.

He waved impatiently at me with both hands. "Well, I don't like it. You're much prettier with your hair down. And why do you keep calling me grandpa?" he harshly added, rolling his head away from me. "I don't understand. And I have a name."

I flinched, as if his words had burned my skin. But as I eyed him, staring off into space with his blankets tucked around his frail body, the burning eased, and I wanted to hug him. Give him the big bear hug I'd given him when I was a little girl. The kind of hugs we gave each other.

When he knew I was his granddaughter, Miss Maddie Renée.

"I'm tired," he grumbled. "Just leave me alone." And he closed his eyes.

I stood and put the book in its place on his nightstand. I'd definitely had enough, too. But guilt lowered my shoulders as I left his bedroom. None of this was his fault; the one thought that kept me going on rough days like today. Barely. And so much for telling him about my day.

Mom, wearing baggy sweatpants and a worn, San Francisco Giants T-shirt, stood in her bedroom doorway as I walked by. "Sweetie, you know he doesn't really mean anything he says." Which meant she must've overheard his harshly spoken comments.

I nodded and shrugged and continued heading for my room.

I honestly knew all of that. Mom was struggling, too, and I had a feeling her saying that was also a reminder to herself. But sometimes he had a way of saying things that made me want to slunk off into a corner like a wounded animal and lick my injuries clean.

"I didn't want to interrupt you two when I got home," she said, following me to my room. "But now I have to know how your first rehearsal as a leading lady went."

I sat on my bed, then tucked my left leg underneath me, and grabbed one of my most prized possessions—a plump, somewhat white teddy bear with big, round, dark eyes, and wearing his original, but now faded, red bow tie. My grandpa had given Buddy to me for Christmas when I was nine.

I placed my chin on his cushy head and hugged him tightly to me.

Mom leaned against my doorframe. "It couldn't have been that bad. With Shane?"

I forced myself to focus on her questions, and I smiled, remembering the funny rehearsal. And the fact I had a date with Barrett Saturday night.

The play and Project Dating Spree would absolutely be great distractions right now.

"No. It was good." The ex, like I figured, had sat with Liam. But also with J.R. and Kassidy. I'd sat between Noah and Taryn, and opposite them. "I didn't feel like a leading lady, since all we did, like usual with Mr. Peters, was sit in a circle on stage and read our parts as if we were performing them, live." A giggle escaped. "But this play is funny. Everyone's into their roles. Liam's going to be awesome as Teddy. He's great at impersonations and accents." And of course the ex had nailed Mortimer's comical and stunned reaction to finding out his elderly aunts were, basically, serial killers.

"Remind me again who Liam is?"

His puppy-dog brown eyes and dimpled smile drifted into my mind, and I recalled what he'd said about getting good at accents because of "not having a life in middle school." Kind of hard to imagine Liam being that awkward back then. But I hadn't exactly been a beauty queen during those *spectacular* years. I also hadn't known I possessed my brown-eyed girl magic. Which didn't come out until high school.

"Well, he's Shane's best friend."

Her eyebrows shot upward. "Oh. But it sounds like you're still friends with him?"

I lifted Buddy's arms, one at a time. "Yeah. We've been in theater and show choir together since freshman year. He was the T-Bird, Doody, in *Grease,* and was Tybalt a year ago."

She slowly nodded. "I think I remember him. On the taller side, dark hair...dimples?"

I laughed. "That's Liam."

She smiled. "He's really cute."

Yeah. He did happen to be the definition of hottie. On top of the fact he was smart and funny, and could act, sing, and dance. *A total catch.*

I frowned at that thought, and said, "Mom, we're friends. He's also Shane's best friend?"

She lifted her shoulders. "Okay. I understand. But if he weren't?"

"No. I'm never crossing the friendship line again." I vehemently shook my head, which rid my mind of where my thoughts had gone. "Been there, done that." And this was the perfect time to tell her, "I do have a date with Barrett Wagner this Saturday night."

Her dark eyes lit up and she laughed. "Wonderful! Fabulous! But who is he?"

I dropped my eyes to Buddy's head. "Another boy in show choir and active in theater. He's also in *Arsenic and Old Lace,* and played Tom the Jock in *Grease.*" I lifted my eyes to hers. "The one who took off his—" I cleared my throat. "He was shirtless a couple times?"

Her eyes widened. "I remember him." She winced. "Is it weird for me to admit that?"

I giggled. "No. It's totally fine." Because he had looked really good.

She swiped her forehead. "Okay. Good to know. But he's pretty cute, too. I approve. What are you two going to do?"

I switched to lifting Buddy's legs, one at a time. "Going out to eat, then a movie."

I'd have to play the movie thing *very* carefully. No sitting in the back of a dark movie theater, since that could give Barrett ideas. Kissing ideas. But I couldn't believe he'd try something like that on a first date. What would be our only date.

"Good. I assume he's picking you up? I'd like to meet him."

I stopped lifting Buddy's right leg.

Shoot. I hadn't thought about the whole Mom-wanting-to-meet-my-dates thing.

What would she think about my serial dating? It's not like I'd be doing anything inappropriate on my dates. But still. She'd probably start asking questions when I reached date three with bachelor number three. And I certainly couldn't tell her about Project Dating Spree. Maybe, after my date with Barrett who *would* be picking me up, I'd arrange to meet my bachelors at the places for our dates. It could work. If Mom didn't need our one car.

"Yeah," I absently answered. "At eight."

"Perfect. Keith has a show," she continued, "but I won't be leaving until 8:30."

Keith being Dr. Keith Radley, her long-time boyfriend who ran the music department at the city college and also played the saxophone in his jazz band.

Mom snapped her fingers. "I'll need to talk to Ruth about being here Saturday night. I hate to ask her, but she has grown quite fond of your grandpa and knows he..." Her voice trailed into nothing.

But I knew how that sentence ended.

Knows he doesn't do well with strangers taking care of him.

"But don't worry about that," she added, and with her "serious Mom face." She straightened. "I'll get it worked out." She gave me an affectionate smile. "Maddie, I'm so happy and excited for you. I know you liked Shane, but it's good you're moving on."

In more ways than just one boy.

"Thanks. I'm definitely ready to move on." Totally the truth, too.

She nodded. "I'll let you know when dinner's ready. And

I'll keep your grandpa company the rest of the night so you can focus on homework and learning your lines."

I did have a lot of schoolwork tonight, but I knew Mom's statement came from a place of concern. At least I no longer felt like crouching in a corner to tend to my wounds.

What really tugged at my heart and soul was that rough days like today would only get worse as he continued to...deteriorate.

Inhale to count four...exhale to count eight...

I squeezed Buddy.

Maybe meditating for a bit would be best before jumping into all my homework.

* * *

I leaned toward my full-length mirror to apply lip gloss. But not too much. I'd also applied a little more makeup than I wore to school because I was going on a date. I did want to look nice for Barrett. But not enough to give him any *ideas*.

I capped the lip gloss and scanned my carefully chosen, appropriate outfit. A light blouse with a faint, flowery pattern that had a mid-high neckline over a pale-pink cami. My skinny jeans were on the snug side, but what skinny jeans weren't? And dark-brown, knee-high boots completed my outfit. Almost. I planned on adding a light, stylish pale-pink jacket.

Totally appropriate. Girly. Innocent, most importantly.

I walked toward my bed and dropped the lip gloss, then lightly ran my fingers through my hair I'd decided to air dry, which made it fall in soft waves. Also very girly.

I picked up my phone since I had another rule to fulfill.

I chose Heather and Noah, but hesitated before choosing Liam's name. Despite his weird reaction, he'd said he wanted to be included in this part of Project Dating Spree. But had he said that out of obligation since he'd been sitting with us? He also could have said it out of guilt.

I sighed and chose his name. I guess I'd soon find out.

I texted, *Barrett should be here any minute. Will check in later. xo*

I swiped my jacket and crossbody phone case, that held two just-in-case twenties, off my bed. I then gave myself one more, swift glance in the mirror.

I nodded at my reflection. And my phone buzzed and chimed with a text from Heather.

And the fun begins! Are you nervous?

I paused.

No racing heart. No tummy fluttering. No clammy, jittery hands. No trying to catch my breath. Come to think of it, I hadn't even felt those things before the ex picked me up for Snowflake Formal. But then, we had been good friends first.

More like and the crazy begins appeared from Noah.

I wrinkled my nose. He needed to lighten up.

I replied, *Not nervous at all*.

The buzzer ripped through the condo and meant Barrett was downstairs. But since Mom made it clear she wanted to meet him, I couldn't go down there. Which I'd warned him about.

I raised my head and marched from my room since the fun really was about to begin.

I hope you have a super awesome time.

I frowned at Liam's reply that seemed *super* sarcastic and closed out of text messaging.

He *and* Noah needed to lighten up.

Mom stood at the open front door. She looked pretty girly herself tonight in a figure-flattering black dress that landed at her knees, black heels and her hair hanging loose.

She smiled at me as I walked toward her. "Lovely."

I shrugged my thanks at the same time Barrett appeared in the doorway.

I froze at his 1000-watt smile. Then my eyes fell to his snug, blue T-shirt that showed off his defined chest, arms, *everything* up top. And my eyes drifted to his equally tight jeans.

I glanced at him as heat hit my cheeks.

"Hi," Mom said with an outstretched hand, "I'm the mother."

He leaned forward to shake her hand. "Barrett. It's nice to meet you."

Wow. I rarely saw him out of the boys' uniform and he looked pretty fantastic in his own clothes. And dressed for a date.

No. This was just Barrett. Bachelor number one in Project Dating Spree.

I slid my phone into my case, then shrugged into my jacket.

"Where are you two going to eat?" Mom asked.

Barrett glanced at me. "I was going to let you decide that."

I stepped toward him. "Thanks!" But it came out sounding like I'd chirped. I really needed to work on that and the whole sounding-like-Barbie thing.

"Well, have fun tonight." Mom focused on me. "Home by curfew."

I nodded and walked until I was within touching distance of Barrett, who smelled good, too. Expensive, but on the lighter side, cologne good. He'd clearly made it a point to look and smell great for our date. For me.

I tried to squash the guilt weaving its way through me.

"It was nice meeting you, Barrett." Mom caught my eyes and raised her eyebrows. Her way of saying, "Behave yourself."

Apparently, Barrett's efforts hadn't gone unnoticed by my *mother*.

I sent her a hasty smile, slipped into the hallway, and motioned Barrett to follow me.

We were silent as we went down the two flights of stairs. The kind of silence that made me want to fill it, but I knew I'd sound like a babbling Barbie.

"You look really nice," he softly said when we walked outside.

The comfortable, humid night air clung to my skin and hair that was probably becoming wavier; the salty, San Francisco humidity another reason I'd let my hair air dry.

"Thanks," I softly replied. "So do you."

He smiled, but it seemed a bit on the shy side. "Thanks. The car's this way."

Serial dater Barrett Wagner actually seemed a bit nervous. Which meant he, most likely, wouldn't try anything during the movie.

I mentally sighed.

"So what are you in the mood to eat?" he asked. "I was thinking we could find a place somewhere close to the movie theater?"

"Sounds *great*!"

Shoot. I was acting like this was my first date with a cute boy. Yes, it was my first Project Dating Spree date. But still. I needed to stop acting like a silly, inexperienced freshman.

He laughed quietly. "Great."

Inhale to count four...exhale to count eight...

When we reached a silver, mid-sized SUV, he stopped us. And his cheeks turned rosy.

"I know I acted weird when you asked me out. But I didn't think you liked me that way, and I" —he laughed— "wanted to ask *you* out. Back in April."

My mouth fell open as I stared at him.

He'd wanted to ask me out back then. When I'd been acting nuts and bitchy.

"But you didn't seem interested in anything like that. Because of everything that happened with you and Shane and...you know."

"Yeah. I do know," I muttered.

I would probably never live down confronting the ex's girlfriend on lip sync competition day. Actions *CruElla* Walker had talked me into as a way to enact her twisted revenge on her now ex-best friend. And Quinn Abbott, who I had really thought was my friend, had simply sat there, silent, while I stupidly listened to CruElla.

Though I'd told the girlfriend at the time I felt much better, I hadn't. Not one bit.

"You definitely seem more like yourself now," he continued as he withdrew the car key from his pocket. He then hit the button to unlock the doors. "I'm glad you asked me out."

I tried to smile before he turned to head toward the driver's side.

I opened my door and stepped sideways into the SUV. And Noah's question from Thursday floated through my mind while I closed the door.

What if one of these guys ends up liking you?

Okay. I hadn't counted on my first bachelor admitting he'd been wanting to ask me out. Since the spring. But I could handle this unexpected, yet flattering, development, especially since he was a serial dater. Which eased some of my guilt. Still, I didn't know what serial dating meant in his world and would absolutely need to stay on high alert tonight.

Chapter Six

Barrett and I stared at each other from our seats at a table in the middle of the restaurant devoted to burgers. Cooking hamburgers, onions, and pickles scented the air.

All around us people were at their tables, and loudly talking and laughing, enjoying their Saturday night that was probably just beginning. Like our night. The fact the restaurant was packed and the seating open were the reasons I'd walked inside. This place was also close to the movie theater.

Barrett took a drink of his Pepsi, and I reached for my chocolate shake.

As I took a long, slow sip of the cold, thick, chocolatey yumminess, I racked my brain for something to say. Weird, too, since it wasn't like I knew Barrett that well. But I also didn't want to get too deep with my questions. It's not that I didn't want to know anything about him, but the deeper, getting-to-know-you questions were reserved for wanting to go beyond one date.

"How's your shake?" he asked.

I swallowed my last sip and said, "It's delicious. How's your—" I cringed.

Had I really almost asked him about his Pepsi?

Fighting a smile, he said, "I think I should've ordered a shake, too. Because it does look really good." He shrugged. "But I'm more of a strawberry shake guy."

I placed my sweating glass on the table. "I'm a chocolate girl. All the way."

Okay. Better.

"So Abby Brewster." He laughed. "Way different character than Marty."

I caught a drip of condensation sliding down the glass with my right index finger. "Officer O'Hara. Way different character than Tom the Jock."

We shared a quick laugh, and I rubbed my damp finger against my thumb.

"Yeah. Fun character." He leaned forward. "I shouldn't tell you this, but..." His face flushed. "You looked really cute in those pajamas you wore. During the slumber party scene?"

My face became as warm as his looked, and I broke our eye contact.

Shoot, shoot, shoot. Heavy flirting was not part of the Project Dating Spree plan.

What were the chances, off all the cute boys at Pacifica Academy, my first bachelor would be someone who seemed to *like me, like me*? And remembered how I looked in my cutesy, pink, summer pajamas months ago?

I needed to take control of this date. This conversation.

"Thank you," I mumbled, but still not looking at him. Though he probably wanted me to comment on how good he'd looked in the show, I asked, "Where do you want to go to college?"

His face returned to its normal color and disappointment filled his eyes. But it had to, without question, be this way.

He sat back. "Santa Barbara. The campus is crawling distance from the beach. You?"

I picked up my spoon and twisted it back and forth. "San Francisco State." Because a state school was all we could afford.

"Staying here. Huh." He nodded once. "I figured you for someone who'd want to go to a school down south. Like LA? Being in the middle of *the* acting world?"

In truth, I wanted to go to UCLA. Because of their phenomenal theater program. But that school and career were not in my stars. "Acting's really just a creative outlet." I dropped my spoon to pick up my shake. "And San Francisco State's a good school."

"Yeah. Totally. And I get what you said about acting. So what are you going to study?"

I took a sip, then said, "Literature, with a minor in theater." Just because I couldn't go to a fancy school with a phenomenal theater program didn't mean I had to give up my creative outlet. And San Francisco had a great community-theater scene.

His blue eyes brightened. "You like to read. Something else we have in common."

I stared into my glass.

Not even a good sign he was keeping track of what we had in common, and not close to the Barrett Wagner I'd expected tonight. Had I misunderstood his serial dating? Could he actually *want* a girlfriend and just hadn't connected with other girls?

The guilt returned and tugged my conscience.

Maybe I should've taken Noah seriously and interviewed him first.

I cleared my throat. "I love reading. What do you want to study?"

"History." He picked up his Pepsi and took a quick swallow. "It's my favorite subject." He set his glass down. "But it wouldn't fit with my parents' plan." He frowned. "They're lawyers and want me to be a lawyer."

That, too, tugged me, since it was clear he *didn't* want to be a lawyer.

Gratitude at the fact Mom had never pushed her love of literature on me filled me up. At the same time, this conversation had turned in the direction of way too personal. But I still felt the need to ask, "What do you want to do?"

"Teach." He laughed. "But college. I couldn't deal with what our teachers deal with."

I laughed, too. But more out of surprise at Barrett's confession. Or confessions. He'd never struck me as a bookworm into History who wanted to teach. Probably because I'd only ever seen the performer side of him.

"That's very cool. And my mom's a literature professor at the city college and loves it."

He hesitated, then asked, "So is it just you and your mom?"

No doubt his way of asking, *Where's your dad*?

I held on to a sigh, then went back to sipping my milkshake that was now almost gone. "Yep." He didn't need to know anything about my absent brother. Or Russell Harrington, our "father." He apparently didn't know anything about my grandpa, either. Which meant I really did have the best friends ever.

He nodded at my simple answer.

And rule eight. Keep the convo neutral.

A waitress then appeared with our food.

Thank you, thank you, thank you.

I set my glass down after she placed my salad, with extra red onions, in front of me. Between the chocolate milkshake and extra onions, Barrett wouldn't try a thing.

* * *

Thirty minutes into the action movie about superheroes, Barrett shifted closer to the wide armrest, separating us. A gigantic cup of Pepsi sat in the cupholder. He'd offered to buy me a drink and popcorn, but the milkshake and extra red onions, which had seemed like such a good idea at the time, were twisting inside my stomach.

I tried to concentrate on the movie I'd chosen for its non-romantic elements. But now he had his left arm and hand on my side of the Pepsi.

I shifted a bit closer to the empty seat on my left side.

Surely he could sense I didn't want to hold hands. Or do anything else. And what about the milkshake and onions? Seriously. Girls didn't drink and eat stuff like that if they planned on kissing a boy. It's not like I'd popped gum in my mouth, either. I didn't even have any gum.

An explosion in the movie lit up and practically shook the theater, and Barrett started to raise his arm.

Oh, my God, oh, my God, this could not be happening.

I leaned toward him, and he lowered his arm so quickly his elbow hit the armrest.

I mumbled, "I have to use the bathroom." I stood before he could reply and, keeping my posture hunched down, carefully avoided other moviegoers reclining in their seats.

I hadn't removed my crossbody phone case when we sat down in our seats in the *middle* of the theater. And now would be the perfect time to send my mid-date text.

How was I going to get out of this? I couldn't avoid his arm all night in a crowded movie theater. Maybe my friends would have a solution.

Rule nine. Absolutely no more movie dates.

I scurried to the closest women's bathroom that wasn't

too busy because of all the movies running, darted into a stall and locked the door. I then pulled out my phone.

So 30 minutes into the movie and Barrett's making a move. Help!

I leaned against the door and closed my eyes.

Inhale to count four...exhale to count eight...repeat...

My stomach gurgled. So much for chocolate milkshakes and extra red onions.

My phone buzzed, and I opened my eyes.

Heather had texted, *Wow. He doesn't waste time. Where are you?*

In a bathroom stall. What should I do?

I told you this would happen.

I glared at Noah's *not* helpful reply as *Your neurotic is showing* appeared. And I snarled at his second not helpful response.

Then Heather's, *You can't hide all night. But I suggest no more movies* popped up.

I released a loud sigh, then typed, *I know that. And, yes, no more movies. Rule 9.*

Tell him you got sick. Guys take girls puking on dates seriously came from Liam.

My eyes widened.

I wasn't exactly feeling well, so it wouldn't be a total lie.

Noah texted, *He's right. He'll run red lights to get you home.*

I like it. Will save Barrett's feelings, too. But what's Rule 8?

I smiled at Heather's message and replied, *Liam, you're the best. Will tell you Rule 8 later. Text you when I'm home.*

My shoulders slumped forward.

Okay. Crisis averted. And all because of Liam, surprisingly enough. But I couldn't help but wonder if he'd actually been on a date where the girl did get sick.

I shook that thought off and went into my thread with Barrett that began when we were planning our date. That would absolutely not be ending the way he clearly wanted. Still, it had to be this way. And he deserved a girl who wanted a cute, nice boyfriend.

I texted Barrett, *I'm really sick and need to go home. Can you meet me out front?* I then added the sad face emoji, which was genuine. Because I did like Barrett and hoped all this wouldn't affect the play or show choir or anything else. But bachelor number two needed to be in no way connected to Pacifica Academy's theater world. I would also need to do *much* better dating-history research on the next boy.

Chapter Seven

I walked into the choir room Monday morning and stopped. Barrett had taken Taryn's seat beside me, and his face lit up when he saw me.

Okay. Hadn't been expecting this, either. Especially after how Saturday night ended. But I gave him my Barbie smile and headed for my seat.

I could totally handle this.

I dropped my backpack and sat. That's when I noticed Barrett taking Taryn's seat had made her decide, I assumed, to sit next to Liam. Which was a good thing. I needed to start working on getting those two together.

"Feeling better?" Barrett asked. "You didn't look so good when I dropped you off."

I'd reached deep into my actress side and pulled off the performance of my life on the rapid drive home; Noah had been right. I'd also practically vaulted from the SUV when he pulled up to my building. Because I desperately "needed the bathroom."

I swung my eyes toward Liam, watching us with an

emotionless expression. And I wanted to smile at his acting ability.

"Did you two go out on a *date*?" Taryn asked with a playful smile.

"Wait," Sloane said, putting down her phone. "Who's dating?" She leaned forward to look at Barrett, then me. "You two?"

Oh, my God, oh, my God. I didn't need Sloane taking this false info to her deranged bestie, Brandy. "It was one date. *No one's* dating," I clarified. I focused on Barrett, whose eyes had dimmed at my words. But I'd spoken the truth. "And I'm feeling much better. Thank you." I smiled tightly. "Chocolate milkshakes and red onions don't go together."

Liam lowered his head, while struggling to keep a straight face.

Barrett laughed. "Yeah. Your salad was covered with them. I've never met a girl who liked onions that much."

Now Liam's shoulders were shaking with quiet laughter.

We needed a subject change. Immediately.

"Well, I think you two would make a cute couple," Taryn added.

Not at all what I had in mind.

I eyed Barrett, whose face had brightened again, then I glanced at Liam, no longer laughing. Or smiling. Because he, of course, knew the truth.

"Okay, everyone," Mrs. Chaplin loudly said from where she stood at the edge of the mini-stage. "We need to talk about what we'll be doing in choir before we start preparing for our Christmas show."

I didn't like Mrs. Chaplin. Not too many of us did. But her timing made me want to leap over the seats so I could throw my arms around her in a gratitude hug.

"Mr. Hathaway and I met before the school year started," she continued, "and he thought it would be a good idea if I added another choir concert to the calendar this year and moving forward." Her nose turned upward, making it clear she didn't agree with our principal. "He thought it would be nice if the student body saw all of you more than twice a year." She gave us a ghost of a smile. "Because you're so talented."

I exchanged wide-eyed glances with Liam, Taryn, and Barrett.

Mrs. Chaplin rarely complimented us, so hearing something like that from our principal made me tingle with pride, since we did work our butts off for her. Especially in the musicals. And the tingle of pride turned into excitement at hearing we'd be doing something new this year that would have nothing to do with Christmas or the big, end-of-year spring show.

"I put much time and energy into the musicals," she declared.

Liam looked sideways at me and his eyes rolled upward.

"As such, we decided to add an October show for the students only—but your parents *are* welcome to attend—that'll be Friday, the nineteenth. We have a lot of work to do. And that's what we'll be focused on until we start preparing for Christmas."

I smiled as my show choir classmates started chattering. Usually we spent the first month or so of school focused on various, really old, boring songs to exercise our voices.

"What's the theme of the show going to be?" Michael, a senior and baritone, asked.

He was also active in theater and had gotten Reverend Harper in the play.

"Please say Halloween. Because I can kill the 'Monster Mash'."

Almost everyone burst into laughter. Even Sloane snickered. Totally rare for her, too.

Mrs. Chaplin frowned at him. "That's good to know,

Michael. Thank you." Her face relaxed when she again focused on the class. "But that was a good question, since Mr. Hathaway also said he thought it would be best if we took a break from *the norm*." Her frown returned.

I sat up.

Could that mean we wouldn't have to sing show tunes?

"He would like this concert to feature appropriate music of *your* choosing, for the additional numbers, that can include mainstream songs."

Cheers and claps exploded around me, and I laughed. Now I wanted to find Mr. Hathaway and give him a gratitude hug. I absolutely loved show tunes. But after doing three spring shows devoted to that music genre, this was a huge, way early Christmas present wrapped in shiny paper with bright-red ribbon. The kind of gift a kid couldn't wait to open.

I shared an excited smile with Taryn, Liam, and Barrett.

"Which leads me to," she again loudly said, "you'll be join-ing, like usual, the concert choir for the bigger numbers of my choosing, which I'm in the process of deciding. The songs will complement the show's overall theme." She crossed her arms and sniffed.

Wow. Mrs. Chaplin's music snobbery was oozing off of her right now.

"But, as I said and like our other shows, you'll have the stage for the additional numbers and, to be *different*," she continued, but with an edge to her voice, "pair up for a duet. Or a small-group, a cappella number. No solos. And this fall show will count as your midterm."

More excited rumbling filled the classroom, and I zeroed in on Liam and Taryn. Then pictured them singing a super cute duet.

Too perfect.

"After you pair up or create a small, a cappella group, your next assignment is to choose an *appropriate* song that must be approved by me before you can start rehearsing." She paused, then said, "Are there any questions?"

Enthusiastic conversations exploded around me. Everyone probably already focused on finding their duet partner or putting together a small, a cappella group. Which sounded like so much fun, too. A soprano, alto, tenor, baritone. Easy enough.

"So does that mean if I choose the a cappella group, we *can* do the 'Monster Mash'?"

Laugher filled the choir room at Michael's question. He'd be a great choice for the baritone. And would probably be a lot of fun to work with.

"No. You cannot choose that song," Mrs. Chaplin answered with a flat expression.

Michael's face fell with what looked liked genuine disappointment.

"You'll have the rest of the period to find your partner or group. Have this figured out by tomorrow's class. Song choices are due Wednesday. Submit lyrics, as well."

She went to her piano, and as I stood to head right for Michael, Barrett faced me.

"Wanna pair up and do a duet?" he asked.

I froze, my butt hovering over my chair. And I knew I had to look like a deer about to face its terrible fate with an oncoming car...yuck.

I slowly lowered myself back to my seat.

Shoot, shoot, shoot. I never should've chosen him as bachelor number one. But it's not like I'd known he *liked* me, liked me.

I pushed my hair behind my ears, but not in a flirty, demure way, and turned toward him. His eyes were so wide with hope, too, that the guilt pushing down on me, to the point I dropped my eyes to my lap, made me feel obligated to say yes. Just to make the lousy feeling go away.

"Or you can pair up with me."

I lifted my head and whipped it in Liam's direction.

"Two old friends finally singing together?" His eyes locked on mine. "I think we'd be great together. What do you think?"

I gaped at him as I tried to find a response.

What was going on here? Two ridiculously cute boys wanted to do a duet with me? And after everything that had happened in the spring?

I knew I should've felt flattered. Elated. But I didn't want or need this attention. Liam needed to pair up with Taryn. And there had to be a girl in here who would love pairing up with our Tom the Jock.

"I think *we'd* be great," Barrett countered, glaring at Liam. "And I asked her first."

My face burned.

Wow. Didn't need them "fighting" over me, either.

I refocused on Barrett while letting go of joining an a cappella group.

Sloane leaned forward. "I'll pair up with you, and we'll be great."

Barrett's face paled and he swallowed.

My already loaded conscience couldn't allow snotty Sloane to pair up with sweet Barrett. He absolutely didn't deserve that torture.

"I think Barrett should pair up with Taryn," Liam offered with a smile in her direction.

I wanted to grip his throat and squeeze until those dimples fell off his face.

She lifted her shoulders. "That'd be cool. But I get if you really want to be with Maddie."

Finally finding my voice, I stood and said, "Mrs. Chaplin, can Liam and I go out in the hallway and talk where it's quieter?" I felt everyone's eyes, including Liam's. I had spoken loudly. But I couldn't exactly lunge for his throat in here.

She nodded distractedly as she focused on the papers she held.

I went for the doorway, and without waiting for him. When I reached the deserted hallway, I walked a few steps, crossed my arms, and turned.

He took a step back and smiled. I guess he'd been right on my heels.

I leaned forward and hissed, "That cute smile of yours won't work! What are you doing?"

He also leaned forward. "Saving you. Again."

I narrowed my eyes. "Arrogance is beneath you, Liam Langley. And I wanted to be in an a cappella group."

"Okay." He nodded. "Then let's go join an a cappella group."

I groaned. "No, *you* need to pair up with Taryn."

He leaned back, crossed his arms, and frowned. "Why is that, Maddie Harrington?"

My arms fell to my sides, and I tilted my head back to stare at the ceiling.

Inhale to count four...exhale to count eight...

"I don't need your help getting a date, if that's what you're thinking."

He'd sounded a tad on the offended side, and I lowered my head.

He stared at me, still frowning.

"I just think you two would make a great couple. Is that so bad?"

He continued staring me. For a second, followed by another. And I sighed. Taryn was so pretty, nice, and talented. Why wouldn't he want to go out with her?

"Don't you have enough going on with the play and *Project Dating Spree*?" He shook his head. "Do you really need to add matchmaker to your to-do list?"

"You don't have to say it like that!" I snapped. And he and

Noah's attitude toward my mission was really beginning to tick me off. "I appreciate you helping me out Saturday night. But it's like you said. You guys are *not* my keepers. And forget I said anything about Taryn."

He looked at the floor, and I moved around him.

"Maddie, what's the big deal about doing a duet with me?" he softly asked.

I stopped, he raised his head, and our eyes caught.

Something flickered deep inside me. At the way his dark eyes pierced mine with an intensity and vulnerability I'd never seen from him. From any boy, for that matter.

"I really think we'd be great together," he murmured, without breaking our eye contact. "Will you at least think about it? Mrs. Chaplin said we have until tomorrow."

I held our gaze for a few more seconds, then looked at a spot over his shoulder.

He wasn't asking anything unreasonable. Out of all the years in show choir and being in three musicals, we'd never sung together. Just the two of us. He did have a great voice, too. Smooth. Powerful. But not in a booming way. We probably would sound pretty good together.

"I'm going to take your silence as a"—he dramatically cleared his throat—"why, yes, Liam," he said in a high-pitched, girly voice. "I'll think about it."

I tilted my head left. "I don't sound like that."

"Are you sure?" he said in *his* voice. "We don't sound the way we hear ourselves." He smiled. "I hear a British accent when I talk, but I know that's not what everyone else hears."

I rolled my eyes. "Yes, Liam. Even though I *wanted* to be in an a cappella group, I'll think about it."

His smile grew, and we headed for the choir room.

It was the least I could do since he had "saved" me Saturday night.

"So Barrett and I did decide to pair up," Taryn quietly said the moment we sat. She glanced at me. "I had to rescue him."

I noticed Sloane's empty seat and my eyes flitted to Barrett, glaring at me.

Another round of guilt pushed me down, and I slouched in my seat. Maybe Barrett and I wouldn't be okay, and I slid a bit lower.

"Sloane wouldn't leave me alone after *you* guys left," Barrett stated. "Did you two work everything out in the hallway?" he crabbily added.

"Man, lighten up," Liam said with a grimace. "This is supposed to be fun."

Barrett responded by standing and walking over to his good friend, Michael.

Definitely needed to tweak some things in Project Dating Spree.

Taryn gave me a half-smile. "He really wanted to be with you."

"Taryn, don't listen to him," Liam grumbled. "You have a great voice. He won't regret pairing up with you."

She smiled shyly at him, which he returned.

I again couldn't understand why he had no interest in Taryn Marshall.

Chapter Eight

"Well," Heather said after swallowing her chip, "I think it's sweet Barrett wanted to do a duet with you. But, yeah, new rule. No more theater or choir boys."

I'd just finished telling Heather and Noah about what happened in show choir.

I peeked at Barrett, sitting at the opposite end of our table with Michael. He hadn't looked at me since getting up and walking away during class. But I planned on talking to him before or after rehearsal today. It's not like I'd meant to blow him off. In fact, it was Liam and Sloane's fault I'd never had the chance to tell Barrett I'd wanted to be in an a cappella group.

I pulled my eyes from him to pick up my Diet Coke.

"But I agree with Liam," Heather continued. "Your voices would sound great together."

I took a quick drink and set the can down.

I still hadn't made a decision about being his duet partner. And, thankfully, he'd chosen to sit with his best friend, the girlfriend, and other friends at lunch today.

"So how many rules are we up to now?" Heather asked.

"Too. Many." Noah gave me a hard look. "Which should be another blinding clue your project is already getting Out. Of. Control."

I glared at him, beyond sick of his bad attitude. "Why is this bothering you so much?"

"Because it isn't right," he said in a lowered voice. "Now Barrett's hurt and pissed at you. And he's my friend, too."

I crossed my arms. "Him liking me was an unexpected twist and *won't* happen again. So would you relax? The other boys I choose won't be connected to theater or choir. Meaning they won't know me. And I can't give up on my mission." I had a point to prove to myself and everyone else. I ripped my eyes from Noah's to glance at Heather. "We're up to ten rules." But saying that out loud made me flinch. Ten rules did seem like a bit much for a dating project.

Noah groaned and went back to his enormous sandwich.

"Well," Heather said, eyeing Noah, "I already have non-theater bachelor two in mind. And we need to find you a bachelor number three to bring to my party."

I laughed. "You're right." Her eighteenth birthday party was next Saturday night. "I definitely have to make your party a Project Dating Spree date."

Noah sat back. "You two are nuts. I think I'm going to go sit with Liam and them."

His comment hung in the air. And anger replaced my humor as it wound itself around my core. My eyes became slits, and he lowered his gaze to the table.

"I can't believe you just said that," I said through gritted teeth.

Heather started reading the back of her little bag of chips.

"I'm sorry," he mumbled. Then he lifted his head, but instead of an apology, I saw confusion. And concern. "You're one of my best friends. But Shane's also my friend. So are

Kassidy and J.R. And I know you don't want to hear this—" He sighed. "Natalie's really cool. And I consider her a friend, too."

I stiffened in my chair as his words scorched my insides.

Okay. He hated Project Dating Spree. And he hadn't said anything else I didn't know. Including being friends with the "really cool" girlfriend. But he hadn't needed to say any of it.

"Since you feel that way and clearly despise Project Dating Spree," I enunciated, "no one's stopping you from eating with them."

Noah shook his head. "Maddie, I don't want to eat with them. But this project of yours..." He shrugged. "A friend has already gotten hurt, and I'm worried you might get hurt."

Silence fell around us. And a burst of laughter came from the other end of our table.

I glanced sideways to find Barrett laughing hard with Michael.

"Noah," Heather quietly began, "you're being really sweet. But does Barrett look like a guy who's upset because a girl he liked didn't like *him* that way?"

More laughter erupted from their end.

Noah huffed. "You got me there." He looked at her, then me. "But no matter what girls think, guys do have feelings. They're just better at hiding them."

Fine. That was fair. But not earth-shattering news, either.

"Look," he said, "you know how I feel about this project, so I'll start keeping my mouth shut. But be careful and stick to your *ten* rules. Okay?"

I relaxed into my seat and uncrossed my arms.

His big, soft heart was in the right place. How could I stay angry with him for being a concerned friend? Though he absolutely hadn't needed to mention his friendship with the "really cool" girlfriend. "Noah, I promise I'll stick to my rules." I sent him a soft smile. "And thank you for being such a good friend."

He nodded, picked up his sandwich, and continued eating.

"Great!" Heather sat up. "So, Madeline, what are your thoughts on politicians?"

I squinted at her. "Um...they do more harm than good?"

Noah laughed after swallowing his bite of sandwich.

"Have you ever thought about dating one? Specifically a president?"

Realization hit, and I leaned toward her. "You think Tyler Bennett should be bachelor number two?"

She giggled. "Why not? He's never had a girlfriend, is the leader of student council, and isn't terrible looking. He's" — she rapidly snapped her fingers— "nerd cute. It's the glasses."

I pursed my lips as I pictured Tyler. Not too much taller than me. Solid, but in a he-takes-care-of-himself way. Light-brown hair. And eyes? He also wore flattering, rectangle-shaped glasses. He was really smart, too. Would probably be our valedictorian.

I frowned.

Would I be able to keep up with his intelligence? I made really good grades, but worked hard for them. Then again, his intelligence might keep us from talking too much. And rule nine was keep the convo neutral. Or was that rule eight? I needed to write down the newest rules during study hall.

"So?" Heather asked. "Maybe you can catch him before lunch tomorrow."

I absently nodded. "He's perfect." I slid my eyes to her. "I'll really have to work my brown-eyed girl magic on him. I haven't spoken to Tyler since freshman English. He was a little socially awkward. But nice." We didn't exactly run in the same social sphere. But the exciting thought of a challenge shot through me, and I sat up. "Okay. Tyler Bennett it is." Hopefully.

* * *

I made a beeline for Barrett after Mr. Peters dismissed us from another funny day of reading lines in a circle on stage. And today we'd made it well into act two.

He grabbed his backpack he'd dropped near the front row seats.

As he hoisted it onto his right shoulder, I said, "Hey."

A completely not brilliant opening. But he hadn't looked at me once during rehearsal. Which meant Noah, darn him, was probably right about Barrett masking his hurt feelings.

The heavy guilt I'd felt during show choir returned to my shoulders. At the same time, I honestly hadn't meant to hurt his feelings.

He turned and adjusted his backpack. "Yeah?"

I stepped closer to him, then glanced left. Where the ex stood at the end of the row while talking with Liam, Noah, Kassidy, and J.R. I also caught Taryn and Michael already heading up the aisle toward the auditorium doors with a few more of our castmates who had smaller parts. Heather was still on stage, and talking with Mr. Peters. So this was as private as it would get.

"Are we good?" I smiled. "I'm sorry about what happened in show choir. And what I never got the chance to tell you is that I actually wanted to be in an a cappella group."

His face relaxed and he sort of smiled. "So you're not doing a duet with Liam?"

Shoot. I had no idea how to answer his question. Except be honest. But I had a feeling my honesty might not help this awkward situation. "Well, I'm not sure. I may have lost my chance to be in an a cappella group because Liam and I were talking out in the hallway."

"Maddie, why did you ask me out?" he asked with a deep frown.

Wow. Another question I hadn't expected. And I sure couldn't answer this one honestly.

"You were all flirty, then acted so...weird on the date." He dropped his eyes to the floor. "I figured you were nervous. But then you made it clear to Sloane and Taryn we *weren't* dating."

Now it was my turn to frown. "Because one date doesn't mean we're dating."

"But I want to date you," he mumbled. "You're really cute, and...I like you." He shrugged. "We have things in common, too. Like we love reading. And theater."

Oh, *no*. How could this have happened? After one Project Dating Spree date? And I had no choice but to let him down as nicely as I could. But nothing would stop him from being hurt.

The thought of being the cause of his hurt made my body become limp. To the point I almost needed to sit.

Inhale to count four...exhale to count eight...

He lifted his head and stepped back. "But you obviously don't feel the same way."

I stared at him, almost desperately. "Barrett, I like you. Really. I'm just not interested in anything serious right now." All of it the truth, too. "I guess I should've made that more clear."

"Yeah," he muttered. "That would've been helpful." He turned and stalked up the aisle.

I quietly moaned as he yanked open an auditorium door and disappeared behind it.

Oh, my *God*. Had I lost another friend? It's not like Barrett and I had ever been super close. Not like I was with Noah and Liam, and had been with the ex. But I hated the thought of us being at odds. Especially since we were in show choir together and in this play.

Liam appeared at my right side, his eyes full of concern.

And I wanted to moan again, because I was getting sick of that look.

"What happened? Is he still pissed about this morning?"

I faced him. "No. And you and Noah will be happy to know Project Dating Spree is off to a pretty rough start."

He stayed silent. A good choice, too.

I took a head-cleansing breath and added, "It'll get better, though. Because my next bachelor is Tyler Bennett. Just as an FYI since you are a part of rule five."

He released a sigh that sounded on the verge of agitation. "You don't have to do this."

I rolled my eyes. "I can't even deal. Not you *and* Noah in one day." I turned and headed up the same aisle as Barrett, but paused to pick up my backpack sitting by the third row.

"Okay," he said, catching up to me. "You win. But, like Noah, I'm here if you need me."

"Thanks," I grumbled, not sounding close to thankful. "Did you need something?"

When we reached the auditorium doors, he opened the right one and held it for me. Which made me smile at him.

"I need you," he answered as he followed me into the lobby.

My steps slowed at the way he said that, and he laughed. A bit nervously, too.

"I mean, I *needed* to ask if you made up your mind? About the duet?"

He fell into step beside me as we headed back into the school and toward the main entrance and exit. The auditorium lobby doors were bolted, except on show days and nights.

I eyed him. And found the stinker trying to use his smile

that must've gotten him out of so much trouble as a little kid. It had probably earned him some dates, too.

"I told you that smile won't work on me."

"Yeah. But you also admitted you thought it was *'cute'*."

I fought a grin. But as we approached the doors, a thought hit me. "Duets are almost always love songs."

He again opened a door for me. "Okay. But singers do duets all the time with people they aren't in love with. So that argument stinks so bad I can smell it."

A giggle escaped when we walked outside into the sunshine. Because he was right.

"What if I asked you again, but" —he cleared his throat— "in my best British accent?" he said, sounding like he was from England. "Girls are complete suckers for accents."

I shook my head, and when we reached the sidewalk, I stopped. Along with all the other reasons it made sense to say yes, there'd never be a dull moment working with him. It's not like Liam could be considered boring. So I sighed and said, "Fine. *You* win."

He waggled his eyebrows. "I knew the accent would work. Talk about songs tomorrow?"

I nodded once. "Absolutely."

He went right, I went left, and a smile teased the corners of my mouth as I replayed him talking in his British accent.

Yep. Girls were suckers when it came to cute boys with accents. Even fake ones.

Chapter Nine

I peeked around the corner to see if Tyler was at his locker, but I didn't see him. A good sign I hadn't missed him since we'd just been dismissed for lunch. Heather had suggested yesterday I should try to catch him now. It would also be the best time to catch him because I had to be at rehearsal right after school.

I wasn't exactly sure how I'd convince super-smart Tyler Bennett to go on a date with me. Especially since I hadn't spoken to him in so long. My sudden interest would probably surprise him. But that's where the brown-eyed girl magic would come in handy.

As I waited, groups of kids passed me on their way to their lockers or down to the cafeteria. Including CruElla and her only evil sidekick, Quinn. I'd hardly seen them since the school year started. Which was beyond fine with me. And their eyes never strayed in my direction as they strutted by me.

I somehow stopped myself from reverting to first grade and sticking out my tongue.

"What'cha doin' there *little lady*?"

I glanced over my shoulder at Liam, his face bright with humor. "Nice John Wayne impersonation."

He laughed. "Thanks. But I'm impressed. Most girls don't know who he is."

"He's my grandpa's favorite actor." *Or was.*

His eyes warmed. "How's your grandpa doing?"

Only Heather and Noah knew how bad he'd gotten since the spring. The three of us had spent a lot of time together during the summer. And I only wanted them to know, especially since I now knew I'd become "clingy" after my grandpa had to move in with us.

I'd never again allow myself to lean on anyone but my mom and best friends.

That thought caused me to raise my chin and say, "He's the same. Thanks for asking."

His gaze became piercing. As if he was trying to see into my head. To find the truth. And something about that gaze made my breathing slow.

He nodded, then stood next me. He stood so close I smelled his mint gum and something fresh. Boy fresh. Maybe his soap? And the same flicker from yesterday, while we talked about being duet partners in the hallway, returned. But heat came with this flicker.

What was wrong with me? Liam was my good friend. Nothing more.

I leaned away from him and looked to see if Tyler had appeared at his locker. No sign of him. Yet.

"Who are you looking for?" Liam quietly asked, close to my ear.

Goosebumps covered my arms beneath my sweater. I took a tiny step forward. "Tyler. I want to catch him before he heads downstairs for lunch."

He stepped away from mc. Thankfully. And he shouldn't have been standing so close to begin with.

"Maddie, do you even *know* Tyler?"

I wrinkled my nose at his exasperated tone. "No. And that's why he'll make the perfect bachelor number two. There will be no chance of any feelings getting hurt this time." A huge priority since Barrett was back to ignoring me. Hopefully he'd get over it by going on a date with another girl who wanted a boyfriend. I leaned forward. "Don't you dare start, either. I'm getting enough nasty from Noah about all of this. And you said yesterday you'd leave it alone."

He ran a hand through his hair. "You're right. Fine. So are you busy after rehearsal? I have an idea for a song, but I was hoping you'd come over to my place so you could hear it."

I peered at him. "What is it? And why can't you just download it to your phone and play it for me later?"

His face became cherry red. "Well, I don't want to do that because you might not like it." He shrugged. "It won't take long, and I don't live that far from here. And I know you don't, either. I could even walk you home when we're done." He paused to take a breath. "What's the big deal?" he mumbled, speaking to the floor.

I glanced around the corner. And there stood Tyler, finally at his locker.

I looked back at Liam, now watching me, his dark eyes almost pleading.

I inhaled, a tad on the shaky side, and said, "It's not a big deal. You just surprised me. Your place after rehearsal is fine." I smiled. "But you don't have to walk me home. I carry mace on my key chain. At my mom's insistence."

He cracked a smile, and I adjusted my backpack straps.

"I'll see you later." I turned from him and headed right for bachelor number two.

As I approached Tyler, forcing his backpack into his locker, I noticed his books and notebooks were crammed onto the two shelves with loose, crumpled paper trying to escape.

The bottom of his locker looked no better, if not worse, because of all the snack wrappers.

I guess genius and incredibly messy disorganization did go hand-in-hand.

I walked up to him and, with a huge smile, said, "Hi, Tyler!" And of course I'd sounded like Barbie. But super perky could work to my advantage.

He stopped fighting with his backpack to look at me, then used his forefinger to push his glasses onto the bridge of his nose. That's when I noticed his eyes were a chestnut brown. He really wasn't too bad looking. Like Heather said, "nerd cute."

"Hi, Maddie," he replied with a trace of wariness. "What's going on?"

Perfect. He remembered my name.

I leaned against the locker next to his and smiled softly. "Nothing. Just wanted to—" That's when an idea hit. How to get him to go on a date with me. Unfortunately, it would include a *tiny* bit of lying. But I was on a mission and what he didn't know wouldn't hurt him. "I just wanted to tell you I'm so happy you got elected president of student council. I voted for you," I added in a flirty whisper. Totally not lies, either.

He smiled, but it seemed arrogant. "Thanks. But it was an easy win since Ella's a bitch."

Okay. Although what he said was nothing but the truth, I hadn't expected Tyler Bennett to drop a bad word. And so easily.

"I'm a little surprised to hear you did vote for me. Because you were in her lip sync completion routine."

Yep. Another stupid choice I would probably never live down.

I laughed. But it sounded more like I'd barked.

Chirping. Barking. Now I needed to work on two animal sounds.

"Yeah." I rolled my eyes. "I never should've been in that competition with her and Quinn." Also totally not a lie. "I'm so glad I didn't vote for her." It had also been super fun seeing her shocked, almost humiliated expression when the results had been announced at the end of last school year.

We'd somehow gotten third place in the stupid competition. But that and Ella's campaign to be the first female president of student council hadn't replaced the fact she was the snottiest, cruelest girl in this school.

I opened my mouth to launch into the next phase of this conversation, but saw the ex and the girlfriend. Walking with their fingers linked as they approached the stairs to go down to the cafeteria. Smiling, he lowered his head and said something that made her burst into laughter.

I narrowed my eyes as they, completely lost in each other, headed down the stairs.

He'd made me laugh like that, too. Especially when we'd been friends.

I hadn't seen *them* very much, either, since school started. I'd never noticed her at his locker. Probably because my locker wasn't far from his. I also always avoided looking at their table in the cafeteria, and there hadn't been any sight of her before rehearsals.

Still, the sting from losing him...his friendship...made me take a sharp inhale.

"So is that why you came over to talk to me?"

Tyler's voice caused me to blink, and I dragged my eyes back to him.

Focus, focus, *focus*.

I brought back my huge smile. "Actually, I was really, really hoping I could sit down with you and talk about politics." I stopped myself from cringing at my first white lie and demurely pushed my hair behind my ears. "I'm thinking about getting into politics in college. Maybe even going to law school?" Oh, my God, oh, my God. I couldn't believe I was lying to this nice, innocent boy who did like politics.

He frowned. "Really? You've never struck me as a girl who would be interested in politics or law school or anything like that. Because of the whole acting and singing thing?"

Acting and singing thing?

I bristled, though I kept my smile in place.

"No offense," he added, then pushed his glasses up.

Clearly Tyler Bennett's social skills hadn't improved since freshman year.

My smile became brittle. "None taken."

"It takes guts to get on a stage and perform. I couldn't do that. And you're not bad."

Maybe socially awkward Tyler hadn't been such a great choice after all. But I couldn't give up since I'd come this far. "Thanks. So about that chat? Are you free Saturday night?"

His eyebrows shot to the ceiling and he drew back. "Are you suggesting we go on a date? This Saturday?"

I batted my eyes twice. "Sure. If that's what you want to call it."

He pushed his glasses up again, and I wanted to suggest he buy a pair of glasses that fit him better. But I simply smiled and batted my eyes two more times.

He angled his head forward and squinted. "Do you need to borrow my eyedrops?"

Oh. Wow. Okay. But if he agreed to this, at least I wouldn't have to worry about him making a move. In fact, I wasn't entirely certain Tyler knew the meaning of that phrase.

He reached into his locker, withdrew his lunch bag, and shut the door. "I always go bowling Saturday nights. But you can join me if you want and we can talk."

I stared at him.

What was happening here? Because nothing about this felt close to an actual date. And bowling? Really? I'd gone bowling once, in seventh grade, and only because it had been our end-of-year party.

"Are we done? I'm starving."

"Um...yeah. But shouldn't we exchange phone numbers?"

He grinned. "Right. Good point." He reached into his right pants pocket, pulled out his phone, and punched in his password. "Add yourself to my contacts, and I'll send you a text later."

With wide eyes, I took his phone.

This was the last time I'd let Heather choose my bachelors.

Chapter Ten

"**B**owling?" Liam said as we approached his front door. Then he burst into laughter.

We stopped, and I wrinkled my nose. "I shouldn't have told you, either. And I only did because *you* asked."

Noah had reacted in the same way after I'd caught him and Heather up at lunch. Liam had again sat at the other table.

He pulled on a straight face. "Do you even know how to bowl?"

"I've bowled." I shrugged. "Once. It's not like it's brain surgery."

He pulled his house keys from his pocket, then brought his eyes to mine. And stared long and hard at me. "No, but you have nothing in common with Tyler Bennett."

I turned from him and his penetrating stare that had lasted a bit too long for my comfort level. "That's not what Project Dating Spree is about and you know it. And there's nothing wrong with that." I pointed at the door. "Can you play this song for me? I have a ton of homework, and I'm still learning Abby's lines."

He paused, then said, "Maddie, you're really killing it as Aunt Abby."

I glanced sideways at him, and he gave me his dimpled smile. Which should be considered hazardous to a girl's mental health.

My shoulders and back relaxed as I fought a grin.

"As someone who's pretty good at accents and impersonations," he continued, as if he were a businessman, "you're nailing Abby's sweet, elderly voice. With the perfect touch of clueless insanity behind it."

His compliment made my insides flush. And to the point the heat reached my cheeks.

"Thank you, Teddy Brewster." I dropped my eyes to the floor. "I am working really hard and like hearing that." In fact, everyone in the cast was nailing their parts. Not surprising, but my castmates being so amazingly good made me want to be that much better.

"You're welcome. And you're going to be incredible." He leaned forward. "Sorry for laughing at you about the bowling."

I nodded, but I also couldn't blame him, or Noah, for laughing. Bowling wasn't exactly on my social activities list.

"Does the nod mean you'll still keep me in the loop while you're on these dates?" He turned and put the key in the lock. "I mean, you might need my genius again."

I huffed while I remembered how my date with Tyler came together. But I did appreciate Liam wanting to still be a part of my safety rule. "I'll definitely keep you in the loop, but it's Tyler Bennett."

"Yeah." He followed me into the condo. "But he's still a guy and you're a really—girl."

I looked sharply at him. And he swiftly turned to shut the door. But before I could question his weird comment, two cats strolled up to us.

I tore my eyes from him to focus on the smaller, fluffy gray one, which sat on its butt and stared up at me. The white, bigger one with short hair rubbed its body against my left ankle with so much zest it toppled onto my foot.

Liam faced me and pointed at the cat, now gazing up at me through blue eyes. "That's Frank Sinatra."

The affectionate kitty started purring. Pretty loudly, too.

"He really likes girls."

I bent down to scratch Frank Sinatra's face. And he purred to the point his body vibrated.

"The one kind've glaring at you right now is Ava Gardner."

I swung my eyes to the gray cat watching me pet her mate, without blinking.

I gave Frank a final scratch and straightened. "Who named them?"

"My mom." He eyed me. "Did I forget to mention insanity runs in *my* family?"

I laughed.

Although we'd been friends since freshman year, I'd never been around Liam's family longer than quick hellos after play and choir performances.

His attention caught on someone coming up behind me, and I turned and found myself looking at Lucas, his identical twin brother. He had shorter hair and, because he'd long ago decided to be homeschooled, wore a white T-shirt and jeans. If not for the hairstyle and clothing differences, and one other significant difference, I wouldn't be able to tell them apart.

Lucas shot me that Langley brother smile, and I said, "Hey, Lucas. How are you?"

Liam had once told me his brother was really good at reading lips.

Lucas signed his response to his brother.

Liam rolled his eyes. "He's fine." He shrugged out of his backpack that he dropped on the floor near the door.

Lucas slapped Liam's upper arm with the back of his hand and impatiently gestured. As if he wanted his brother to continue.

Liam sighed. "And wants to know what you're doing here with his loser brother."

Before I could reply, Lucas signed something else. While wearing an impish smile.

I glanced at Liam.

His eyes widened and he rapidly signed back.

Okay. Something weird was going on here.

"Are you two talking about me? Because that's not cool." At that moment, Frank rolled off my foot and onto his paws.

"No. It's nothing," Liam replied while focused on his brother. "He's just being a *dick*."

Lucas released a quick, but loud laugh.

Frank sauntered down the hallway, and Ava watched me a few seconds longer before turning and following him.

"Where's Mom?"

Lucas signed, and Liam's face relaxed. "She's at the store, and he's going to his girlfriend's house." Then Liam signed while glaring at his brother, and without speaking. Again.

Lucas winked at me and waved goodbye, a little too innocently.

The second he left I crossed my arms. "*What* was that all about? Because I know you two were talking about me."

"Maddie, it was nothing. Really." Without looking at me, he slipped his hands into his pockets. "He thinks you're cute. That's all."

I leaned back, and my face burned at the surprising compliment. And at getting snarky with him. Them. But it's not like I'd known what they'd been saying. "That's so sweet." I smiled. "And you can tell him I think he's—"

Liam's head shot up.

Shoot, shoot, *shoot*.

Giving me a totally phony confused look, he angled his head forward. "Tell him what?"

Great. How was I going to get out of this hole I'd created because of my stupid, big mouth? I certainly couldn't finish my sentence.

"Maddie Harrington," he teased, "were you about to say you think my brother's cute?" He gave me a pretend serious look. "I hate to break it to you, but he's crazy about his girlfriend."

I narrowed my eyes. "Thanks for clarifying that."

"No problem. But I'm sure you've noticed we look a lot alike." He waggled his eyebrows. "And since you think *he's* cute— "

"Liam Langley, are you going to play that song for me or not?"

He laughed. "Yeah. Come on."

He headed straight, and I followed him.

I needed to watch what I said around him. Because he really was a stinker. But remembering the brotherly exchange between Liam and Lucas made my mind rewind to *my* close relationship with my brother. Before Bradley had left. With barely a backward glance.

Just like Russell had left *us* when I was a baby.

I clenched my teeth and shoved both selfish jerks from my mind.

We walked into a great room. Sunlight streamed through the windows lining the back wall. To the right was their living room, full of furniture with plump cushions, all facing a fireplace with a big T.V. hanging above the mantle. To the left was their kitchen that had a massive island counter with a few barstools.

"This is really nice," I murmured as I continued to follow

him right, toward the fireplace with deep shelving on both sides.

When we stopped, I zeroed in on pictures displayed on the mantle. There were many of Liam and Lucas at different ages, their smiles huge and goofy while they had their arms hooked around each other's necks. But the two pictures of his parents —the brothers inherited their dimples from their mom— dressed in full uniform made my eyes widen.

"Your parents are in the military?"

"Were in the military. They're retired Marines," he added, with pride in his voice.

Okay. Wow. Silly Liam, who could do accents and impersonations with the skill of a veteran stand-up comic, was from a military family.

"I'm enlisting in the Marines, too."

I whipped my head in his direction and my mouth dropped open.

How had I not known any of this? We'd been friends for three years. Not *super* close friends. Come to think of it, I hadn't really started hanging out with him outside of school until Shane and I stupidly crossed the friendship line last December. Still, Liam hadn't hung out with us too much. Probably because he'd been single even then. For some odd reason.

He reached out and placed his bent, right forefinger under my chin to close my mouth. "Why do you look so surprised by that? Is it because I'm a" —he smoothly slid left with his arms out and gave me a smile worthy of Satan— "*debonair* song and dance man?" he finished in a thick, French accent.

I frowned. "Maybe. I just can't believe I didn't know all this about you." I hesitated, then asked, "So, are you joining because of your parents? Or is it more than that?"

"They're a big part of why I'm enlisting." He closed the gap he'd created with his dance move. "But I also want and need to serve my country." He straightened. "It's important. And there's the GI Bill."

I guess there was that. But still. I couldn't imagine this incredibly sweet, funny boy with the cute, dimpled smile being sent thousands of miles away and into a...war zone.

My soul hitched at the way too vivid image. Then our eyes locked, and my breath caught in my throat at his now familiar, piercing gaze.

Right. Okay then. We needed to get back to why I was here.

"Well, it's admirable you want to join the Marines. Like your parents. Surprising. But admirable. And I mean that. Seriously."

Oh...my...*God*.

He grinned. "Thank you. And I mean that. Seriously."

I ripped my eyes from his and this time they landed on the nearest shelves, packed with records. Rows of vinyl with a fairly new record player sitting on a lower shelf.

"That's a lot of vinyl. Is that why we're standing here?"

He stepped forward and withdrew a record on the same shelf as the player. He faced me and held the record, in a clear, protective case, as if it were a sign. "My parents are super old school. A lot of the vinyl, including this, has been around *way* longer than we have. But the player's newer since vinyl is making a strong comeback." He rolled his eyes. "Like my dad predicted. Right after they gave me my first iPod when I turned eleven."

I read the brownish cover. "Frank Sinatra?"

He released a quick laugh. "My parents love him. Especially my mom."

I smiled, remembering how Frank Sinatra the cat had introduced himself to me. Maybe Liam got his silly side from his mom?

"Anyway," he continued as he turned toward the player,

"they were playing this record last night, and I...noticed for the first time there's a pretty cool duet on here." He lifted the player's cover. "It's an old song, but short and easy. Since we don't really have time to learn something long because of the play, I thought it might be a good choice."

After he slid the record out of its cover, I reached out to take it from him, and he gave me a tight smile.

He seemed so nervous, and I said, "Liam, relax. My mom likes Frank Sinatra, too. So did my grandpa."

He placed the record on the platter, then gave me a questioning look.

And that's when I realized I'd used the past tense.

I sighed and shrugged and decided to be honest with him since he'd been so honest with me the last few minutes. "He doesn't know who that is anymore. Or John Wayne. Or...me."

His expression transitioned into sadness, followed by concern.

I looked away.

Liam was just being a good friend, but I hated that look when it came to my grandpa.

"That's really rough," he mumbled. "When did that...happen?"

I frowned at the floor. "April. And Heather and Noah are the only other ones who know. But they stopped asking about him a while ago." I cleared my throat. "I don't talk about it since I never have anything good to say."

He stayed silent, until, "Maddie, I'm also your friend and it might help to talk about it."

Been there and done that, too. And it had earned me almost nothing in return.

I raised my head. "Thanks. But I'm fine. Really."

He slowly nodded before tearing his eyes away from me. "So the song's called 'Somethin' Stupid' and he sings it with his daughter. Which is weird," he added with a cringe.

He pressed the power button and carefully placed the needle on the spinning record. Seconds later acoustic guitar drifted from nearby speakers, followed by other instruments, then father and daughter started singing.

We stood there, listening to the first verse which smoothly led to the...pretty sweet "Somethin' Stupid" part. But Liam had been right. It *was* weird a father and daughter were singing a I'm-in-love-with-you song. And her part was lower than I was used to, but not impossible for me. Could be a nice change, too.

During the instrumental break, I glanced at Liam, staring intently at the spinning record.

"Liam, stop worrying," I said above the music. "I really like it." And I honestly meant that. "But it is weird they're singing this together."

He barely smiled as they started singing again. And not even a minute later it was over.

He hit the power button, and silence fell. Until he turned toward me and shoved his hands into his pockets. "So do you, maybe, want this to be our song?" His eyes became round. "I mean, our song for the show?"

I caught his eyes and said, "Stop acting weird." Seriously. What was wrong with him? "It's a great choice because of all the reasons you said. And Mrs. Chaplin will totally say yes to this. But do you think we'll find an arrangement since it is old?"

He shrugged. "You can find anything on the Internet."

"Okay. Then we're set." I stepped back. "Do you want to print the lyrics for Mrs. Chaplin? And us? Or do you even need them?" I asked, giving him a playful grin.

"My *parents* love Frank Sinatra, smartass." He shot me a pretend dirty look. "I'm more of a Coldplay and Imagine Dragons kind've guy. But, yeah, I'll print the lyrics tonight."

"Great. Then I'm going to go home."

This time he followed me as I headed for the front door.

"I'm glad you like the song. I wasn't sure what you would think of it. Since it is old."

"It's classic," I corrected him. "And I'll bet no one else will choose a song like it."

"So, we'll be classic and original." He opened the door for me. "Are you sure you don't want me to walk you home? It's not a big deal."

Liam Langley. Cute, funny, smart, talented, and a gentleman.

Yep. The definition of a total catch.

Hmm. Not good I'd been noticing Liam like that lately. At all.

I stepped out of the condo. "That's sweet of you, but I promise I'll be fine. I'll pull out my mace before I leave your building. See you tomorrow," I threw over my shoulder.

I jogged down the steps, but I couldn't stop my soft smile since that had been...fun. Then my smile vanished at the thought. And at the thought of something happening to him. After he became a Marine—wow. Liam's parents were retired Marines and he wanted to enlist instead of going to college after we graduated. His choice was brave. But also scary.

I pushed the upsetting images into the deepest part of my mind. Along with the fact I'd been noticing him way too much. Which was so stupid and totally wrong.

I liked Liam. I'd always liked him. But only as a *friend*.

When I paused at the downstairs door to dig out my key ring that also held my mace, I focused on our cool, *friendly* duet that would probably stand out during the show. Because it would be classic and original.

Chapter Eleven

assidy read Aunt Martha's line, which ended the play. She then raised her head, glanced at me, sitting beside her, and we giggled. The rest of the *Arsenic and Old Lace* cast closed their blue playbooks and laughed, too. Because the last act was pretty funny.

Mr. Peters sprung from his cross-legged position in the center of our circle on stage. "Excellent work! I love that each of you has really embraced your roles in this play." He turned in a slow circle to smile at each of us. "So, your homework this weekend is to continue perfecting your roles and get some rest since we'll be starting blocking on Monday."

Kassidy and I, along with everyone else, stood. She and I headed for the stage right stairs. The only person missing from our rehearsal today had been Heather, who'd had an eye doctor's appointment right after school.

"I've been meaning to tell you," I said as we went down the stairs, "J.R. has been so awesome as Jonathan." We laughed. "He can do dark and deadpan surprisingly well."

"Yeah, it's a little scary." She shrugged. "But I guess we all have a dark side."

I nodded, since that was totally the truth, and we walked toward where we'd dropped our backpacks at the first row.

"You have to be going to Heather's birthday party next Saturday, right?" she asked.

Barrett, Michael, and Taryn surrounded us to get their backpacks.

I tried to catch Barrett's eyes, but he, talking to Michael, didn't even look at me while he swung his backpack onto his shoulder. Then the three went around us to walk up the aisle. Taryn, however, did send us a friendly wave goodbye.

I frowned at Barrett's back, since his continued attitude seemed a bit ridiculous. Why was I being punished for simply being honest with him? And how much could he *like* me? He hardly knew me.

"Maddie?"

I blinked and looked at Kassidy, watching me.

Right. She'd asked me about Heather's party.

"Yes," I answered, forcing myself to forget about Barrett. "I'm definitely going."

Noah, J.R., the ex, and Liam stood not too far away from us, laughing together, and a thought occurred to me. The ex and the girlfriend had to be going, too. But unlike the *Grease* cast party, where I'd stayed—more like hidden—outside with Heather, Noah, and a few other castmates, this time I'd be myself. Social. Especially since Heather had invited half our class. There would be plenty of kids to hang out with who weren't a part of the theater world.

"Fantastic!" Kassidy gave me a bright smile and stepped closer. "So do you have a date? Because I know someone who thinks you're really pretty."

I stared at her.

Another boy in this school actually liked me? Or had at least noticed me.

"A popular someone who plays soccer with Justin and Meg's boyfriend, Owen."

I absently nodded.

A popular jock had noticed me?

I couldn't stop my smile as flattery fluffed my ego. But only a little bit. "Who is it?"

Her smile deepened. "Nicolas Costello. Bryan's cousin?"

Bryan had been "King of the School" before he graduated last year. And his tall, dark, and head-turning cousin had noticed *me*?

I stood there, blinking like a dummy as I wrapped my brain around the thought.

"He asked me about you. When no one else was around." She lifted her shoulders. "I told him I'd talk to you. Because he thought it might be kind've weird if he came up to you out of nowhere and asked you out."

I mentally cringed when I remembered that's exactly what I'd done to Tyler.

"And I thought if you didn't already have a date for Heather's party..." Her voice trailed into nothing. Which snapped me out of my daze.

She couldn't be implying I go to the party with Nicolas, her, J.R., and *them*. And even if she weren't, Nicolas would probably want to hang out with them, especially his soccer buddy.

I shook my head. "You're so sweet. And I'm really flattered Nicolas is interested in me. But I can't go with him and hang out with all of you."

"Maddie, I totally get it. But Nicolas is cool. And I have a feeling he'd just want to hang out with you. Get to know you?"

Shoot. I couldn't go on another date with a boy interested in me, considering what had happened with Barrett. My project *wasn't* about making connections. Though I didn't know Nicolas, he was friends with Kassidy and J.R., who I also called my friends.

"Kass," I softly said, "I'm just not interested in anything serious right now and don't want to give Nicolas the wrong impression."

Her face drooped. "Okay. I understand," she mumbled. "I'll break it to him gently."

Before I could express my thanks, Shane appeared at my side.

I froze, and he gave me a tentative smile.

"Hey. Can I talk to you for a minute?"

I again fell silent while Kassidy stepped back.

"I'll see you guys later." She dashed off toward J.R., waiting for her at the end of the row with Noah and Liam. Who had his piercing gaze locked on me before the four of them started up the aisle.

I forced my eyes back to the ex whose expression had turned serious. Something was definitely up with Liam and his best friend. Unease crept up my back and settled itself onto my shoulders. "What do you need?"

He sighed. "Liam told me you were at his place, because of the duet you two are doing for that choir show. And I asked him if you'd mentioned how your...grandpa's doing."

I gritted my teeth and lifted my chin.

Liam effing Langley wasn't going to live long enough to make it to blocking on Monday, much less the choir show next month. "He had no right to tell *you* what I said."

His blue eyes dimmed. "He's worried about you. And I am, too." He leaned forward. "I know how hard all of it has been on you."

I should have appreciated his words. His concern. Especially after all the rotten that had happened between us. Some of that had been a result of my horrible choices, too. But I could only find anger at him knowing the truth. And Liam's big, traitorous mouth.

"And now it has to be—"

"I'm fine!" I snapped. "And I would really appreciate you and your best friend not talking about me. Behind my back."

He frowned. "It wasn't like that. He's your friend. And I am, too. If you'll let me be your friend again," he added under his breath. "Maddie, it doesn't have to be like this."

I picked up my backpack and lifted it onto my shoulder. Then I faced him. "Yes. It does." I smirked. "And, just for the record, I'm not that *clingy* girl anymore."

His expression became emotionless. An expression I'd seen many times after our numerous arguments over everything and nothing. And in that moment, I wanted to take back asking him to Snowflake Formal. Because we hadn't worked as a couple, and I...missed his friendship.

I gave him my back and marched up the aisle. But when I emerged from the auditorium, I started shaking. I wasn't sure how I'd stop myself from wringing Liam's neck the next time I saw him.

* * *

So I tracked down an arrangement. We can start rehearsing. Tomorrow after school?

I glared at Liam's text. As if everything between us was super fantastic.

Boys were so *stupid*.

I put down my playbook and swiped my phone off my bed. *No. You're a traitor with a BIG mouth.*

Not exactly a brilliant comeback, but I smiled triumphantly as my response hit our thread.

I went back to focusing on Abby's lines in act two. Then

my phone began to vibrate before bursting into its ambient, rippled ringtone.

I glanced at the screen and closed my eyes.

Inhale to count four...exhale to count eight...repeat...

My phone stopped and I opened my eyes. When was the last time I'd meditated? Maybe I needed to take a break from my lines and try to clear my head.

My phone again started to vibrate and ring, and my shoulders sagged.

Darn, Liam, and his persistent side.

I dropped my playbook, grabbed my phone, and answered, "What do you want?"

"Maddie, he asked *me*," Liam replied. "And I was honest. What the hell's wrong with that? It's not like Shane doesn't know what's going on."

"You had no right to tell him what I told you. As *one friend to another*," I added. "And is that how it's going to be? I tell you something personal, and you run and tell your best friend?"

My grandpa bellowing something about not being a baby, followed by a clatter of what sounded liked several dishes shattering against the hardwood floor, made me freeze.

"No, it's not going to be like that," Liam edgily said. "I'm not your enemy. And Shane isn't, either."

I scrambled from my bed and said, "I have to go. I'll call you back." I hung up before he could reply and raced from my room.

When I reached my grandpa's bedroom doorway, I halted. At the sight of his wide eyes and slightly open mouth as he stared at Mom, standing by him where he sat at the little table where he always ate his few meals. And at her feet were the messy remains of his dinner. Tomato soup with a grilled cheese sandwich surrounded by two broken dishes, a shattered glass that looked like it had been filled with water, and a spoon.

I glanced at Ruth, standing at the foot of his table, who was focused on my mom. And that's when I noticed Mom was wearing a good portion of my grandpa's tomato soup.

"I'm...I'm sorry, Meredith," my grandpa stammered.

My eyes grew at hearing him say Mom's name. He'd been calling her Molly, too.

"I don't...know why...what happened." He looked up at her stunned face.

Her face relaxed into a patient smile. "It's okay, Dad. We'll get this cleaned up."

"I'll get this all cleaned up," Ruth warmly said as she stepped forward. "You just go take of yourself, honey."

Mom nodded, and I wanted to hug Ruth. She'd started staying later to help us with his dinnertime.

Mom carefully turned, since the front of her blue T-shirt and pajama bottoms were splattered with tomato soup. Our eyes caught, and that's when I noticed hers were glistening.

My chest became so tight I struggled to fill it with air.

Ruth dropped to her knees and began gingerly picking up the larger pieces of the broken dishes while my grandpa stared at his hands, resting on his lap. And looking like a child who knew they'd done something they shouldn't have.

I fought my tears as Mom walked silently by me.

I had to do *something* to help them, to help my grandpa, so I headed for Ruth. But she glanced at me and smiled. Though there was clear sadness behind her smile.

"You go on back to your homework, honey. I'll get this cleaned up in no time."

I glanced at my grandpa, still focused on his hands, then gave Ruth a tiny nod.

Blinking rapidly, I spun toward the doorway and raced

after my mom. She was just stepping into her room, and I said, "Mom?"

She turned toward me, her eyes a little clearer. "Sweetie, I'm fine." She sighed. "But I am going to go crawl into the bathtub with a glass of wine. Will *you* be okay?"

I shrugged, nodded, and suddenly realized what I really wanted to do tomorrow after school. And it had nothing to do with learning lines, other homework, or rehearsing the duet with Liam. "Since you and Keith don't have plans tomorrow night, do you think we could hang out?" Her face brightened, and I added, "Maybe get a pizza, make those gooey brownies we love, and watch *Pride and Prejudice*? The BBC version?"

She smiled. "It's a mother-daughter date. A long overdue date." She gestured at her clothing. "I'd give you a big hug right now, but that'll have to wait until later."

I tried to smile, and my phone buzzed and chimed with a text. From Liam.

Is everything okay?

No, I wanted to scream. *Not even a little bit.*

"I need to get into the tub, and you need to answer that. I'll check in with you later." Mom stepped farther into her room and closed the door.

I headed back into my room and dropped to my bed's edge.

I certainly couldn't tell Liam the truth, even though a huge part of me wanted to call him and unload everything. But he'd proven he couldn't be trusted. So frustration and sadness and worry engulfed my insides. All three emotions for my grandpa *and* mom. She was publicly shouldering all of this with an amazing, brave attitude. But I had a feeling when she was all alone, like right now, her bravery melted with the rapidness of ice under a desert's sun.

My lower lip quivered and I grabbed Buddy from his spot against my pillows.

I hugged him to me and closed my eyes. I squeezed him so tight his black, plastic nose dug into my chest. Then my phone again started vibrating and ringing. I cleared my throat and answered, "Liam, I'm fine. I spilled some water and had to clean it up."

There was silence on his end, then, "Maddie, you can talk to me."

Which probably meant he didn't believe my big, fat lie. And I tried to ignore the guilt making its way to my shoulders, since he was reaching out to me. But I stayed quiet.

"I really didn't think telling Shane the truth would piss you off," he quietly continued. "But I promise it won't happen again. Okay?"

He sounded genuinely sorry, and his soothing voice made my body relax. "Okay." That didn't mean I'd sit here and spill what really happened. And remembering why he originally texted, I added, "I can't start rehearsing with you tomorrow. I have plans with my mom."

Silence followed my statement, until, "That's cool. What about Sunday? I know you have your...bowling date with Tyler on Saturday."

Because of the way he said that, I envisioned him rolling his eyes.

"Yes," I stated. "I do have my date with Tyler on Saturday. But Sunday will work."

A date I really wasn't looking forward to, but I certainly couldn't tell him that. Or Noah.

"Great," he mumbled. "We'll figure out a time later." He paused, then said, "Are you sure everything's okay?"

I squeezed Buddy at the sound of Liam's voice, back to soothing. And the urge to tell him what happened overwhelmed me. To the point I opened my mouth to free the truth. But fear stopped me. "Everything's fine. But thanks for asking," I softly added.

"Yeah," he said on a breath. "See you tomorrow."

We hung up, and the guilt at lying to him weighed me down. Especially since he'd sounded like he truly wanted me to open up to him. And talking about everything *did* help. But I'd learned the hard way my family...rottenness...was way too much reality. Even for me.

Come to think of it, my real world could have been the true reason Shane had called me clingy. I'd clearly relied on him too much, at a time when we'd been—what had we been back then? Not a couple, but not friends, either. Though he'd tried to be a good friend. Until I'd stupidly put my trust in Sloane, CruElla, and Quinn. Then he'd basically stopped talking to me. Followed by him getting together with her.

I rested my chin on Buddy's cuddly head.

I had incredible friends now. But I was strong enough to handle all of this on my own. I also had plenty of distractions. Though the thought of my upcoming date with bachelor number two made me wrinkle my nose.

Chapter Twelve

My eyes followed the blue bowling ball rolling... rolling...right into the gutter. Again.

I glared at the pins, standing tall at the end of the lane. But if they'd been cartoon pins, they would've burst into laughter at my *spectacular* bowling ability.

"You don't bowl very much," Tyler said from behind me.

I plastered my Barbie smile on my face before facing him. "Nope." And it's not like I felt ashamed of that fact, either. Even though "my date" had a near-perfect score. He also seemed to know several of the other Saturday night regulars, bowling on our left and right sides. On top of knowing some of the employees.

I still couldn't figure out if that was really cool or really sad.

"You're aiming the ball too much to your right," he continued. "I could help you with that. If you want," he quickly added, followed by pushing his glasses up his nose.

What I really wanted was something to drink and food. But Tyler had yet to offer to buy me those two things. And though he was simply bachelor number two of Project Dating

Spree, it would've been nice to see some common courtesy from him.

"Thanks for the offer," I said with a shrug, "but it's all good."

He nodded, as if he'd fully expected my answer, and picked up *his* bowling ball from the track. A black ball with the Distance Speed Time Formula in bright white font on the side. He then stepped up to the lane, paused, took two steps toward that stupid line you couldn't cross and, in that perfect bowler's stance, released his custom-designed ball.

My eyes fell to his backside. Despite his social awkwardness, he did look good in jeans.

His ball plowed through the pins and his latest strike ended our second game.

Cheers exploded on both sides of our lane.

"You're on fire tonight, Bennett!" some guy said from the left us, and above the loud, Top 40 music and other nearby pins being struck down.

Their pins clearly weren't laughing at them.

Tyler smiled and waved at the guy while I dropped to a plastic seat.

Between the blaring music, explosions of pins being toppled, and smell of roasting hot dogs, my head tightened. And I envisioned the homemade lasagna Mom and Keith had been making when I left. She hadn't said much about my date tonight with a different boy. Probably because she'd seemed giddy about having our condo somewhat to herself and Keith...yuck.

I shook those thoughts from my head.

I hadn't eaten because I'd believed Tyler would've had enough sense to buy me dinner. But the thought of eating the bowling center's food made my tummy lurch. Unless they sold those soft, buttery, gigantic pretzels. With cream cheese.

Ooh. Yes, yes, yes.

"So, are you hungry?" I asked as he sat beside me.

"No. I always eat before I come here." He grimaced. "The food in this place smells disgusting, so it can't taste good. And I never eat that crap. It's terrible for you."

I somehow held on to a huge, dramatic sigh.

Perfect. A socially awkward boy who also happened to be a health nut. But it explained why he was in such good shape.

"Thanks for asking, though." He pushed up his glasses. "Ready for round three? Or do you want to have that talk first?"

Right. The talk. Also known as how I'd ended up at a loud, smelly bowling alley with him on a Saturday night. My comfy bed, pajamas, and *Pride and Prejudice*, which I'd decided to read for the third time after Mom and I had watched the best movie version, were feeling like a much better option than *this*. But my conscience would never allow me to dart out of here.

I tried on a pleasant smile. "Actually, I'm starving. And thirsty." I stood.

Thank God I'd again had the sense to stuff two twenties into my crossbody phone case.

Surprise hit his eyes. "You didn't eat before you came here?"

In that moment, sympathy for Tyler's dating cluelessness erased my irritation. I kept my smile in place and said, "No."

He also stood. "Okay. Well, I'll talk to some of these guys until you get back." He gestured toward the other, nearby bowlers. "Then we'll talk."

If not for my sympathy toward his cluelessness, I probably would've laughed.

I turned and headed for the snack-bar area. That, of course, had a line four people deep.

I stopped behind two giggly girls who looked about thirteen or fourteen. They wore skin-tight jeans and tank tops, way too much makeup and, based on the smell radiating from their tiny bodies, too much sickeningly sweet perfume.

The tightness in my head became a full headache.

I pulled my phone from its case. I needed to send my check-in text to Heather, Noah, and Liam. Who, for some reason, hadn't replied to my "I'm heading out" text from earlier. I'd tried to ignore my silly disappointment, but Liam had been a little distant yesterday during show choir. He'd also eaten at the other table again. In fact, the only day he'd eaten with us all week had been Wednesday. Not normal for him, either. Maybe I'd hurt his feelings Thursday night by not opening up to him. And though I did *really* appreciate and like knowing I could talk to him, I was determined to handle everything going on with my grandpa by myself.

His distance aside, he'd told me he wanted to be a part of these texts, so I went into the thread I'd started.

Our brilliant student council president doesn't know the meaning of a date.

Hopefully Liam would text back this time. We were supposed to start rehearsing our song tomorrow. Something I was actually looking forward to, especially after this night.

The line moved forward, and I scanned my surroundings.

What was I doing here? And I remembered Liam's "you have nothing in common with Tyler Bennett" statement from the other day. I'd meant my reply to his comment, but I now understood what he'd been saying. Tyler was so far out of my social sphere, I'd gotten myself into a different type of uncomfortable, Project Dating Spree situation. Standing in line to buy myself a snack and drink while my so-called date chatted up his fellow, Saturday night bowlers.

Laughter bubbled out of me. The two girls eyed me cautiously as my phone vibrated and chimed with a text. From Heather.

Liam's silence shouldn't have mattered this much. But it felt like he was ignoring me. Which I didn't like one bit.

My smile faded and I sighed as I read Heather's message.

And maybe that's why he's never had a girlfriend. But you're okay? Not hiding in a bathroom stall?

I rolled my eyes, though I totally deserved that, as Noah's reply hit.

What did you expect? It's Tyler Bennett.

I walked forward while I frowned at yet another I-told-you-so text from him. Then *Good one, H. Lol!* came in. Also from Noah effing Sanchez.

Not in a bathroom stall. Waiting in line to by myself food and a drink.

I flinched at how absolutely pathetic that sounded. I should've faked something just now, so I could be on my way home. To my bed, pajamas and book, and wow did that make me sound like a 19th Century, Jane Austen heroine. But could that be considered a bad thing at this point?

Really? came from Heather.

It was my turn at the counter, so I slipped my phone into my back jeans pocket and ordered my soft pretzel, thank *God*, and an enormous Diet Coke. As I carried my pretzel, but without cream cheese, and drink to an empty table, my phone buzzed a couple times.

Hope that one of the messages was from Liam made me set everything down and go for my phone.

Noah had texted, *Ouch.*

Of course. And Liam had texted. Finally. But just to me.

So that means you won't be out late and can come over around 11?

I grinned at his message as my shoulders sagged with relief. I guess his funny reply meant we were fine after all. He also, unlike Noah, hadn't pulled the I-told-you-so card. Even though he had warned me about going out with Tyler. If he were here, I would've hugged him. And imagining myself in Liam's arms that had to be warm and strong and *safe* caused me to pause.

Where had that come from?

With shaky fingers, I typed *I'll be there. Do I need to bring anything?*

I sat and forced myself to focus on my pretzel. But as I ripped off a piece and chewed the stale bite, I couldn't stop envisioning being in Liam's arms. Or his dimpled smile the stinker knew how to use. Or his voice Thursday night that had been so soothing. And his voice made me think of his adorkable accents and impersonations.

Just you. And your great singing.

His unexpected, yet super sweet compliment caused heat to rush through me. I then remembered the other, recent times I'd reacted to him in the same way.

Oh, no. History could not be repeating itself. With my ex's best friend.

"There you are. I didn't know you were—oh."

I raised my head and found Tyler standing at my table. And I lost my thoughts at the sight of him scowling at me.

"You're doing that *thing* girls do," he said, his voice now full of surprising hostility.

I glanced at my pretzel. "I'm eating?"

I lifted my eyes, and he antagonistically crossed his arms.

"You're texting a friend and, when you were done eating, you were going to come back with some lame excuse as to why you had to *suddenly leave*."

I sat up. At not only his totally false accusation, but his beyond snarky tone.

His overreaction to finding me like this made me think that had happened to him. Many times. And, as bitchy as it was, my assumption didn't surprise me. But still. That's not what I'd been doing. "Tyler, I was texting a friend about meeting up with him tomorrow—"

"So, you're here with me while making another date with someone else?"

I laughed. And, yes, it sounded like I'd barked. But my reaction fit this moment. "You call this a *date*? Seriously?" My voice had risen to near screech. I felt numerous eyes watching us as his face darkened to a shade favoring scary. "I'm sitting here, by myself, and eating food I also bought."

He pushed his glasses up his nose. "I paid for the lane."

"Only because you got here before me and started bowling!" I snapped.

A couple sitting nearby winced. Which added to my feeling of righteousness.

"I thought you, of all the girls at that fucking school, would be different," he ground out. "But you're no better than the other phony, stuck-up girls who prance down the hallways."

Oh. Wow. He did not throw me into a category of Pacifica Academy girls that, most likely, contained Sloane and Brandy, and CruElla and Quinn. And I never pranced.

I stood. "You don't know anything about me." I leaned forward. "And for how supposedly *smart* you are, you have no idea what a date is." I failed to add, *Maybe that's why girls always ditch you during dates.*

I caught that couple, and other people sitting at tables near us, trying to muffle their laughter at my dig. An extremely honest and well-articulated dig.

I straightened in triumph.

My phone, still on the table, buzzed and lit up with a text.

He sneered at me, then my phone. "Nothing's good enough for you immature high school girls." He stepped back. "I can't wait to graduate and go to Berkeley. And be around *real* girls."

I narrowed my eyes into slits.

Who was this angry, irrational boy standing in front of me and making a scene at his favorite, Saturday night hang out?

"Tyler, I can promise most college girls won't think of *this* as a date, either." I heard a bit more muffled laughter as I swiped my phone off the table, then grabbed my un-touched drink. I'd lost my appetite for what was left of my pretzel. "I'm going home." A place I never should've left to begin with. But at least I'd driven myself.

I threw a mental, heartfelt thanks up and into...the sky outside of the ceiling.

"Big surprise there," he muttered. "Have a nice life, Maddie Hammarton."

I halted.

Our genius, student council president didn't even know my last name.

"It's *Harrington*," I loudly said to his back as he stalked toward the lanes. "And I never should've voted for you!" Not that I would have ever voted for CruElla. But at least I'd made my feelings clear on what I thought of him.

He kept walking, and I turned on my heel and stalked toward the exit.

Once outside, I paused and closed my eyes.

Inhale to count four...exhale to count eight...

My phone went off again and I opened my eyes. Heather had been the one who texted first, while Tyler was sneering at me. Liam's message was second and part of the group thread.

She'd texted, *Liam, got anything for our damsel in distress?*

Heather had meant it as a joke, but I still frowned. Until I read Liam's reply.

Nope. Our MH can handle our student council president.

I smiled and typed, *Yes. He's a big, dumb jerk. I'm going home. Text you when I'm there.*

Then after texting them, I would take another shower.

Wash off the stinky food, those girls' perfume I smelled on myself, and Tyler's arrogant nastiness. I just hoped Mom and Keith wouldn't be upset when I walked into the condo. I'd have to shoot her a message before I left.

I went in the direction of where I'd parked our Prius.

Okay. Project Dating Spree had turned into more of a bust than fun, and after only two dates. So the thought of going on a third date destined for nowhere didn't interest me. For reasons that included I couldn't shake the thought of being wrapped in a certain, cute boy's arms. A boy who knew *me*, and never would have treated me—or any girl—like this. Ever.

Darn it.

I absolutely couldn't be *liking* another good friend.

Chapter Thirteen

"Hey." Liam flashed his dimpled smile.

All I could think to say was, "Hey."

I walked into the condo, and he closed the door behind me.

I'd taken my time heading here. A stroll that had been full of deep breathing to control the uncomfortable combo of nervousness and excitement I couldn't believe I was feeling. For Liam. And at this moment I had no clue how to act around him. Except take it one second at a time.

"You ready for this *little lady*?" he asked in his John Wayne impersonation.

Please, please, please stop being so freakin' adorable.

But I smiled. Then my tummy flipped when I noticed how good he looked in his blue Coldplay concert T-shirt, jeans, and...bare feet.

Oh, wow. Super cute and casual Liam wasn't the worst way to officially start my Sunday.

I looked at the floor.

I hadn't rolled out of bed until almost 10:00, since I'd read until nearly 1:00 in the morning. So I'd only thrown on a pair of old jeans, a T-shirt, and light, zip-up hoodie and pulled my hair up into a loose knot. I had washed my face and brushed my teeth, but I suddenly wished I'd taken more time with my appearance. Then again, this was *not* a date. Just two friends getting together to rehearse a required duet.

"Hi, Maddie. It's really nice to see you here."

I lifted my head.

His mom strolled up, wearing her huge, dimpled smile, and a red and gold San Francisco 49ers jersey. A cute curvy girl, with dark curly hair and wearing a 49ers shirt, was with her. But before I could greet them, Frank Sinatra appeared at my feet and rubbed his body against my leg. And he again collapsed onto my foot, which he started vigorously rubbing with his head.

"We need to stop meeting like this," I said to Frank, now purring.

Liam's mom eyed her pet. "Oh, my. You are one *shameless* kitty."

Frank rolled right, paused, then rolled back onto my foot. And his purring became louder.

"I think he'll need a drink and cigar when he's finished," Liam said in a voice I didn't recognize.

"Cary Grant." His mom smiled at him. "Nice." She looked at me. "My son. The next Robin Williams."

Liam ran a hand through his hair. "Mom, his life didn't have an awesome ending."

She sighed. "Very true. But you know what I mean."

The girl thrust her hand in my direction. I grasped it, and we shared a quick handshake.

"I'm Willow. Lucas's girlfriend."

I returned her warm smile. "I'm Maddie. Liam's friend." Because that's all we were. But I held on to a sigh as I glanced down the hallway that led to the great room, and was the direction they'd come from. "Where's Lucas?"

"He's at the store with their dad. Getting food for the game." Her smile deepened. "I'm *so* excited to meet you."

Oh. Well, that seemed like a strange statement.

"Are you ready?" Liam asked while taking a step backward.

His mom bent down and scooped her cat into her arms. "Have fun. And you have my permission to close the door if we get too rowdy." She shrugged. "Game days around here are never dull. Especially if we're losing. Which we normally are," she grumbled.

Liam turned left, and I followed him.

"I *so* hope I'll get to see more of you!" Willow called out.

My steps faltered at her second strange comment, and I couldn't stop myself from asking, "Why do I feel like I'm the first girl you've ever had over?" I didn't exactly hate that idea, either.

"Yeah, I don't know," he answered around a tight laugh. "They're weird."

We approached a doorway, and I stopped. Curiosity had gripped me. I also tried to catch his eyes, but he was focused on the floor. "Seriously, Liam. What's up with that?" I'd never known him to have a girlfriend, on top of the fact he rarely dated. "Did some girl break your heart and now you're anti-dating?" My tone had been friendly, but his eyes stayed on the floor. Which told me my question may have hit close to home. And a growl inched up my throat at the thought of some idiotic girl breaking amazing Liam Langley's heart.

Amazing.

He finally brought his eyes up to mine. "Why the sudden interest in my personal life, Maddie?" he asked, followed by that darn smile of his.

My face became hot. "I'm just curious. It's not like you're repulsive."

My words hung between us. And I managed not to cringe as he raised his hands.

"Whoa. *That* was the best compliment ever."

I avoided his eyes and added, "And for some reason you rarely date."

He lowered his hands. "Just because I *rarely* date doesn't mean I'm anti-dating." He walked into his room. "And maybe I do like a girl."

My eyes widened.

He couldn't like someone. Especially since I'd never seen him around a specific girl at school, outside of girls who were his friends. Still, jealousy fueled my march into his room. I joined him at his desk, sitting against the wall. "Who do you like?" I asked. More like demanded. "Does she go to P.A.?"

He opened his laptop. "Yes. So I downloaded the father-daughter version of the song and the arrangement. My computer is hooked up to pretty good speakers, too."

I leaned toward him. "Liam Langley, you're really not going to tell me who you like?"

He faced me, and our eyes connected. But his were tinged with frustration.

I was definitely being way too demanding and nosy. Still, I had to know who he liked. And would she even appreciate every singing, dancing, adorkable, hot part of him? *Like I would.*

Shoot, shoot, *shoot*. I was officially screwed.

"Maddie Harrington," he said, leaning toward me, "it's none of your business."

His sharp words stung my soul, and I drew back.

He sighed. "Sorry. I'm not trying to be a dick. But I haven't said anything because I *know* she doesn't like me that way." He pointed at his laptop. "Can we get back to this?"

Oh. I guess that explained his defensive, secretive behavior. But darkness swirled through me knowing Liam was crushing on some stupid girl at school. Who didn't deserve his attention.

Inhale to count four...exhale to count eight...

A little better. But not much.

"Yes," I answered. Because I wasn't here to talk about his personal life. I still felt the need to grudgingly add, "I'm sorry she doesn't like you the same way."

He replied by staying focused on his computer.

Okay then. It's not like I wanted to continue this wonderful conversation, either.

As he brought up the songs, I noticed his bulletin board. He'd pinned a few red and gold United States Marine Corps logos around the phrase "Semper Fi." I was about to ask him what the phrase meant when some photos caught my attention. I leaned in for a closer look—I froze.

One of the pictures was a group selfie. Of the ex, the girlfriend taking the selfie, Liam and...oh, my God.

"Is that *Bree*?" But I'd sounded like I turned into a mouse and squeaked.

He straightened, reached out, and plucked the photo off his board. "Oh, yeah. I forgot this was up there." He opened a desk drawer, dropped the picture inside, and shoved the drawer closed. "We went hiking with them over the summer."

I stared at him. And the image of our theater friend Bree, who'd graduated last year, hugging his side as the four of them smiled at the girlfriend's phone, branded itself into my brain. "We?" I faintly said. "You and Bree were together?" They'd never seemed interested in each other as more than friends. Or maybe they had, and I hadn't noticed, being too caught up in my own rotten drama. And I guess I'd been way wrong about him never having a girl over here.

"Sort've."

Well, it didn't get any vaguer than that. So I asked, "When did that happen?" Because they couldn't have gotten together at the end of the school year. I hadn't been that out of it. Or had I? Then I remembered Liam asking me to prom as friends and my bitchy response. "Did you end up going to prom with Bree?"

He frowned. "No. We ran into each other over the summer and...one thing led to another. It wasn't serious or anything." He slid his fingers into his jeans pockets. "I mean, you know she got into Carnegie Mellon. And we're still friends on social media. But that's it."

I forced my mouth into a smile. "Sounds like a summer romance to me." But remembering the picture of all of them, super happy and out together on a beautiful, Bay Area day, caused jealousy to flare inside me.

My jaw tightened as I glared at his bulletin board. And the flare grew to a wildfire when I remembered how I'd spent my summer. It hadn't been miserable, but it had been nothing like his. Theirs. Mostly lazy days, getting lost in one book after another. Or reading a classic to my grandpa. Or hanging out with Heather and Noah, and even my mom. Or meditating.

"I know that's how it might sound," he mumbled, "but it wasn't like that."

I lifted my chin. "Well, it sounds like you two had fun. Whatever happened didn't ruin your friendship so, okay." But images of them having *fun*, since they'd looked pretty cozy in that dumb picture, engulfed my brain. "We need to start." And I needed to get a hold of my imagination and ridiculous jealousy. Because I had no right to these feelings that weren't fair to Liam. Who'd done absolutely nothing wrong.

I looked around to search for a place we could rehearse. And that's when I noticed his neatly made bed to the right of us. Not a wrinkle in sight. No casually discarded clothing or shoes anywhere. Even the few school books and folders on his desk were perfectly stacked. He'd also hung a Marine Corps wall flag over his dresser, across from his bed.

The room of a future Marine raised by Marines.

I shook my head and asked, "So where are we going to do it?"

He raised his eyebrows.

Oh...my...*God*.

He unleashed his smile. "On the floor. Will that work?"

Right. That smile should be against the law. Actually, the entire Liam Langley package should be considered illegal.

"We need to be near the computer so I can easily start and stop the music," he continued, facing his desk. He picked up a couple sheets of paper and handed one to me. "The lyrics."

Good. Back to business. But between his smile and quick, surprisingly naughty comeback, my *everything* was at the temp of burn.

I dropped to the floor and crossed my legs.

How was it possible this girl he liked didn't like him back? She had to be nuts. I had clearly sunk into crazy, too. A different kind of crazy. And it was all his fault.

He went around me to close his door.

Okay. I could totally handle being alone with him. In his bedroom. With the door closed.

"My mom wasn't kidding when she said they get *rowdy* during games. But what she didn't say is that she gets the loudest." He sat in front of me and crossed his legs. "Do you want me to play the actual song again?"

"No. Let's do it first, then—" *Shoot*.

I stared at my paper as silence settled around us. Until he cleared his throat.

Of course the stinker wasn't going to let my totally embarrassing second slip go.

"Maddie," he said in a lowered voice, "are you trying to tell me something?"

The way he asked that made me want to answer with tossing my paper aside and throwing myself into his arms. But as all the heat returned, I said, "Will you just play the song?"

He turned toward his desk.

I concentrated on the lyrics while fighting the urge to turn the paper into a fan.

"What happened with Tyler?"

I blinked and raised my head to find him frowning at me. I'd texted them when I got home, but called Heather to tell her everything that had happened.

I spilled the details, and as I told him about Tyler's nastiness his face became dark.

"He really said all that to you?" he asked when I finished. "What a fucking dick."

I laughed, since I rarely heard him drop F-bombs. And his reaction pretty much matched Heather's last night. "He's definitely that." At the same time, a part of me felt sorry for Tyler and his utter cluelessness.

Liam sighed. It sounded a bit edgy, too. "Maybe this *project* of yours isn't working. I mean, you did handle yourself with Tyler, but he was an asshole to you. And Barrett..."

I'd already accepted everything he'd said and let go of Project Dating Spree. But all I could tell him was, "Yeah. My project didn't go the way I thought it would and there won't be a date three." And that's all I'd say to Heather and I-told-you-so Noah when the time came. "We need to start rehearsing." So I could leave and focus on the fact Liam and I were good friends. And the last thing I wanted was to lose *his* friendship.

Meditating. Yes. That's exactly what I needed to do when I got home.

Our eyes caught, and he opened his mouth. Then he stopped and again faced his desk. A couple seconds later the familiar music drifted from speakers hooked to his computer.

He'd wanted to say something, but I sat up, tightened my diaphragm and focused on my paper. He also sat up, and we waited for the break. Then sang the opening lyrics. Until I croaked. As if I'd turned into a frog.

He looked at me. And we burst into laughter.

No. I couldn't lose this closeness with him.

"What the hell was that?" he asked around a laugh. "Do you need some water?"

"I'm not used to the low key." I cleared my throat and pointed at his computer. "Hit it."

He did just that, we waited, and we started singing a second time. And while wearing a smile that matched his, I lost myself in the song.

Chapter Fourteen

I stood at my locker and took a long swallow of cold water to ease my stinging throat. That had started stinging after going through the song several times with Liam so I could get used to singing what was really an alto part.

Liam. Who I couldn't stop thinking about because I'd really liked being alone with him yesterday and getting lost in our singing. Which officially made me the dumbest girl ever for reasons that now included he liked some other freakin' girl.

I sighed, twisted the cap back onto my reusable bottle and stuck it into a side pocket of my backpack. Then I sneezed.

"Bless you."

I raised my head at the deep, unfamiliar voice. And I found myself staring at brown eyes framed by dark eyelashes any female on this planet would kill to have.

"Hi. I'm Nicolas Costello." His mouth curved into a flirty grin. "And you're *the* Maddie Harrington."

I sniffed and somehow stopped myself from swiping my nose.

I tore my eyes from his to glance at my surroundings.

Pacifica Academy hallway. Kids at their lockers and

walking by us while chatting and laughing. And, yeah, it was Monday morning, and I was at school. Not still sound asleep in my warm, comfy bed.

I slid my eyes back to *the* Nicolas Costello, standing at my locker.

"So, you're probably wondering what I'm doing here," he said, his smile turning shy.

And that voice. The deepness matched his entire *hel-lo* factor. But it wasn't his voice I wanted to hear right now.

His smile dipped a fraction. "Are you okay?"

That's when I realized I'd been standing there like an idiot, staring at him, and had yet to respond to anything he'd said. "Yes!" I replied. More like chirped. "I'm great. You?"

I mentally moaned. No, I wasn't interested in him. That didn't mean I wanted to start the day with a hefty does of humiliation, either.

He laughed. "I'm okay. It's Monday." He stepped closer. "This is a little embarrassing, because I know Kassidy talked to you about me last week. And she told me what you said." He released a quick laugh. "But I'm here to see if you'll reconsider? Your friend's party sounds like fun, and I think we'd have...fun." He flinched.

I smiled at his surprising nervousness. Because Nicolas could get any girl he wanted, in and outside of this school. And here he was with me at my locker, wanting me to "reconsider" going to Heather's party with him. Seriously, *was* I still sound asleep?

My nose twitched, I turned, and sneezed. Loudly into my locker.

"Bless you," he said again, and I heard the smile in his voice.

I sniffed twice.

"I hope you're not getting sick."

I faced him, smiled, and had to sniff again as snot tried to slide out of my nose. "I'm totally fine. It's probably allergies." But even as I said that, my stinging throat and twitchy sinuses made doubt creep through my muddled mind.

Wouldn't that be super fantastic. After going on a lousy Project Dating Spree date with Tyler *effing* Bennett, I get—no. I wasn't getting sick.

"So what do you think?" Nicolas again gave me his flirty grin. "It's just a party. And if we decide we can't stand each other, we'll call it a night." He leaned forward. "But I don't think that'll happen. Do you?"

Okay. He was dangerous with a capital DANGER. And though I was flattered by his interest, it was another boy's dark eyes, illegal smile and total hotness I wanted to be around at Heather's party.

So much for never again *liking* a good friend.

I also had to suck it up and be honest with Nicolas. Well, mostly honest. I had no choice but to hold on to my feelings for Liam. I didn't even want Heather and Noah to know since liking Liam was complicated and embarrassing.

I pushed my hair behind my ears. "Nicolas, I'm flattered you want to go to Heather's party together." I hesitated before adding, "But I meant what I said to Kassidy last week. I'm just going to go with friends." At least that part wasn't a lie. But seeing his face and shoulders fall with disappointment made me want to sigh.

I seemed to cause that reaction in boys after being honest with them. For the most part. Still, I'd learned the hard way I couldn't lead Nicolas to believe I was interested. No matter what Tyler thought, I wasn't a snotty, mean girl. And, hopefully, he wouldn't tell anyone about Saturday night. I didn't need *another* personal disaster ending up in the school's gossip mill.

"Is it because you think I'm one of those arrogant jocks?" he softly asked. "I swear I'm nothing like my cousin."

Yeah. Bryan hadn't earned the title of "King of the School" by being super down-to-earth. But he had thrown some cool parties during his reign.

I gave Nicolas an encouraging smile. "It's not that. I promise. And you don't seem anything like Bryan." Relief filled his eyes, and I lifted my shoulders. "I just want to focus on friendships. With it being our senior year?" Again, not a total lie. And I tried to ignore the image of Liam's irresistible face as it drifted through my cloudy brain.

"Okay." Nicolas's grin returned. "Then how about we go, but as friends?"

I gaped at him. He couldn't be serious. Considering he could walk away and ask a random girl to Heather's party. Who would not hesitate to shout her yes.

"That might actually be a better idea, since we don't know each other at all."

My nose decided at that moment to—I turned and again sneezed into my locker.

Shoot, shoot, shoot. I could not be getting sick. I also desperately needed to blow my nose. Which meant we needed to wrap this up so I could get to class and a box of tissues.

"You're sweet," I said, then sniffed. "But that still sounds too much like a date."

"It won't be a date and here's why," he persisted, still wearing his grin. "We can meet at her place. I won't even compliment you on how great I'm sure you'll look."

I laughed softly.

"There won't be any touching," he continued, "and no long, epic stares from across the room if we get separated. Just talking. While we're standing around with other kids. I won't even ask you to dance. If there's dancing." His grin faded. "But not asking you to dance might be hard since I've noticed in the musicals, and during the lip sync competition, you're a great dancer."

The competition hadn't been my finest moment as a long-time dancer, so he was using every weapon in his arsenal to get me to say yes. And I couldn't stop the flattery from surrounding me. As yet another oncoming sneeze tickled my sinuses. His straightforward statements seemed genuine, too. What would be the harm in meeting up at her place and hanging out as friends? It's not like we wouldn't be surrounded by our classmates.

"What do you think? Because I think you want to say yes."

I sniffed the sneeze away before saying, "Okay. I'm in." And none of it meant we had to spend the entire night in each other's company. Like we would if we were on an actual date.

His face lit up. "That was *the* best sales job of my life." He pulled his phone from his pocket. "What's your number? In case you change your mind between now and Saturday, and I have to go through another sales pitch."

I fought a smile at Nicolas being so down-to-earth to the point of polar opposite of his cousin. And I gave him my number.

He smiled, then sent me a text. "I think we'll have a great time, Maddie." He stepped back. "But only as new friends, getting to know each other."

Hmm. Hopefully I wouldn't regret this.

He turned and disappeared behind several kids.

Okay. I could totally handle hanging out with Nicolas while not pining for Liam. Who would be pining for some other girl who also had to be going to Heather's party.

The sneeze I'd tried sniffing away exploded from me.

And I was absolutely not getting sick.

* * *

Heather sat beside me in the cafeteria while I blew my nose. For what felt like the hundredth time that morning. As I wiped my nose, I noticed her glasses were gone. "You're wearing contacts. And look amazing." But I cringed at how not nice that may have sounded.

I'd always thought she was striking with her bright-red glasses. But without them, her green eyes stood out against her olive complexion and dark hair.

I looked pointedly at Liam and Noah, sitting across from us, quietly inhaling their sandwiches. But when they caught my wide-eyed, agree-with-me look, they stopped chewing long enough to grin and nod at Heather.

She blushed. "Thanks." She pulled a bag of chips from her lunch bag. "I didn't wear my contacts on Friday because I wanted to spend the weekend trying to get used to them. But they're still driving me crazy." She glanced at me and paused. "And I hate to say this, Madeline, but you *don't* look amazing. Are you getting sick?"

I'd been asked that question by Sloane and Taryn during show choir, and Noah had asked during our class together. "No. It's just allergies—" I turned and sneezed into my right arm.

Of course.

I quietly blew my nose.

"Bless you." Heather opened her chip bag. "So I heard from a couple kids in concert choir Mrs. Chaplin chose cool, mainstream songs for the big numbers for your show next month. Like a Bruno Mars medley? And a Fun. medley? What's going on with her?"

Our uptight, song snob of a teacher had surprised all of us this morning by announcing the music the choirs would be singing together.

Liam and I locked eyes, and we shared a smile. Which made my heart skitter, and for the second time since he'd decided to sit with us today. But I also hadn't known what to say to him in the last few minutes. It was probably a good thing he seemed absorbed in his lunch.

"Yeah," Liam replied, dragging his eyes from mine to Heather. "But the song changes are Mr. Hathaway's choice. Not hers. And the songs aren't new." He shrugged and went back to his sandwich. "But better than show tunes."

"Agreed," I said. More like croaked. And gurgled.

"Well, that sure sounded *darn* healthy," Liam said in a thick, southern drawl.

I wrinkled my nose at him, then looked away and sneezed again.

"Bless you. And he's right," Noah offered. "You sound as bad as you look."

"Thanks. And I'm not getting sick." I placed the used tissue in my left sweater pocket and grabbed a fresh tissue from my right pocket.

"You better not be getting sick," Heather whined. "Because you *cannot* miss my party."

"Heather, I'll be there," I insisted. With my hoarse voice.

"Okay." Her face brightened. "So have you chosen a bachelor number three?"

Yes. But he's my friend, my ex's best friend, and likes someone else.

I couldn't say that, but I could mention my friendly non-date with Nicolas. All of us would be hanging out together at some point during her party. And I didn't even feel like getting into abandoning my project. Especially while the main reason I'd let it go sat across from me.

"I've decided not to bring a bachelor. Though Nicolas Costello asked me to your party."

They stared at me, their mouths hanging slightly open. And I didn't know whether to be flattered or offended by their reactions. So I sniffed twice and wiped my nose.

Heather laughed. "Maddie, I love you to pieces. But I'm

pea-green with envy that one of the *yummiest* boys in this school asked you to my birthday party." Her eyes widened. "I also can't believe you said no to Nicolas *Wow* Costello. You have to be the first girl to tell him no."

Liam rolled his eyes and went back to his sandwich. But was he fighting a smile?

"You really are getting sick," she mumbled. "And not thinking clearly."

I lowered my tissue and was about to clarify we'd planned to meet up and hang out as friends when Noah leaned back in his chair.

"Heather, you're acting So. Awesome. Can you two talk about this when we're not here?"

She pulled out a chip. "You and Liam are total hotties and you know it. But you're like having two more brothers, and I already have three." She looked at me. "Please back me up. I know you feel the same way about these two."

I did feel that way about one of them. And not the one eyeing me right now. In fact, in the three years I'd been friends with Liam, he'd never felt like the brother Bradley *used* to be. But Noah definitely felt like having a sometimes annoying, younger brother.

"Thanks for that," he muttered. "I guess."

And thank you, Noah, for that interjection.

I focused on Heather. "Don't be too disappointed. He's still going to your party." I shrugged. "We're meeting up to hang out as friends. It's a non-date."

Liam had been about to take a bite out of his sandwich, but stopped and lowered his food to the table. "You and Nicolas Costello are meeting up at the party to hang out as *friends*." He stared at me through confused, narrowed eyes. "You can't be serious."

I straightened at his offensive tone. And at the way he was looking at me. Like I'd let him down or something. Which made no sense at all. In fact, he almost sounded jealous. But that didn't make any sense, either, since he liked some mysterious girl around here.

"What's the big deal? And you don't have to be so snarky!"

"And Nicolas doesn't have girls as just friends!" he snapped back. "So you might as well consider him a *project* date." He shoved his food into his lunch bag. "I need to finish my math homework. I'll see you guys later." He stood and left.

I turned and sneezed into my arm. I then put away yet another used tissue to grab a fresh one. *What* had just happened here?

"What's his problem?" Heather asked Noah.

He swung his eyes to Liam stalking away and back to us. "Don't know. But he was right about Nicolas not having girls as friends."

I blew my raw nose. "Nicolas knows I'm not interested in dating him." But maybe he'd hidden his arrogance behind his charm? And maybe I was clueless and too trusting.

Noah shrugged and leaned toward the table to pick his sandwich back up.

Great. I'd gotten myself into another dating mess while the boy I wanted to be my actual date for the party was now mad at me. But why? I hadn't done anything wrong.

Chapter Fifteen

J.R. and Shane, or Jonathan and Mortimer, raced across the stage and dropped into metal chairs. They glared at each other for a few seconds. Then Shane's eyes widened, and he leaned slowly away from J.R., who held his dark, deadpan stare. Until his mouth trembled, followed by shaking with laughter. Again. Which made Shane laugh. Again.

I released an impatient sigh. "Would you two pull it together?" It came out hoarse and less than forceful due to my borderline laryngitis I'd woken up with this morning. On top of my aching throat and head and body. "I'm tired of rehearsing this scene."

The boys stared at me, their humor replaced with wariness.

I reached into my sweater pocket for another tissue since my nose hadn't stopped running since Monday. And because of how utterly crappy I felt, I hadn't slept well the last two nights. Another reason for my bitchiness.

I swiped my red, sore nose and caught Kassidy looking at

me much like the boys. "I'm sorry," I hoarsely grumbled. "I feel awful." Completely obvious and a huge understatement.

The boys' faces relaxed into sympathy and they nodded.

Kassidy reached out and placed her hand on my forehead. "Maddie, you're really warm. And you've gotten way worse since Monday." She removed her hand. "You shouldn't be here."

Right. Because I could afford to miss school and rehearsals. But that bitchy thought added to my feeling of overall terribleness since Kassidy seemed worried. And spoke the truth.

"Okay, everyone." Mr. Peters stood from his cross-legged seat near the stage's edge. "Let's call it a day. But really great work." He walked toward me, concern radiating from his eyes and expression. "I'd like to talk to you for a second."

Kassidy, J.R., and Shane walked around us and toward the stage right stairs. My eyes then caught Heather, Noah and Liam, the rat who'd barely spoken to me since Monday, focused on me from where they stood at the front row. Of course they were looking at me just like Mr. Peters and Kassidy, and even J.R. and Shane. After I apologized for snapping at them.

"Maddie," Mr. Peters quietly said, "I appreciate your dedication to your role and this show. And you've been, without question, wowing me since rehearsals started."

I tried to smile at his compliment. But it hurt even to do that much.

"But you can now barely talk and, very likely, have a fever." He gave me a sympathetic smile. "Which means you're contagious and that Kassidy's right. You shouldn't be here."

My shoulders drooped. "Mr. Peters, you know Abby is in almost every scene in this play. I *have* to be here. And it's just a bad cold." Even though I did really want to be at home, in bed, curled under my soft sheets and comforter since I'd been fighting a chill all day.

"Yes," he admitted. "But you can miss a rehearsal. And bad cold or not, you need to stay home tomorrow. I'd stay home Friday, too, if you can. And hopefully by Monday you'll be feeling much better. So, go home and get some rest."

He turned and walked toward the stairs.

After a few seconds, I sluggishly followed him. I wasn't sure I had enough energy to lift my backpack, much less wear it the block and a half to my building.

Heather, Noah, and Liam still stood at the front row seats, but were now wearing their backpacks. And that's when I noticed Liam, giving me a tentative smile while holding mine.

"Will you make it home okay?" Noah asked. "You look like you're about to Fall. Over."

In fact, that's exactly how I felt, but before I could assure him I'd be okay, Liam stepped up to my side.

"I'll walk you home," he murmured. "Since we don't live that far apart."

I stared at him and wanted to vehemently protest him doing such a thing after basically ignoring me for two-and-a-half school days. But I again couldn't find the energy. I also didn't really have the voice to vehemently protest anything. And, despite his irritating behavior, a burst of coziness shrouded me at him offering to walk me home. While carrying my backpack.

"Aww." Heather batted her eyelashes at Liam. "Tell me again how you don't have a girlfriend?" she teased as we headed up the aisle.

"I'm picky," he mumbled.

Was I the only person who knew he liked someone? Well, Shane probably knew. But those two were like brothers. I guess it also didn't make much sense for him to announce to all his friends he liked a girl who didn't like him the same way.

I didn't know how long he'd liked this dumb girl, either, but he needed to move on to someone else.

Someone like me.

But that impossibility only added to my overall feeling of yucky.

Heather's mom was waiting for her in their SUV in the pick-up zone when we walked outside into the warm, late summer evening. But the warmth wasn't enough to absorb my chill. I needed my heaviest sweats and sweatshirt.

"I'm guessing you won't be at school tomorrow, so I'll text you," Heather said, going straight for the SUV. "You *must* get better by Saturday."

Right. But at this moment I couldn't work up enough effort to think about her party. Or even care. I just wanted my bed so I could at least suffer in comfort.

"I'll text you later, too." This from Noah as he also went straight, but to cross the street. He lived in a building we could see from where we stood.

I turned left, and Liam fell into step beside me.

We walked in silence until I cleared my throat, which hurt to the point I cringed. "Thanks for doing this, but you didn't have to."

"It's not a problem," he answered, mimicking my hoarse, almost non-existent voice.

I rolled my eyes, but released a giggle. Which also hurt. But then I frowned, remembering his confusing, borderline silent treatment the last two days. "Actually, I'm mad at you because you've been mad at *me* since Monday."

He sighed. "Maddie, I'm not mad at you." His eyes flitted to me. "I just think you going to Heather's party with Nicolas as *friends* is a way for you justify another one of your dates. And I don't think it's a good idea."

I stopped walking, which made him stop. "Well, Mr. Know-It-All, it isn't," I said as strongly as I could. "He's friends with J.R. and Kassidy. Who I trust. So he can't be a bad guy."

"You're right. He sits with them—us—at lunch and seems *awesome.* But you have to know he wants to be more than friends with you."

I crossed my arms. "I told him I'm not interested in being anything but friends. And how would you know what Nicolas wants?"

"Because I'm a guy," he shot back. "And he's not good enough for you. This project of yours isn't, either." He shrugged. "Noah's right. It isn't you, and you have nothing to prove."

I stayed silent as his super sweet statements penetrated my full-of-ickiness head. He'd never liked Project Dating Spree, either. But these comments seemed more protective than his usual, Noah-type attitude. Especially his comments about Nicolas. That still, strangely enough, sounded a tad on the jealous side. So weird, too. But, maybe, he *was* giving up on this other girl?

He looked right. "It's only my opinion. As your friend."

Those last three words devoured where my mind had gone.

Of course. Just one friend protecting another friend.

He frowned. "Maddie, what is this project, with all your rules, really about?"

I returned his frown. "You of all people know what that project was all about. And no matter what you say or think, I meant what I said on Sunday. Nicolas isn't a third Project Dating Spree date." Seriously, why wouldn't he believe me? Because of some ridiculous guy thing?

"Fine. Whatever." He ran a hand through his hair. "And I've apologized for what I *shouldn't* have said that day. It was a stupid, dumbass mistake. But you've made your point." He lifted his head toward the sky. "This just in," he said in a booming, broadcast news voice, "Madeline Harrington is *not* clingy. I repeat, Madeline Harrington is not—"

"Liam Langley, I don't think you're cute. Or funny," I stated while glaring at him.

He leaned forward. "I only said the truth."

I started walking, more like marching, down the sidewalk. I wasn't even in the mood for this stupid conversation. Or him, for that matter. Because he wasn't listening to me. And I didn't think he was cute or funny. At least, right at this moment I didn't think those things.

He caught up to me, and we walked in unison.

But my tummy fluttered when I remembered him stating so confidently he didn't think I was clingy. Had never seemed to think that. Still, he was way overreacting to my non-date with Nicolas, who I could handle if Liam ended up being right about his intentions.

When we reached my building, I stopped at the front stoop steps and held out my hands to take my backpack.

"I'll walk you inside."

"*Liam*," I groaned, "I appreciate you carrying my backpack and walking me home. But you're not my boyfriend."

Oh. Wow. Hadn't meant for that bitchy comment to come out. Even though I'd simply spoken the ugly truth.

"You're right." Without looking at me, he handed over my backpack. "I hope you feel better soon." He turned and headed back the way we came.

I swung the heavy bag onto my shoulder and moaned. I couldn't even deal with any of this. I needed to focus on getting back to one-hundred percent so I could go to my best friend's big, eighteenth birthday party.

Chapter Sixteen

Mom, carrying a steaming mug, walked into my bedroom. Then Keith appeared in my doorway and gave me a broad smile. His salt-and-pepper hair matched his thin beard. And his smiles always reached his brown eyes. Mom had lucked out with him, also divorced but with no kids. She deserved Keith after years of being a single, hard-working mom.

"How's our teen sicko feeling?" Keith asked.

He was trying to make me laugh, which he could normally do, but I wrinkled my nose.

He nodded. "Whoa-kay. Good to know." He stepped back. "Think I'll go finish dinner." He shared a wide-eyed glance with Mom before leaving.

I curled up into a tighter ball against all my pillows between my headboard and me, and refocused on *Pride and Prejudice*.

She set the mug down on my nightstand. "A peace offering of green tea with honey."

"Thanks," I hoarsely mumbled, without looking at her.

My phone, beside me on my bed, buzzed and chimed, and

I set my book down. The message had to be from Nicolas, since I'd felt obligated to text him. With my rotten news.

That sucks. But if your mom changes her mind, text me. I don't care how last minute it is.

I typed, *She won't. But I hope you have fun tomorrow night.*

Not the truth at all. But only because I wouldn't be going to the party.

Mom sat on my bed's edge and sighed. "Maddie, I know you're upset about missing Heather's party. But Dr. Randolph said—"

"I know, Mom. I was there?" What was left of my voice had cracked on my last word.

Bad infection. Meds for ten days. Lots of rest so I could go back to school on Monday.

She narrowed her eyes at my snarky tone.

"I'm sorry. But she's one of my best friends and it's her eighteenth birthday."

"And I'm sure Heather understands."

She did understand. Though she'd been extremely bummed when I'd broken the news to her during our Face-Time chat after Mom and I returned from the doctor's office.

My phone again buzzed and chimed.

Won't be as much fun without my really cute "date." He'd also added the winking emoji.

Thanks for being so nice about this.

I rested my forehead on my knees, buried under three layers of blankets.

Okay. Maybe Liam had been right about Nicolas's intentions. Which meant it was probably a good thing I couldn't go to her party. And did I really want to be around Liam while he pined for another girl? Still, this was so unfair, and I could only blame myself. For meeting up with Tyler *effing* Bennett at that germ-filled bowling alley. It had to be where I caught this nasty infection, because I *never* got this sick.

Another text hit my phone, and I lifted my head to glance at the screen.

Why wouldn't I be? Feel better.

"Who are you texting?" Mom asked.

I placed my chin on my knees. "Nicolas. We'd planned on meeting up at her party." I dropped my phone.

"You had a date with this boy?"

I groaned. "It was a total non-date, because we don't even know each other. We were just going to talk and hang out. You know?"

She frowned. "Not exactly, no." She angled herself to fully face me. "But I'd love for you to tell me what's going on with you and all these dates with different boys."

Oh. Perfect. She chooses now, when I'm feeling lousy times one hundred, to ask me about my dating spree. Which I would never call it in front of her.

I shrugged. "Just having some fun." But not really. "Because it's my senior year?"

Her eyebrows reached the ceiling.

I rolled my eyes. "Mom, it's not like *that*. They were just dates. Not a big deal."

Her face relaxed. "So you're trying different boys out? To see if there's a connection?"

My face became warm and not from my fever.

I didn't know how to answer her questions, since Project Dating Spree had been about going on a date and moving on. To prove I wasn't clingy and absolutely didn't need a boy for anything. But I couldn't tell her that. And now I liked the wrong boy, who I hadn't heard from since he'd walked away Wednesday afternoon. Even though other friends had checked on me the last couple days. And boys called *girls* moody and unpredictable?

"Mom, don't overthink it. I'm enjoying my senior year, and I promise I'm not doing anything bad." But then Barrett's disappointed face floated through my mind. He also still wasn't talking or looking at me.

I frowned at my phone, remembering Nicolas's disappointment and flirty reference to our "date." Like Barrett, his hope at having something more with me wasn't my fault. But I'd still somehow given them hope. And someone had gotten hurt. Like Noah predicted.

"Okay," she said. "I just don't want you or anyone else to end up with hurt feelings."

Right. I lowered my eyes to a crease in my comforter as guilt increased my aching.

"I sent your brother an e-mail today. To let him know how your grandpa's doing." She sighed. "I did try calling. I also wanted to ask him about that news he'd mentioned in his last postcard. But it went right to a generic voicemail. So I didn't leave a message."

I sat up to grab my mug of tea. And my aching body filled with relief at the subject change, even though it was about my worthless brother.

"Do you even have the right e-mail address for him?" I grumbled into my tea.

The rat bastard was far away in Vancouver, Canada, doing God knows what, while we were here with *my* grandpa. And a wave of anger rolled through me.

I clenched my teeth.

If Bradley *effing* Harrington were standing here, I'd probably punch him.

"It didn't bounce back," she murmured. "And I was extremely honest with him about everything. But who knows when I'll get a response since he's terrible when it comes to e-mail."

Yes. Something I'd learned the hard way after he left us without hesitation. To go "do his own thing for a while."

I sipped my tea and closed my eyes as the hot, semi-sweet

liquid slid down my raw throat. Heaven in a mug, which also eased my anger with Bradley.

Mom mentioning my grandpa, and that she'd been honest about his condition in her e-mail to my brother, made me ask, "How's grandpa been this week?" It seemed weird asking her that, since he was right down the hall. But after getting sick, I'd stayed out of his room.

Mom and Ruth had made it clear the last thing he needed was to get sick, too. It's not like I could disagree with them, either. So Mom had taken over reading to him in the evenings.

Her dark eyes dimmed. "He's been quiet. And he's back to calling me Molly." A sad laugh escaped her. "I have to admit it was nice hearing him say *my* name last week. Even under those circumstances."

Her dim eyes became shiny, and I stared into my mug.

I wanted to throw my arms around her. Give her the hug she seemed to need. And that I also needed. But being sick, I couldn't do that. Still, Keith was here. I cracked a smile at knowing he would give her the big hug I couldn't give her. That her dad couldn't give her, either.

My smile disappeared as my eyes became wet.

I had a strong feeling my grandpa was who she *really* needed to hug. So did I, for that matter. Especially feeling as icky as I did. He'd been such a great hugger, too. He'd given the kind of hugs that made me feel safe and warm and loved and, on bad days like today, made everything shift back into rightness.

I rapidly blinked my eyes to stop the tears. At my grandpa's condition. My mom's pain she hid very well. My brother's selfishness. At missing rehearsal yesterday, and missing out on Heather's party. At not being able to free my feelings for Liam. And at feeling so yucky.

Mom stood. "Think you'll be hungry for Keith's famous garlic chicken?"

I grimaced. "No. But I'll warm up some soup later if I do get hungry." I tried on a smile. "I promise you and Keith won't know I'm here."

She laughed, which was nice to hear. "We're going to eat dinner on the couch and find a movie on Netflix. So if you need anything, just ask."

I nodded, settled back into my pillows, and eyed my book.

I needed to start working on all my homework Noah had dropped off this afternoon, right before Mom and I left for my doctor's appointment. But I was to the part in *Pride and Prejudice* where Mr. Darcy was about to profess his love to Elizabeth. Despite her nasty reaction, it was one of my favorite scenes ever in a book or movie.

I switched the mug to my left hand and picked up my book.

Yes. Escape. That's what I wanted and deserved after this rough week. I also had all weekend to get caught up on my schoolwork. It's not like I'd be going anywhere.

Chapter Seventeen

"**S**weetie?"

I looked up from my horrible math homework spread out on my desk at the sound of Mom's voice from my doorway. I wasn't sure what was worse. Being sick and stuck at home on the night of Heather's party, or those two things with the addition of math homework from hell.

Actually, all of this sucked.

She smiled. "You have a visitor."

I frowned, because I hadn't heard the buzzer.

"A pretty cute visitor," she whispered, followed by a soft laugh. "He arrived right as I was letting myself into the building."

Well, that explained why I hadn't heard the buzzer. But a cute boy visitor? I wasn't exactly in the shape to see anyone, much less a cute boy—my eyes widened.

Oh, my God, oh, my God. It couldn't be *him*.

"Who is it? And you didn't let him in here, did you?" I glanced at my heavy, pink hoodie sweatshirt and black, baggy sweatpants. I'd also, after a quick shower, pulled my damp hair into a messy ponytail.

"You look fine. And you have told me this boy is just a friend."

Which meant it was him.

Mom stepped aside, and Liam appeared from behind her.

His eyes lit up when he saw me. "She's *alive*!" he said in some weird, exaggerated voice.

I stood, gave him my back, and did the only other thing I could to escape this total humiliation. I dashed toward my walk-in closet, ripped the door open, and shut myself inside.

What had Mom been thinking, letting him into our condo *and* my bedroom...doorway?

I leaned against the door. The only light in the closet came through the opening at my feet. And that was pretty dim since that light came from my desk lamp.

Okay. I liked that he was, for some reason, here and did want to see him. But not like this.

Knock, knock, knock.

"Go away." A thought occurred to me, and I added, "Shouldn't you be at the party?"

"I'm on my way there. I stopped by to drop something off for you. And you'll love it. I promise. But you have to come out here," he added around a laugh.

I faced the door. "Thank you for whatever you brought. Really. But you can go now."

"Maddie, as Noah would say your neurotic is showing. And it's just me, so open the door." He laughed. "It's not like I haven't seen you in pajamas before."

Right. The slumber party scene in *Grease*. And those had been skimpy compared to what I currently wore. Still, this situation was real, and I looked disgusting. And the thought of *Liam* seeing me like this made me release a soft groan.

"I don't care. I'm not coming out of here until you leave."

I heard him loudly sigh, then, "Fine. You win. I'll text you to see if you liked my gift."

My shoulders sagged from relief. And I waited for what felt like at least a minute before slowly opening the door. I poked my head out and...no Liam.

I walked out of my closet, closed the door behind me, and stepped forward to scan my room for whatever he'd brought.

Liam appeared and leaned against my doorframe, and of course while wearing his huge, dimpled smile. "I can't believe you fell for that."

I narrowed my eyes. "You rat bastard."

His humor transformed into pretend hurt. "Ouch, Maddie. That hurts. Right *here*." He pointed at his heart.

I stomped toward my bed and yanked out one of my four emoji pillows I'd been using behind my real pillows. And proceeded to turn and toss Crazy Face. Right at his head.

He ducked as he walked into my room, and I grabbed the other one with its tongue sticking out. And hurled that pillow at him.

He leaned left. "You should know I got an A in dodgeball back in the day."

I threw the eye-rolling pillow at him, and his hips went right.

"How many of those do you have back there?"

I grabbed the last one, tossed it, and the pillow hit him right in his cute face.

He dropped to my floor and laid there. As if my poop emoji pillow had killed him.

Hoarse giggles ripped out of me. But then I started coughing, and I quickly raised the neck of my sweatshirt to cover my mouth.

Mom walked into my room while holding Crazy Face and Eye Roller. They must've landed in the hallway after missing their intended target.

Her eyes fell to Liam, sprawled on my floor, and she stepped over him. "If you two can't play nice, Liam will have to leave," she said in a mock stern voice. She dropped the pillows on my bed, stepped over Liam again, and left.

I coughed once more and lowered my sweatshirt. "Get up you freak."

He opened his eyes, rolled onto his right side, and propped himself up on his elbow. "Pretty good, huh? I owe that performance to playing Tybalt a year ago."

I rolled my eyes. But when they settled on him again, stretched out on my floor, propped up and seeming so relaxed, I realized how incredibly *hot* he looked tonight.

My eyes landed on his stylishly messy hair. Followed by his puppy-dog eyes bright with humor and totally illegal smile. I then zeroed in on the black, thermal shirt *hugging* his firm chest and waist. And equally snug, dark jeans.

My insides hummed.

"Maddie Harrington, did you just *check* me out?"

I faced my bed. "No. Of course not." But my hoarse voice made that come out weak.

Trembling, I crawled into bed. And my trembling had nothing to do with all the energy I'd used tossing those pillows at him.

He looked good enough to devour. He also had to taste as good as he looked.

My heart battered my chest while I buried myself under the blankets. I also covered half my scalding face. "So what did you bring me?" I asked with as much indifference as I could manage.

He stood, now smiling as if he'd become the devil. He then reached toward my desk and picked up a covered, medium-sized bowl.

He brought it to me, and I took the...warm bowl from his hands.

"You'll need a spoon. Do you want me to grab you one?"

I lifted the bowl to my nose that wasn't quite as drippy

and inhaled. My empty tummy rumbled. "Is this chicken noodle soup?"

He puffed out his chest. "Homemade chicken noodle soup. Not that crap from a can. It's an *old, family recipe*," he added in a gruff, old-man's voice.

I laughed. Was there a voice or person he couldn't impersonate?

"My mom made it when I told her how sick you've been," he quietly added. "And I thought I'd drop the soup off on my way to the party. I also wanted to see how you're feeling."

I lifted my eyes from the bowl and they connected with his.

He smiled, but this one held affection.

My still achy body relaxed against my pillows, and everything inside and around me became warm as we held our long stare. And it hit me. Shane had given me thoughtful gifts for Christmas, my birthday, and Valentine's Day. But this bowl of homemade chicken noodle soup was the nicest...present?...a boy had ever given me.

I dropped my eyes back to the bowl.

Liam needed someone like me, and I needed him.

"Based on your sharp aim with that last pillow," he teased, "my diagnosis is that you'll be back at school on Monday and ready to conquer the stage as Aunt Abby."

I nodded absently. "Yes. And thanks for the soup."

But how would I get him to notice me when he liked someone else? I also no longer cared about history repeating itself or that he was Shane's best friend. Because Liam had latched on to something deep inside me. And crossing *this* friendship line seemed so tremendously right. I'd gotten closer to Liam in two weeks than I had with Shane in three months.

"Yeah. Of course. Do you want me to get you that spoon before I leave?"

I glanced up at him. "You're leaving?"

He raised his eyebrows before justified confusion took over his face.

No. He could not go to Heather's party, looking as incredible as he did, and be in the same place with that dumb girl who, thankfully, didn't like him back. Just the thought of him being anywhere near her caused jealousy to surge through me. To the point I tasted its nasty bitterness. Which was so irrational, stupid, and selfish. I probably also deserved a hard, theatrical slap to the face. But I couldn't help my feelings.

Still, I had no choice but to say, "Of course you're leaving. I think I'm just tired of being cooped up in this place. And being sick." Not lies, either.

"I'm going to go get you that spoon. I'll be right back."

Good. Yes. Distance. Time to get control of my thoughts with deep, meditative breathing. In fact, maybe that's what I needed to do once he left. I hadn't mediated since Sunday. When I'd been unsuccessful at clearing my head of all things Liam Langley.

I lowered the bowl to my lap and closed my eyes.

Deep inhale to count four...exhale to count eight...repeat deep inhale...

My neck and shoulders relaxed even more during my second long exhale.

"Here you go."

I jumped and my eyes flew open. I took the spoon he held out and mumbled, "Thanks."

He turned and went straight for my desk. Where he grabbed my chair and rolled it to beside my bed. He then straddled the chair and rested his arms on the back.

My mouth inched open. "What are you doing?"

He shrugged. "I'm hanging out with my duet partner."

Oh, my *God*. I didn't think I was being that obvious. Or needy. But something I'd said had clearly changed his mind about leaving for the party.

"I did shoot Heather and Shane a text before I got your spoon. To tell them I wouldn't make it."

An odd combo of guilt and excitement shimmied through me. And maybe, just maybe, he had given up on this girl? At the same time, I didn't like the thought of both of us missing Heather's big party. So I felt obligated to say, "Liam, you didn't have to do that. I didn't mean to guilt you into staying."

"You didn't."

"But what about Heather? You didn't hurt her feelings, did you?"

"I don't know. All she texted back was that." He looked over his shoulder and pointed at my sticking-out-its-tongue emoji pillow on my floor.

I giggled. At least, it kinda, sorta sounded like a giggle.

He angled his head toward the bowl. "You should eat that before it gets cold."

I wrinkled my nose at him, then pulled the lid off the bowl and dropped it on my nightstand. But my everything was popping at the fact he wouldn't be leaving. To the point I wanted to unleash a goofy smile. But I dipped my spoon in the soup and—oh. Yummy. Way better than that crap in the can. The warm, lightly seasoned chicken broth slid down my still raw throat, and I moaned.

He laughed. "Did I forget to mention that soup is actually a miracle drug?"

"It tastes like it." I swallowed another spoonful and my eyes drifted to him, watching me with a look I couldn't interpret. So I quietly asked, "What did Shane say?" Not that it mattered one bit. But I was curious since his best friend *had* suddenly chosen to skip the party and hang out with me. His ex.

Liam's gaze turned piercing, and my breath stalled.

A gaze I was beginning to crave with the same intensity of just being around him.

"What would he say? You and I are friends, hanging out here instead of at a party."

His words might as well have been a bucket of frigid, Bay water dumped on my head.

I went back to spooning soup into my mouth. Until a question appeared in my mind. "What's wrong with you?"

He sent me a deep frown.

Okay. That had come out a tad on the bitchy side.

I lowered the bowl to my lap. "Sorry. But I have to be honest with *you* about something that's been on my mind."

He hesitated before saying, "Okay."

I sighed, paused, then said, "You don't get Project Dating Spree, and I don't get why you're pining for a girl who doesn't like you back." There. I'd said it. Then quickly added, "It seems like such a waste since it's our senior year. And I think you should let her go and move on." *To me. Because I* know *we'd be great together.*

Hmm. Something about that seemed so familiar.

A long, thick silence followed my honesty.

I stared at my soup. I had spoken a bit harshly. But maybe that's exactly what he needed to hear. And it's not like he hadn't been super honest with me on Wednesday.

He started picking at the top of my chair. "I'm trying to let her go. But I like this amazing girl. *A lot.*" He released a soft laugh. "Who has no idea she's amazing."

The dark side of my personality caused hatred for this unknown "amazing" girl to ignite. I spooned soup into my mouth. To stop myself from growling like a rabid dog.

"But it's a good thing she doesn't like me that way," he continued, "since I don't think it's a good idea for me to get close to anyone. Especially since it's our senior year."

I lowered my spoon and glanced at him, still picking at my chair. "Liam, why would you think something like that?"

After several seconds, he brought his eyes to mine. And

my breath became lodged in my throat at the sadness filling his dark eyes usually lit up with laughter and mischief.

"Because I'm enlisting in the Marines."

Oh...my...God. That part of this had never crossed my mind. At some point after graduation, he'd be leaving his family. His friends. Then what?

His sadness reached out and grasped my soul. The overwhelming urge to put aside my bowl of soup to wrap him in my arms for the hug *we* needed caused my trembling to return.

Becoming a Marine was in his blood and admirable. But I couldn't stop the selfish thought of *why him?*

"It's the reason I *rarely* date and have never had a real girlfriend."

Of course. And it's probably why he'd picked Bree as a "summer romance." She'd gone to the other side of the country for college. There'd been zero expectations.

"Anyway," he said, running a hand through his hair, "thanks for listening."

I sighed and murmured, "Thanks for sharing." Though he hadn't said anything I wanted to hear, at least I now understood where he was coming from. And knew without question we were destined for no more than what we had. Good friendship.

Disappointment filled my bloodstream, and my eyes blurred.

Inhale to count four...exhale to count eight...

"Thanks for staying with me, too." He did have a way of making me forget *my* world. Another reason I liked being alone with him. Like we had on Sunday at his place.

I blinked until my blurry eyes cleared.

"No thanks required. So who's your friend?"

I caught him pointing at my bear, propped up against the wall.

"Buddy." I sniffed. "My grandpa gave him to me when I was nine."

He again folded his arms on my chair's back. "Okay, Madeline. It's your turn." Our eyes locked. "It looked like your grandpa was sleeping when I got here. But how's he doing? Really?"

I carefully shifted more onto my right side, so I could better see him. I then let Liam into that part of my life.

Chapter Eighteen

I giggled for what had to be the hundredth time as I listened to Liam reading *Pride and Prejudice* in a British accent. He'd even changed his voice for the female characters, while keeping the accent. Between this, and unloading everything going on with my grandpa, an unfamiliar, yet much-needed sense of peace had settled itself around me.

My eyes had drooped several times while listening to him. But I didn't want to miss a second of my peacefulness. Or this incredibly special alone time with him. That would never happen again, outside of us rehearsing our duet. And I had no idea how I would get through *that*.

Mom had checked on us a couple times. I'd also caught her aren't-you-two-cute smile.

Yep. All of this was pretty cute, sweet, and though it was getting kind of late, the thought of him leaving made me pout.

"Keep going?" he asked, in his normal voice. "Or did I lose you?"

I slid my eyes to him and smiled.

No. I wouldn't let him go until he absolutely had to leave.

"You didn't lose me. But aren't you tired of reading out loud in a British accent?"

He shook his head. "Nope. I could do this all night." He smiled. "But I could switch it up if you want." He cleared his throat. "Go for the accent from down under?" he said in a thick, Australian accent. "*What d'ya say*?"

I giggled. Again. "How do you do all that? The accents and impersonations?"

He shrugged. "I'm not sure. It's always been pretty easy." He bookmarked the page. "But I wasn't kidding when I said I had no life in middle school."

Something I still couldn't believe considering how freakin' good he looked tonight.

My face warmed as he gently tossed the book on my bed.

"I mean, I had friends," he continued, "but girls didn't look twice at me because I was skinny and had braces." He cringed, clearly remembering his awkward stage. "And Lucas has always been scary good at playing video games." He rolled his eyes. "He happily kicks my ass. So, I became a real loser back then and got into watching movies."

I grinned. "You're not even a loser. I'd rather read than watch T.V. or be on my phone."

He turned to look at my bookcase, on the right side of my desk, crammed with books I'd read or planned on reading. Someday.

"I can tell." He swung his head back to me, his smile again affectionate.

I tried to squash the flutters as I asked, "What about Lucas? Did you two look *identical* during the horrible, awkward years?"

He nodded. "We went through awkward together." He frowned. "But he did get his braces off a month before me. And loved reminding me every damn day of that month, too."

I laughed, and I realized I knew almost nothing about his brother. "Who's older?"

His smile came back. "Me. By nine minutes. And I remind *him* as often as I can."

Wow. For some reason, I'd expected him to say Lucas was the older brother. Then more questions about Lucas swirled through my mind. Kind of personal questions, too. But Liam didn't seem to have a problem with sharing and something had definitely shifted between us tonight. And just because I couldn't have what I really wanted with him, didn't mean we couldn't be better than good friends. So I asked, "Is it hard for Lucas? With you being...you. And him..." I lost my voice while his smile slowly formed a sad line.

Okay. Maybe my question had been too personal.

"When we were little. Before he—we—learned sign language." He paused, then added, "But our parents sent him to a school for the deaf that specializes in working with really little kids until around age seven. And we were learning sign language, too."

I sat up and pulled my knees to my chest. "So why did he want to be homeschooled?"

He frowned. "He had a hard time being in a regular classroom. Didn't like the extra attention he got. Especially from most of our classmates." He huffed. "And he *really* didn't like relying on me to interpret." His eyes drifted to a spot on my bed. "The school brought in an interpreter. But he didn't like that, either. Still too much attention." The corner of his mouth lifted in a smile. "But now he's ready for a college classroom. So, yeah. It all worked out."

Yeah. Everything had worked out, but I couldn't help but ask, "Is it hard for you? Especially since you're in theater and choir, and can do all the accents and stuff?"

He rested his chin on his arms, again folded on the chair's back. "Sometimes."

Oh. My heart slowed. And there came the strong urge to put my arms around him.

"But Lucas once told me he can *feel* music. If that makes sense?"

I gave him a soft smile and nodded. "Totally."

"And he's been familiar with all our shows," he continued. "I mean, he's seen the movie versions of the plays and musicals we've done. And read *Romeo and Juliet,* and *The Crucible.*" He smiled. "He and Willow are reading *Arsenic and Old Lace* together and they love it. Can't wait to see it." He laughed. "And my parents, being into really old movies, and actors and actresses, bought the movie version. Which we've watched. It's pretty good, too."

I nodded. "I can relate. My mom's a literature professor at the city college and is also into really old movies. And actors and actresses. But we've owned that movie for a long time. And you're right." I played with the corner of my blanket. "It is a good movie."

"You've watched it, too," he said with clear appreciation. "Cool. And your mom's job explains why you love to read. And why you're reading *Pride and Prejudice.* For the third time."

I peeked at him, and his smile grew.

I'd shared that info when he'd caught me mouthing some lines while he read.

"You also have a sappy, romantic side. That no one seems to know about." He straightened, his expression becoming full of...pride. "Except me. And I'll guard your secret with my life," he said in his Teddy Brewster-Roosevelt voice.

I giggled. Yet again. Seriously, how had I never noticed his overall adorableness the last three years? But the answers came fast.

Because we were friends. Then I'd stupidly developed a crush on his best friend.

I shoved that thought to the back of my mind and asked, "Where does Lucas want to go to college?"

He rested his chin back on his arms. "He and Willow are actually going to go to the city college." He glanced at me. "Guess that means they might have your mom."

"Yeah. Probably." And I smiled at the thought.

"So, what are *your* big plans next year?"

I sighed. "Just San Francisco State. Where I'll be majoring in lit and minoring in theater."

Our eyes came together, but his seemed full of surprise. Like the way Barrett had looked at me after I told him the same thing.

"Lit makes sense. But why not major in theater? Maddie, you're good." He held our gaze as he added, "Better than good. You can act, sing, *and* dance."

I tingled and shivered at his compliments. While fighting another goofy smile. But I managed to say, "We can only afford a state school. And San Francisco State isn't exactly known for being a theater school. Not like UCLA."

His eyes dimmed.

"It's a good school. And I don't see the point in going to a state school somewhere else." I paused, then added, "I also don't want to leave my family."

He slowly nodded, and I went back to playing with the corner of my blanket.

"I get it," he murmured. "My parents have their military-retirement income. My dad also has a pretty good job, being in charge of security for some corporate VIP. But it doesn't make us rich. And between what they're paying for P.A. and having to pay for almost all of my brother's college tuition...yeah. I'm going to need the GI Bill."

I kept my eyes on my fingers, flipping the corner back and forth, while a strong question burned inside my brain. To the point I couldn't ignore it. "Aren't you scared? About joining the Marines? Especially now?" It's not like we lived in a super happy world, where everyone loved and tolerated each other.

He stayed silent for so long, I finally lifted my eyes to chance a glance at him. And he was again watching me with a look I couldn't interpret.

"Maddie," he softly said, "I'd be lying if I said I wasn't scared." He looked away. "My parents definitely saw a lot of...ugliness."

His words filled the space between us. And picturing *him* surrounded by that ugliness—no. I couldn't and didn't want to go there.

"They were incredible Marines." He brought his eyes back to mine and gave me a quick smile. "I will be, too. Because being a Marine is what I'm meant to do. And I'm excited about it. But it *won't* be easy to leave," he added.

Right. Okay then. How could I say anything else?

I tried to smile as I asked, "What does Semper Fi mean? I saw it on your bulletin board when I was there last week."

His gaze once again turned piercing. "It's the Marine Corps motto, and is Latin for 'always faithful'."

We held our stare for several seconds. Until he tore his eyes from me.

"All this is reminding me, you have an older brother."

I blinked and lowered my head.

Oh. Wow. Hadn't seen that one coming.

"Is he in the military? I mean, he's never around. And you seem a little sensitive about the topic."

Only because I hate the thought of sweet, amazing you joining the military.

But I certainly couldn't tell him that, and his choices had nothing to do with me. Or anyone else, for that matter.

His phone loudly quacked twice, then stopped. His eyes stayed centered on me, though.

Too sweet. Like everything else about him. But I said, "Nice text message tone."

"I didn't hear a thing."

"Liam, you can get that."

He narrowed his eyes. "You're avoiding."

Totally the truth, but I narrowed my eyes. And we held this long stare for many seconds.

He dramatically sighed. "God, you're stubborn," he muttered. "Fine. I'll check my phone. But we're not done." He reached behind to remove his phone from his right, back jeans pocket.

In that moment, I remembered Heather. I'd been so caught up in Liam and this awesome, unexpected time with him, I hadn't once thought about her party.

I picked up my phone lying beside me and texted, *How's it going, party girl?*

As I waited for her reply, I eyed Liam, rapidly texting.

I wanted so badly to ask who texted him, my mouth watered. Or maybe my mouth was watering due to my side view of his butt curved perfectly from him straddling my desk chair. Something I'd noticed while he'd been reading and had tried *not* to continue noticing.

I dragged my eyes from the view as her response hit.

Totally a blast! But I miss you. She'd even added the crying emoji.

I miss you, too. Glad you're having fun.

I probably should've added *Wish I was there.* But as much as I loved her, that would've been a total lie.

Liam bailed at the last minute. Jerk. And Shane wouldn't tell me why. Two jerks.

I cringed as I dropped my phone. Still, why the secrecy? To save Heather's feelings? Which made sense. But I guess that meant I'd eventually have to tell her why "Liam bailed."

A part of me still couldn't believe he'd chosen to stay. Even though the party had to be a million times more fun than hanging out and talking with sick, yucky me.

Amazing wasn't a strong enough word to describe Liam Langley.

"Okay. Done." He slipped his phone back in his pocket and, once again, gave me his undivided attention. "What's the story with your brother?"

I hated this topic as much as my grandpa's illness. But after being honest with Liam about my grandpa, it seemed so natural and effortless to say, "My brother, Bradley, *is* never around. But it's not because he's in the military."

He nodded. "So where is he?"

I hugged my knees. "Right now he's in Vancouver with some girl he's been seeing. But he's been all over the place since he left right after graduating. Five years ago. He hasn't been back since." I smirked. "He's great at sending us occasional postcards, though."

Liam's eyes flashed with shock. "What's his deal?"

"He's turned into our worthless *father* who left us when I was a baby, because he wasn't interested in being a dad or husband."

I froze.

Wow. I'd never said that out loud. When directly asked about Russell, my reply was "He's not around." But instead of embarrassment at sharing the truth, relief swept through me and escaped in a soft puff. Just like it had after I'd opened up to him about my grandpa.

Liam's mouth hardened.

"My grandpa has always been more than just a grandparent," I added.

His eyes and face softened, and he opened his mouth to say something. But then Mom appeared in my doorway.

"I hate to break this up," she slowly began, "but it's getting late and you need your rest."

Liam shook his head and stood. "Yeah. It is pretty late."

No, no, no. Not yet.

Mom left, and he released a quick laugh.

"You need to be back at school on Monday. Because it'll suck if we have to rehearse without you again, Aunt Abby."

I couldn't stop my goofy grin at his latest, tummy-fluttering compliment.

He grabbed the chair and pushed it back to my desk. He then made a beeline for my doorway, and my soul withered at seeing him leaving like his cute butt was on fire.

"Liam?"

He stopped and looked at me with raised eyebrows.

I couldn't say *Thanks for the best sick day ever.* At the same time, I couldn't think of an adjective that would accurately describe this night. "This was..." *Darn it.*

"This was..." he teased as his mouth curved into his illegal smile. "Get better, okay? I also need my duet partner back." And he left.

My shoulders drooped and I wrinkled my nose at the empty doorway.

I reached left, grabbed Buddy, and hugged him to me.

How was I going to control my feelings for Liam from this day moving forward?

Chapter Nineteen

I cleared the steps to the second floor and veered left.

I wound my way through kids walking in the hallway as I found a certain someone's locker. But I sighed when I didn't see him, so I kept heading in the direction of my locker located in a different hallway.

Against my common sense, I'd wanted to start Monday with his cuteness.

I'd tried *not* to think about him as I fell asleep Saturday night. And while getting caught up on my schoolwork Sunday. And especially while reading *Pride and Prejudice*. But the memory of him reading to me in a British accent, and in the high-pitched female voices, had made me giggle numerous times yesterday.

Liam had grabbed a hold of me, and I couldn't shake him loose. Which I absolutely needed to do. But how? Fall back on Project...yuck. Still, I had to do something to get past these feelings for him. Keeping a friendly distance from him would work. But that thought made me glower as I avoided two laughing boys hogging the middle of the hallway. Friendly distance was also impossible since we were duet partners.

I really was undeniably screwed.

"Maddie!"

I stopped and turned right, in the direction of the now familiar deep voice.

Nicolas stood at his open locker and smiled. He had a nice smile, too. But nothing like—stop it, stop it, stop it.

"Hey, Nicolas." I stepped toward him.

"You're feeling better." His dark eyes with killer eyelashes warmed.

Wow. An entire week had passed since he'd found me at my locker and, despite my sneezing and drippy nose, convinced me to meet him at Heather's party to hang out as friends. That prompted me to ask, "Did you have fun Saturday night?"

He shrugged. "It was cool. But would've been more fun with my *date*." He winked at me.

Okay. Fine. I'd fallen for his charming "it won't be a date" pitch. But it's not like I'd been thinking clearly a week ago.

"So, now that you're feeling better," he said, "wanna try again to meet up as *friends*? This Saturday night?" He smiled a bit shyly. "I don't want to wait that long, but I know you have rehearsals after school through Thursday. And I have plans with my family Friday night."

I had to give Nicolas Costello credit for persistence. But he wasn't who I wanted to go on a date with Saturday night. And I certainly wasn't going to use him, who clearly did want more than friendship with me, as an escape from my reality.

I gave him a half-smile. "Nicolas, I know you want to be more than friends. But that's not what I want." His face fell with disappointment while guilt again clung to my conscience. "I'm sorry. Really. And, as it turns out, I...really like someone else."

But my life would be so much easier if I did *like you.*

He slowly nodded, then peered at me.

I waited for him to react like Barrett had that day in the auditorium. Then again, I wasn't sure I deserved a reaction like that since Nicolas had sought *me* out for a date. Even after Kassidy told him what I'd said, about "not being interested in anything serious."

Where had that conviction gone in the last couple weeks?

"Is it Liam?" Nicolas quietly asked. "Is that who you like?"

I froze for a handful of seconds as he watched me, his eyes full of curiosity. Then my mouth inched opened while my brain filled with, how could he possibly know I liked Liam?

I stepped closer to him. "How do you know that?" I mumbled, because there were so many kids around us at their lockers. "No one knows that."

He gave me a tight smile. "Liam and I were cool until last Tuesday. When he overheard me telling Kassidy at lunch that I was looking forward to hanging out with you Saturday night." His eyes dropped to the floor. "He hasn't said a word to me since."

Oh. Okay. Kassidy and Liam had never told me about that conversation. Sure, I'd been sick and out of it and beyond cranky and—that wasn't even important.

"It really makes me think he likes you, too," Nicolas added.

My eyes widened.

No. It couldn't be *me* he liked.

But as I stared into Nicolas's locker, my mind zeroed in on Liam and his behavior the last few weeks. All the compliments. Barely tolerating Project Dating Spree. His reaction when I told him about my rotten date with Tyler. His reaction when I'd told him about Nicolas. Him carrying my backpack and walking me home last Wednesday, when he'd said my project and Nicolas weren't good enough for me.

Could it be me he liked?

He had shown up at my place with soup and stayed with me on the night of my best friend's birthday party. Listened to me talk about my grandpa's deterioration, and my other family drama. He'd really opened up to me, too. And there was the whole insisting we be duet partners. Because we'd be great together—oh, my *God*.

I pressed my lips together and looked down. Then I remembered the Monday afternoon in April, following our first full dress and tech rehearsal for *Grease*. When he'd *nervously* asked me to prom. And though he'd tossed in "as friends," my response had been a bitchy, "Thanks, but no thanks." In so many words. Because I'd been in such a dark place.

His face had fallen with disappointment, just like Barrett's and Nicolas's, and I had yet to apologize. But what Nicolas had said and Liam's behavior had to mean one unbelievable thing.

I was the "amazing girl" he liked. Who he thought didn't like him the same way.

I closed my eyes as stupidity surrounded me and stole the air from my lungs.

And he also thought it was best I didn't like him back. Because he'd be leaving.

"Did I say something I shouldn't have?"

Slow inhale to count four...exhale to count eight...

"Maddie?"

I opened my eyes and lifted my head to find Nicolas watching me with concern.

"Um...no." I stepped back. "Thanks for being so cool about this."

I whipped my head right to see if Liam had finally made it to his locker. Because we needed to talk in private. ASAP. But an agitated sigh escaped when I didn't see him.

Where was he? Especially with it being so close to eight.

I tore my eyes from his locker to look at Nicolas, still watching me.

He smiled. "Thanks for being honest, Maddie." He leaned forward. "I'll keep my mouth shut about you and Liam." He laughed. "If I'd known he liked you, I never would've asked you out. Because he's cool and cracks me *up*. All those voices and accents he can do?"

I smiled absently. Because my brain was working hard to absorb the fact Liam Langley liked me as much as I liked him. And had liked me since April?

"I'll see you later," I said before turning away from him to head to my locker.

Okay. I'd catch him before show choir. And suggest we have lunch, alone, in the library or on the rooftop since the weather was sunny and warm. But what would I say once we were alone? There were definitely things going against us crossing the friendship line. And would he want to, even knowing I liked him?

I don't think it's a good idea for me to get close to anyone.

I wasn't certain that was a good idea for me, either. But if we didn't clear the air, our friendship could fall apart under the pressure of *not* saying anything.

Right. I could do this. Be honest with Liam. Who I totally adored.

* * *

I sat when we finished going through the Fun. medley we'd be singing with the concert choir during the show, placed my song sheet on my lap, and crossed my arms.

"What's up?" Taryn asked from her seat beside me. "Still not feeling well?"

"No," I mumbled. "Not really." And because my voice was

still on the hoarse side, I couldn't join the singing. Just like last week. I'd also been trying to catch Liam's eyes.

We were back to sitting in our formal choir arrangement, meaning he was in the next section and sitting with his fellow tenors. But he hadn't once glanced in my direction since I walked into the choir room with a couple minutes to spare.

The only time in the last few weeks he'd acted *this* distant was after I'd mentioned my non-date with Nicolas. Maybe he was now regretting our Saturday night? Then again, he had left my doorway while wearing his illegal smile. His behavior today was too effing weird. But class was nearly over, and he wouldn't be leaving without talking to me.

"That was better than last week," Mrs. Chaplin said from near the edge of the mini-stage. "But I am disappointed with your enthusiasm level. It's not nearly good enough."

I stared at my song sheet and wrinkled my nose. We could bleed the lyrics while singing and it wouldn't be enough for this woman.

"I need to get you going on the choreography in the next week," she droned, "but I can't do that until you give me your best with the music. I also need to start hearing your duets, and those of you in an a cappella group. Get it together, show choir."

I glanced at Taryn, who glanced at me, and we rolled our eyes.

"You're dismissed. Please leave your song sheets on your chairs."

While flinging my backpack onto my shoulder, I tried for what felt like the hundredth time to catch Liam's eyes. But he was doing the same thing with his backpack.

Fine. I'd wait right here since he had to pass the soprano section to leave the choir room.

"I'm sorry you're still not feeling well." Taryn smiled. "But it'll be great to have you back at rehearsal this afternoon." She laughed. "Rehearsal was kind've long on Thursday since Mr. Peters focused on the few scenes you aren't in."

I smiled at her as Liam, talking with another tenor, headed for us.

My heart began pounding my chest.

Inhale to count four...exhale to count eight...

He stopped beside Taryn. "Ready?" he asked her. Before sliding his eyes to me. "Hey." He nodded at me. "How are you feeling?"

Shoot, shoot, shoot. Something was definitely up with him.

"Well, I'm better. Not a hundred percent." My voice had cracked on those words. I pointed at my throat. "Obviously. And it's so sucking I can't sing with you guys. I miss it."

Great. I'd sounded like a babbling buffoon.

He shrugged. "You'll get there. But you do sound better." He refocused on Taryn. "We should go if we want to catch Yates before class."

She smiled at him, and I straightened.

"Liam, I really need to talk to you."

He could not leave with Taryn right now.

He frowned. "Can it wait? Taryn and I need to talk to Yates about our project."

He and Taryn had partnered up on a project for American Government. When did that happen? I'd only been gone for two days.

I held on to a sigh. "Sure. How about lunch?"

His eyes darted to Taryn and back to me. "I can't. We're going to start doing the research for our project at lunch. Because we can't after school. You know, rehearsals."

He was telling the truth. But between his cold greeting and obvious disinterest in talking to me, I knew when I was also being blown off. But why? I hadn't seen or talked to him since he left my place Saturday night.

"Maybe we can talk at rehearsal. If there's time." And with Taryn by his side, he strolled out of the choir room.

I gritted my teeth.

What the *freak* had just happened?

Chapter Twenty

Heather landed at my left side while I loaded my backpack with what I'd need that night.

"We're mad at you," she declared. "We would've had lunch with you on the rooftop. If you'd told us where you were sooner."

"Yeah," Noah said from behind Heather. "It's not like you to be anti-social at lunch. What's going on?"

I'd wanted to pout in solitude over Liam's three-sixty change.

Of course I couldn't say that. Though I wanted to tell my best friends about my feelings for our friend, it'd be wrong on so many levels to tell them before telling Liam. If I could get him alone long enough to have the conversation that had turned my tummy into a series of tight knots. Especially after his strange, cold attitude earlier.

I shut my locker door and faced them. "I needed to be alone. To get caught up on some reading for English." Which I had done, but I couldn't remember anything I'd read.

"Hmm," Heather murmured, eyeing me. "I'm not sure I believe you. You seem a little down and distracted today. Is it because you were gone two days? You do look and sound better."

I tried to smile. "Thanks. And, yeah. That's probably it. We need to get to rehearsal." Which really meant I had to get to the auditorium, corner Liam, and tell him we *needed* to talk. No matter my knotted tummy and his mysterious mood.

We walked together, rounded the corner, and headed for the stairs.

I glanced at Liam's locker, but he wasn't there. Probably already in the auditorium. A good thing, too, if we could get there quickly.

"So," Heather said, "I saw you with yummy Nicolas this morning. Did he talk you into going on a date with him? He'd be such a perfect bachelor for Project Dating Spree."

Noah groaned. "Heather, seriously? Can you say stuff like that when I'm Not. Around."

She waved her hand, as if shooing him and his words away. "Oh, be quiet. But you, Madeline, need to answer my question."

I sighed and played with my backpack's dangling strap. "He wanted to. But I said no. And, I'll be honest, I'm done with Project Dating Spree."

Heather and Noah stopped walking, then I stopped. And I almost laughed at their vastly different expressions.

"Finally," Noah said around a laugh. "And I think that's So. Awesome."

"No, it isn't," Heather stated with a deep frown. "You've only been on two dates. That's not a dating spree. Okay, so the first two didn't work out the way you wanted. But what about Nicolas? I *know* one date with him would've absolutely made up for the first two."

Noah faced her. "How do you *know* that? And it sounds like you're the one into Nicolas."

Her cheeks turned bright pink.

I giggled. "Why don't you ask him out?"

Between Heather shedding her glasses and wearing her long, dark hair loose more often, she was easily one of the prettiest girls in this school. Even Nicolas Costello would be a fool not to give her a chance.

She lifted her chin. "We're not talking about me right now. I want to know what changed your mind about Project Dating Spree. And so suddenly?"

Noah and I shared a quick *o-kay* look before we began walking again.

Sadness filled me up, though, since it seemed clear our best friend didn't see herself as beautiful. And possibly didn't see herself as good enough for Nicolas.

I pushed those thoughts aside to concentrate on what she'd asked. I couldn't tell them about Liam. Not yet, at least. Maybe never, considering his behavior today and what he'd said Saturday night. But I could be honest about what I'd realized Friday night while talking to Mom.

"Heather," I began as we approached the stairs, "Noah and Liam were right." I shot Noah a don't-you-dare-say-a-word look. But he fought a smile while we went down the stairs. "Barrett's still not talking to me. I'm not sure if he ever will again. And that date with Tyler was not only terrible, but I ended up the sickest I've been in a really long time." Speaking the truth did feel like a hard, theatrical slap to the face.

Project Dating Spree, which I'd intended to be fun, had brought me nothing but ickiness. As well as occasional contention with Noah. And Liam. But for extremely different reasons.

Heather stayed silent until we entered the hallway that ended at the auditorium's lobby.

"Well," she mumbled, "when you put it all out there like that I *suppose* I understand." She glanced at me. "So, does that mean you aren't going to get a date for the dance next month?"

Right. Our first dance of the year always fell in October and before Halloween.

I shrugged. "I don't know." But Liam and his adorable everything appeared in my mind with such force I had to catch my breath. Then again, we seemed eons from going to a dance together—my steps slowed when I again recalled Liam asking me to prom.

He never would've asked me without first talking to Shane. Then I remembered Liam's vague answer to how Shane responded to him hanging out with me instead of going to Heather's party. And there was the text he'd received while we were talking. It could've been anyone from Liam's circle of family and friends. But I had a strong feeling it'd been from his best buddy.

I stopped.

Shane knows Liam likes me.

"What's wrong?" Heather asked.

Determination, and not just a little irritation with the best friends, filled every part of me.

Yep. Liam Langley and I had *a lot* to talk about before this day ended.

I squared my shoulders. "Nothing. Let's go."

The second we entered the auditorium, I found Liam. Not surprisingly, he was talking with Shane, Kassidy, and J.R. near the front row seats.

I directed my determined steps toward him. But as soon as I reached the front row, Mr. Peters rushed up to the stage and his eyes brightened when he saw me, followed by a swift smile.

"I see our Aunt Abby is with us today," he said. "Welcome back."

Almost everyone clapped, and I froze while my face warmed to the temp of boiling.

What was this all about? I'd only missed one rehearsal. At the same time, my castmates missing me caused the same cozy feelings I'd experienced Saturday night in Liam's company to return and heat my soul. Then flattery tickled my ego.

I smiled as I shrugged out of my backpack. I also looked at Liam, facing the stage. Ignoring me. And my smile vanished. Seriously, what was his problem all of a sudden?

"And because Maddie is back, I want to focus on act two today. Everyone seems to be struggling with this section. So, I need Abby, Martha, Jonathan, Einstein, and Teddy on stage."

Okay. After rehearsal I would pounce on Liam.

Two extremely long hours later, which wasn't even normal when it came to play rehearsals, Mr. Peters called it a day. There'd been so much stopping and starting over. Some of that due to Mr. Peters and his "vision." But more due to Liam and Shane making everyone on stage with them burst into laughter. Even me a couple times.

Mr. Peters had definitely cast the right boys as Teddy and Mortimer.

I went for the stage right stairs as Kassidy went left with her boyfriend, Shane, and Noah. And Liam actually followed me.

Okay. A much better sign. Now I just needed to get us alone.

"So, I know you wanted to talk to me," he said, following me down the stairs. "But it won't take long, right?"

I halted at the bottom of the steps, and he stopped in front of me.

Oh. No. He was *not* doing this to me a second time.

"Because Shane's brother's at his place with his Chevelle that has a new, badass engine."

I crossed my arms.

The old-car thing I'd never understood. Or honestly cared about. Also known as something that had greatly separated

Shane and me. And how perfectly awesome was it that the old-car thing happened to be interfering with me needing to talk to Liam at this moment.

Not even happening without me making my feelings clear.

"You're not seriously blowing me off again."

He borderline glared at me. "I didn't blow you off. Taryn and I had to talk to Yates about our project. We made plans on *Friday* to work on it at lunch today." He gestured at himself with both hands. "And I'm standing right here, so what's up?"

What was left of my patience with him and his baffling, bad attitude with me snapped with the force of a sun-dried twig. I leaned forward. "I'll need longer than sixty seconds of Liam Langley's precious time."

He sighed. A bit impatiently, too. "Well, can it wait until—"

"No! It can't wait. You big, dumb jerk." I took a deep, shaky breath and enunciated, "Because I know it's me."

Understanding flashed through his eyes. But then he broke our eye contact to cross *his* arms. And a tad too defiantly for my nonexistent patience.

"You know it's...what? What do you know, Maddie?"

If I didn't like his cute face so much, I'd probably punch him.

"Playing dumb is beneath you, Liam."

At that moment, Shane walked up and stood beside his best freakin' buddy. "Are you ready?"

Liam and I held our heated stare. And it took every ounce of my self-control to not say *If you leave right now, I'll* never *look at or speak to you again.*

After several more seconds of our stare down, he ripped his eyes from mine to look at Shane. "I'll have to see the engine some other time. But tell Gabe I said hi."

Perfect. Liam did still have his common sense.

The friends shared a long look. Something resembling

understanding flickered through Shane's eyes, too, before he stepped back and nodded.

Yep. He knew. And the burst of irritation from earlier flared through me again. To the point I started trembling.

"Okay. See you guys tomorrow." Shane turned from us and walked swiftly up the aisle.

That left me, Liam and...I glanced at the house. No one in sight. I then glanced at the stage and also saw no one. Which meant we were finally alone.

A thick, tense silence settled between us while we didn't look at each other, but I wasn't going to be the first one to speak. Especially since he'd been such a jerk today. The boy who thought I was amazing. And I had yet to *sink* myself into that compliment, or any of his others from the last couple weeks, because I'd been so distracted by his three-sixty. I'd also been trying to get us to this moment. Where everything was now out in the open. Ready for us to—

He stepped forward, cupped my face, lowered his head, and pressed his lips to mine.

Chapter Twenty-One

I jolted and opened my mouth to—but that made our kiss *really* begin.

My head became light. Fuzzy. As did everything around us. And my trembling increased. So much so I reached up and clutched the front of his polo shirt. Which brought him closer.

The bottom part of his soft pants brushed against my bare legs. Then white heat rushed through me. The fuzzy world started to spin. And continued spinning even as we, in no hurry at all, brought our kiss to an end.

He lifted his head while still cupping my face.

I pressed my lips together.

Yummy.

"Whoa," he murmured as I slowly opened my eyes.

I blinked until I'd cleared the fuzziness. And *whoa* didn't even begin to describe that kiss.

He smiled, then released a quick laugh. "I've been wanting to do that since you asked me 'where are we going to do it'."

I nodded as I tried to get a hold of my head. And our surroundings. Where were we?

He was still cupping my face, but I looked around us.

Right. Okay then. We were alone in our school auditorium. At least, I hoped no one had seen us. Because an earthquake could've hit, made this building crumble around us, and we wouldn't have noticed a thing.

"Maddie?" he asked, his voice tinged with concern. "Everything okay?"

I raised my eyes. That immediately locked with his, filled with an odd combination of affection and apprehension. Because we'd been in the middle of something.

"No. I mean that kiss was…Well, you know. You were there," I added under my breath.

He fought his cute smile. And I suddenly and surely wanted to kiss him again.

But I said, "I'm still mad at you for being such a jerk today." I didn't want to take two steps back, to put distance between us so I didn't wrap my arms around his neck and kiss him a second time, but I did just that. And his arms fell to his sides. "Liam, what's going on? And have you *liked* me since April?"

He slipped his hands into his pockets. "I saw you with Nicolas at his locker this morning and it…pissed me off." He frowned. "And I didn't just have a fucking awesome kiss with a girl I've liked for months who has a date with another guy. Did I?"

The kiss had been freakin' awesome. His jealousy over Nicolas explained his coldness today, too. And I guess he had, for some reason, liked me since April.

Okay. First, we'd deal with the Nicolas stuff. Then we'd get into the other, way more important things going on here. With us.

I crossed my arms. "Well, it just so happens, Mr. *Jealous,* I was on my way to my locker, hoping to see you, when Nicolas caught me. And, yeah, he did ask me out again. But I told him no." I leaned forward. "Because I like you, too."

He raised his eyebrows. Seconds later his face became crimson and he looked away.

"I think you owe me an apology, Liam Langley."

He lifted his head and gave me his illegal smile. "Can I show you I'm sorry?"

Between his smile and cute question, everything in me tingled. Then burned as I remembered our kiss. But as tempting as he was right now, I needed him to be serious. "That smile won't work. And I know Shane knows. He's the one who texted you Saturday night. Right?" Probably to see how things were going between us. And this whole thing probably should've been classified as weird. But I'd shared more with Liam in a breath of time than I had with Shane in the few months we were together.

"Yes." He stepped toward me. "But don't be pissed at him. He hasn't done anything wrong. And you two never worked as a couple. I know it, he knows it, *you* know it. Everyone knows it."

If he had said that to me in the spring, I probably would've kicked him. Even knowing then it was nothing but the truth. As a couple, Shane and I had brought out the worst in each other. But I'd been in such a fragile place, I hadn't been able to let him go. Or accept the fact he'd moved onto...Natalie. A girl who did make him happy.

Just like Liam made me happy. And vice versa.

"So, this might be a dumb question," he said, "but how did you figure it out?" He paused, then added, "But I guess I wasn't being super subtle. Especially after you started that *project*."

I let those comments go, along with my stupidity, and said, "Nicolas."

His eyes widened.

"He told me you stopped talking to him because of our *non-date* for Heather's party and assumed it was because you liked me. You owe him an apology, too, by the way."

He avoided my pointed stare.

"Then everything you've been doing and saying the last couple weeks made sense."

Our eyes came together, and his gaze turned piercing.

Everything around us blurred once more.

I cleared my throat. "What happens now?" Maybe a ridiculous question after that world-spinning kiss. The kind of kiss every girl on this planet deserved to experience over and over again with a boy she couldn't stop thinking about. But his honesty from Saturday night was a conversation we couldn't avoid.

An auditorium door opened, and Mr. Peters and Mr. Lowry walked inside. But stopped the moment they saw us, still standing by the stage right stairs.

Oh, my God, oh, my God. If they'd walked in—I flinched.

"What are you two still doing here?" Mr. Peters asked.

"Just talking," Liam easily answered. "We're leaving."

We headed for our backpacks, swung them over our shoulders, and speed walked up the aisle and out of the auditorium.

"Shit," Liam mumbled the moment the door closed behind us. "That would've been *way* more awkward if they'd walked in five minutes sooner," he said in a gruff, southern accent.

I laughed, since he'd, in his endearing Liam way, expressed what I'd been thinking.

He waggled his eyebrows. "Good. You still think I'm funny. And cute?"

I shook my head. "Liam, we have to talk about this."

His shoulders wilted. "Okay. You're right." He sighed. "Yeah. Shane knows everything. Because I talked to him about asking you to prom."

Just like I'd figured.

He opened the door for me, then the second door, and we stepped into the warm air.

"But asking you, even as *friends*, was a dumbass mistake," he softly continued as we, in unison, jogged down the stairs. "You weren't ready for that. So I…let you go."

The way he said those words, and the fact they were so honest, made my soul ache.

"I wasn't ready," I murmured. "But I didn't have to be a bitch to you. I'm sorry. Really." And could it be the boy I was meant to be with had always been right *here*?

"It's fine. You weren't exactly yourself back then."

We headed in the direction of my place.

"I thought I could handle us staying friends. It's like I told you Saturday." He glanced at me. "I've been trying to convince myself it was better you didn't like me the same way."

Because he's leaving in less than a year to become a Marine.

Right. That reality I still couldn't imagine.

"But I can't stay away from you."

My steps faltered, as did his, and we faced each other.

His newest and extraordinary compliment replaced where my mind had gone, and I shivered. "Well, I really did give up on Project Dating Spree. Because of you," I quietly added. I then gave him a pretend dirty look. "But I'll bring it back if you keep acting like Mr. *Jealous*."

He nodded. "Yeah. Got it." He laughed. "I love knowing you like me, too." He peered at me. "It was my mom's chicken noodle soup that changed your mind. Wasn't it?"

I grinned. "It definitely helped."

"Which means I need to find out what the hell she puts in that soup."

I laughed, but then his expression eased back into serious.

"Maddie, I'm still not sure *us* is a good idea."

My smile slipped. Because I wasn't sure, either. There was

so much on the line. Our friendship. Our hearts. Our souls. But the thought of not being *with* him, after all the honesty we'd shared and our fuzzy-head kiss, made the risky choice crystal clear. And him leaving to become a Marine didn't have to be faced right now. It was only September.

"Was that your crummy way of asking me out on a date?"

He frowned. For about two seconds. Then slowly revealed his dimpled smile.

"You really don't know me very well." He tilted his head in the direction of my place. "Come on. You have to have as much homework as I do tonight."

Okay. He was super sweet for walking me home again. But disappointment at the fact he hadn't asked me out on a date caused me to fight a childish pout.

Chapter Twenty-Two

I put *To Kill a Mockingbird* aside and started to unfold myself from the comfy chair beside my grandpa's bed, but stopped when my eyes settled on him, sound asleep. Him sleeping was the only time I saw his face free of tension and wariness.

I pulled my legs up and hugged them to my chest. My mind then drifted to Liam and everything that had happened between us earlier. Especially our unexpected, *whoa* kiss.

I smiled as that unforgettable memory caused the white heat to rush through me. Again.

Wow. Liam Langley. The boy I'd been friends with for three years. The boy I'd shared the stage with for numerous plays and choir concerts. The boy I thought I'd known pretty well. But, like he'd said before walking me home, I didn't know him very well.

I still couldn't believe I was the amazing girl he liked when I remembered how awful I'd acted in the spring. Though he clearly didn't seem to be holding the awfulness against me. Come to think of it, no one seemed to be holding any of that against me. Even Shane. And the fact it didn't bother Shane that his best friend liked me, could be another way of him trying to get us back to friendship.

My smile faded.

The weirdness between Shane and me and…Natalie… combined with Liam admitting he wasn't sure "us was a good idea," could be why he hadn't asked me out. Maybe he needed time to process what had happened today. Especially since pursuing an *us* probably wasn't the smartest, best idea. But still. What about our *whoa* kiss? He'd also basically admitted he'd liked me since April. So what was he waiting for?

I sighed.

Darn him for kissing me like he did. Though I had definitely kissed him back. And now I couldn't imagine never kissing him again. Or having his cuteness all to myself. But so *not* in a clingy, possessive way. Project Dating Spree was over, but that Maddie would never come back.

I lifted my eyes to my grandpa sleeping peacefully, the urge to tell him about Liam overwhelmed me; the words on the verge of release since this was the only time I could talk to him. And though he'd never remember Liam if I introduced them, the desire to have my grandpa know him caught my soul and hung on for dear life.

He'd been in the army. Under different circumstances, he and Liam would have so much to talk about. He'd probably laugh, loud and hard, at Liam's John Wayne impression, too.

My grandpa's infectious, rowdy laugh filled my head. A laugh I hadn't heard in forever. And never would again. Just like I'd never feel the warmth and strength of his bear hugs. Or hear him call me his Miss Maddie Renée. But the thought of having *my* grandpa back with me one more time made me close my eyes, and I held tight to the hope. And memories.

Mom was stretched out on the couch with her laptop and absorbed in grading papers. Ruth had left for the night after making sure he ate at least half his dinner.

I opened my eyes and they settled once more on his peaceful face. I then rested my chin on my knees and quietly said, "I have to tell you about this boy I really, really like." I paused, then added, "But it's kind've scary. Because there's so much at stake."

* * *

"Ciao, *Bella*."

I paused at hearing his close greeting in a lowered, *hot* Italian accent, then looked right.

I'd, of course, looked for him at his locker the second I'd walked upstairs and hadn't seen him. But here he was, beside me at my locker. And giving me an exaggerated, smoldering grin that made me want to drop my backpack, grab the folds of his sweater and kiss him.

Unfortunately, we were at school, surrounded by other kids, with a couple of teachers nearby, talking. So all I did was return his exaggerated grin and say, "Ciao, *Casanova*."

He laughed. Probably at my somewhat hoarse and terrible attempt at an Italian accent.

"That was pretty cute. And Casanova, huh?" He leaned forward. "I guess my kisses do have that effect on girls."

I rolled my eyes, even though giddiness flew through me, followed by a giggle. He obviously wasn't regretting any part of yesterday afternoon.

Maybe *us* wouldn't be so scary after all? But remembering our kiss and my slightly hoarse voice made me say, "I'm not sure we should've—you should've—done that. I'm still not feeling one-hundred percent." Though I'd never, ever take back that kiss.

His smile vanished and he leaned back. "That's why I woke up with a sore throat."

I gaped at him.

No. He couldn't be sick. Not now.

He burst into laughter. "I can't believe you fell for that, too. Wow. I'm really good."

I wrinkled my nose at him and faced my locker to continue grabbing what I needed. But thank God he wasn't sick.

"You told me on Saturday you were taking serious meds." He leaned against the locker next to mine. "And, honestly, that wasn't on my mind yesterday. Especially after *that*."

I dropped my math book into my backpack while fighting a big, goofy grin, since he also still thought our kiss had been *whoa*. Something I needed to know, considering yesterday hadn't ended the way I'd hoped it would.

"I have something very important for you."

The mischief in his voice made me glance back at him as he held out a *paper* note? That looked folded a million times.

I grasped the note. "What is this?"

Now he rolled his eyes. "What does it look like?" He straightened. "And I expect an answer by show choir." His smile dipped. "I wish I could have lunch with you today. But Taryn and I still have research to do on our project. Then we have to start putting it all together."

Oh. That project. Still, I wasn't sure if we were at the point of announcing to our friends—what? That we *liked* each other? And our kiss was no one's business.

Confusion replaced all my giddiness, so I had to ask, "Liam, what are we doing?"

"Read what I wrote." He placed his head beside mine. "You won't be disappointed."

And there came that rush of white heat at his warm, minty breath on my ear.

I gripped my locker door with my free hand.

Inhale to count four...exhale to count eight...

He lifted his head, pointed at the note, and left.

I shook my head. At irresistible him. Then laughed since I

couldn't remember the last time I'd received a paper note from anyone. He had folded it a million times, too. And when I reached the point where the paper was unfolded, my hands shook as I read what he'd written.

Dear Maddie,

No. That wasn't my "crummy way of asking you out on a date." But I couldn't ask you on the sidewalk, right near school. After that kiss?! So I came up with this idea. Because I've never given a note to a girl I liked.

Will you <u>please</u> go out with me Saturday? Friday won't work. If your voice is back to normal, we really need to rehearse our song. (Hint, hint.)

Liam

I smiled and hugged the paper to my chest.

Maybe we weren't terribly smart for jumping into something this risky. But there was too much chemistry between us we couldn't ignore. He clearly felt the same way, too, and I trembled from excitement at seeing him later.

So the moment I walked into the choir room, I headed right for him. Our eyes came together. And when I reached him, sitting in the back row of his section, I said, "Yes. To both."

His smile inched into illegal, and I turned away. Before I did something really insane and totally against school rules. Like sit on his lap and pick up where we left off in the auditorium yesterday afternoon *before* I stepped away from him. But not being able to do what I wanted would give me something to look forward to this weekend.

Chapter Twenty-Three

I paced in front of my mom, sitting on the couch. I couldn't stop shaking as my heart pounded inside my chest.

I paused and closed my eyes.

Inhale to count four...exhale to count eight...

A little better. But not good enough since Liam would be here any freaking minute.

"Sweetie, why are you so nervous?" Mom asked. "You've known Liam a long time. And you two were together yesterday after school."

I've known Liam as a friend *for a long time.* And today we were going on an actual date. Our first date. Three o'clock seemed like an early start time for a date, too. Especially since he'd asked me yesterday, as we stood outside my building, what time I'd have to be home.

I sighed and mumbled, "I don't know, I don't know, I don't know." I picked up my pacing. "Yesterday was all about rehearsing. That doesn't count."

He had walked me home. But only gave me a quick kiss on

my *cheek* before he left. And after two hours of rehearsing our song. We'd also come up with some easy, fun choreography, since we couldn't just stand on the stage and sing. I needed to ask him about his song choice, too. *Somethin'* about the lyrics, combined with everything he'd confessed on Monday, told me he hadn't been completely honest about why he'd chosen that particular song. At the same time, he couldn't actually feel that way about me. We only knew each other as good friends. For now.

"I think this is wonderful." Mom laughed. "You two were so cute a week ago, I told Keith if you didn't have a real date by now, I'd have to wring some sense into both of you."

Okay. Even my mom had noticed Liam liked me as much as I liked him.

I continued pacing. And shoved that thought into the back of my mind.

"I also have to admit," she slowly said, "I think it's pretty big of Shane to be okay with this. There are rules against this sort of thing," she added, and I heard the smile in her voice.

I stopped and faced her. "Yes," I quietly admitted. Because that's all I could do. "He's been really cool." Liam had told him to keep his mouth shut about us and our date, since we'd agreed we didn't want to deal with the gossip. Yet. So we'd used our acting abilities to stay just friendly all week. And Shane had done a convincing job at acting like he had no idea what was going on between Liam and me. I should've thanked him, too, but I didn't know how. After how I'd acted? And what I'd done to Natalie?

No. I had other things to focus on right now. Like him. And us.

The buzzer shattered the silence, and I jumped.

He was here. This was happening. We were really doing this.

"I'm going to meet him downstairs," I said. "Have fun at Keith's show."

"Thanks. You also have fun." She gave me "serious Mom face." "But not *too* much."

I rolled my eyes, though a little zing went through me at the thought of having too much fun with illegally adorable Liam.

I raced out of the condo, quietly closed the door behind me since my grandpa was taking his afternoon nap, then jogged down the two flights of stairs.

My shaking multiplied when I saw him through the long, glass portion of the door.

His face brightened in surprise, and not just a little excitement, when he saw me coming down the stairs and *darn it.* He looked totally edible in a snug, slight V-neck, black T-shirt that showed off his defined arms I rarely saw because of our dumb school sweater. And with his jeans clinging to his lower body...Yep. Illegally adorable.

Mom never had to know if we did have too much fun tonight.

Taking a shaky breath, I opened the door, and he went down a step.

"Hey." He smiled up at me, his dimples in full force.

And I had absolutely no idea how I'd be able to behave myself around him, in public, for the next several hours.

"You could've buzzed me in," he added as I closed the door behind me.

I shrugged, then laughed. More like barked.

Oh, my God, oh, my God. Not the barking. Not with *Liam.*

Quiet inhale to count four...exhale to count—that's when I noticed him checking *me* out.

With the weather being sunny and in the seventies, late

summer and early fall the city's summertime, I'd chosen my black, mini-jean skirt, a dark pink, cold shoulder top, and my cutest pair of black sandals. I'd also shoved a light sweater into my black, backpack purse, along with my sunglasses and phone. That I *wouldn't* be using unless the world ended.

"*Ciao, Bella,*" he said. In his hot Italian accent.

Also known as the best greeting I'd ever heard in my life.

I joined him on the step. He grasped my hands and pulled me into his arms. My shakiness eased into peace as his arms tightened around my waist. I rested my head against his shoulder, took a deep breath, and my head became hazy from his cologne. Not too strong or too much. Just enough to make me want to be this close to his neck. The rest of the day and night.

"Your Italian accent is definitely my favorite," I murmured as my eyes drifted shut.

We didn't really have to go anywhere.

"I'll have to remember that. And speaking of accents," he said, leaning away from me, which forced me to lift my head from his shoulder. "What's your best accent?" He laughed. "Because it's not Italian."

I grudgingly stepped out of his arms. "I don't know. Why?"

He clasped my right hand, our fingers linked, and I had to stop myself from sighing. And swooning. From all of this feeling so incredibly *wow.*

We leisurely walked down the stairs and headed right.

"It's part of my big plan." His eyes drifted down and up me. "You look perfect."

Every part of me zinged and zapped at his second compliment as I said, "So do you."

"Thanks." He stopped us. "But I should've told you to wear comfortable shoes, since we're going to be doing *a lot* of walking. Do you want to change them before we—"

"Liam, I'm a seventeen-year-old girl dressed for a real first date." I gestured at myself. "I'm not ruining what you just called 'perfect' by putting on my Nikes."

He nodded. "Yeah. Got it."

We started walking again, still hand-in-hand, and I asked, "What's this plan of yours? And why do I need a good accent?" I looked around as we headed east. "Where are we going?"

He squeezed my hand. "So many questions and you still haven't answered mine."

I frowned. "Maybe British?"

"Let's hear it."

I paused to think about what to say, then, "I feel tonight will be positively *brilliant*."

He whipped his head in my direction. "Madeline Harrington, that was positively *brilliant*," he finished in his British accent.

I giggled. "Thanks. But what are we doing?" I whined, but in a playful way.

He released my hand, slid his arm around my waist and hugged me to his side. "Okay. Here's my idea."

* * *

"Favorite play we've done?" he asked as we, with our fingers tightly linked, walked along the Embarcadero after getting here by riding the packed California Street cable car. All a part of his plan we'd worked out in detail while riding a city bus to catch the cable car. He'd also admitted he'd come up with his idea because he "hated driving in the city and dealing with parking."

"Definitely this year's play. And *not* because I'm Aunt Abby," I added. "It's pretty funny, and I like that it has such a small cast. You?"

"Agreed. But I liked *Grease*, too. "

I stayed silent, and he squeezed my hand.

"Maddie, I know you wanted Rizzo and weren't yourself back then," he quietly said. "But you *did* look pretty hot out there in your pajamas and singing 'Freddy My Love'."

Hearing *him* say that caused my entire body, already hot from the sun, to heat up to desert temperatures. My bare shoulders were especially taking the full force of the sun, making the salty Bay to the right of us shimmer. Because of my top, I'd have weird tan lines by the time the sun set. But the perfect, early fall weather only added to this perfect first date he'd planned.

Still, I suddenly needed one of those bottles with the fan that blew the mist of cool water.

"Thanks." Him noticing me in *Grease* and asking me to prom had happened in the same month. So I said, "It sounds like you started *liking* me in April." *For some reason.*

He sighed. "Yeah. But it wasn't that bullshit, I'm-into-my-best-friend's-girl thing."

I slowly nodded. "Okay." Being around Liam and Shane for three years, I believed him.

"I mean, not while you were together. And I've always thought you were beautiful—"

I looked at him and smiled as his face turned the same color as my bare shoulders felt.

He laughed. A bit nervously, too. "But we were friends, you know?"

"Yep," I murmured. But remembering his reasons for never having a real girlfriend made me ask, "What changed?" I turned away to focus on the Bay. "And there's no way it could have been my *magnificent* behavior and attitude."

He stopped us and angled me toward him. But I lowered my eyes to the sidewalk.

"That kind've was it. Because I...know what you're going through. With your grandpa."

I swiftly lifted my head, and our eyes collided. Though his were full of empathy. A much better emotion than that horrible sympathy. And his interest in and concern for my grandpa shifted to a connection that far surpassed simple friendship.

I grasped his other hand and squeezed both. "Tell me about it."

His eyes drifted away from me. "My dad's parents passed away from Alzheimer's three summers ago. Really close together. Lucas and I were close to them before..." He shook his head. "They never lived with us, though." His sad eyes caught mine once more. "Maddie, I can't imagine what that has to be like."

I lowered my head, then frantically blinked. Because I would not cry. Even though Liam truly understood. But breaking down is what clingy Maddie would've done. And had done, way too much, in March and April.

"I've been wanting to say all this to you since *March*." He huffed. "But you and Shane were breaking up. And I didn't think that would be the best time to talk to you."

No. That would not have been the best time to talk to me.

"Then you pulled away from all of us and started hanging out with—"

"*Please* don't remind me." I wasn't sure I'd ever get over my stupidity trusting CruElla and her bestie, Quinn. "And I'm sorry for pulling away and being a total bitch and not being in the competition with your group." Also known as first-place winning Drew and Crew.

They'd almost begged me to be in their routine, but I'd aligned myself with the enemy. Who'd lashed into *me* because of our—her—third-place tie with Bryan Costello's group.

He pulled me into his arms.

I hugged him as tight as I could while snuggling his shoulder.

"Liam, I'm so sorry about your grandparents. *I* can't imagine what it must've been like watching two grandparents go through that." My voice cracked, and he squeezed me. Which seemed to strengthen our connection even more.

"So I guess you could say," he slowly said, "I've really liked you since March."

I smiled into his shoulder.

"It seemed like you needed *me*."

Warmth exploded deep inside me and spread right to my heart. Apparently, we really did need each other.

"And I'm sure this isn't breaking news, but I didn't really want to go to prom as friends." He paused, then added, "I didn't end up going."

I moaned and leaned away from him. "Liam, I'm so sorry about that, too."

He grinned. "Don't be. Because you'll make it up to me his year, right?"

I returned his grin and batted my eyes twice. "Maybe."

He shrugged. "I know how to change that to a yes, brown-eyed girl." He lowered his head to my ear. "I'll ask you again, when you're least expecting it. But in my Italian accent."

I shivered.

Okay then. We'd blown past risky and into the point of no return.

"Oh, honey, let's ask these two!"

Liam raised his head and looked left.

Right. We weren't alone on the Embarcadero, in the city of San Francisco.

We released each other and stepped apart.

"Excuse me," an older woman said, wearing a fanny pack that stated "City by the Bay" and holding her phone, "would one of you mind taking a picture of me and my husband?" She pointed to a heavyset man, standing by the concrete wall; the glistening Bay behind him.

Liam eyed me and raised his eyebrows. His way of saying "Show time."

I nodded once, and we faced the woman.

Chapter Twenty-Four

"Sure. Love to," Liam answered in his British accent.

The woman's eyes widened. "You're from England. Are you tourists, too?"

"Yes. We're on holiday." I snuggled his side and gazed up at him. "For our anniversary."

He winked at me, and we focused on the woman, now squinting at us.

Laughter bubbled inside my chest and went up my throat. But I swallowed it while keeping my lovesick, angelic expression in place.

She tilted her head to the right. "Forgive me for saying this, but you two look awfully young to be so far away from home. And celebrating an anniversary." She continued scrutinizing us. "My husband and I have two children about your age. They're still in high school."

We laughed and squeezed each other.

This was going pretty much the way we'd predicted.

"Yes, well," Liam answered, gazing at me, "I did tell her she looked positively *brilliant* before we left our hotel."

I pressed my lips together, lowered my head, and my shoulders jolted as I fought my giggles. Which made him gently pinch my side.

I cleared my throat and looked up.

"We're actually taking a bit of a break," he continued. "Before we head off to university."

Oh, my *God*, he was scary good at improv. And in a British accent.

The woman's face relaxed. "Oh, well, good for you. Where in England are you from?"

"Brighton," we said in unison.

She pursed her lips. "That sounds familiar. I feel like I've heard that place mentioned in a book or movie. Where is Brighton?"

"South of London," I replied. "On the coast. Are you familiar with *Pride and Prejudice*?"

The woman's face lit up, and Liam glanced at me, his eyes full of affection and...pride.

I *was* killing my British accent.

"I love that book." She laughed. "But I think almost every woman says that."

"Where are you from?" Liam asked.

I smiled at how politely and perfectly British he'd asked his question.

"Colorado. Denver," she clarified. "We'll be here through Fleet Week. Will you be here that long?"

I stopped myself from wrinkling my nose. Fleet Week would be going on a week from today and turned the city into pandemonium. Especially Fisherman's Wharf, which was where we were slowly headed.

"No," he said. "Leaving Monday."

"Barb, are they going to take the damn picture or not?"

Liam looked down, his shoulders shaking, and I gently pinched his side.

The woman sighed. "It's been a long day and someone's a

little tired from all the walking we've done." She opened her camera app, handed me her phone, and darted to her husband.

I followed her, with Liam beside me.

"This charming couple is from *England*," the woman said, cozying up to her husband against the wall. "Behave yourself." She focused on me. "Whenever you're ready."

I snapped a few shots of them with the Bay as their background. She then headed back to us, and I returned her phone.

"Thank you so much for doing that," she said. "I hope you two enjoy the rest of your trip, and get home safe and sound."

"Yes." Liam grasped my hand. "You as well. Cheers then."

We walked away.

After several seconds, Liam glanced behind us. "Okay. They're going the other way."

We looked at each and burst into laughter.

"That was *so* awesome," I managed to say. "I can't wait to get to Fisherman's Wharf and do that again." I shook my head. "You were perfect."

"So were you." He released my hand and put his arm around my shoulder. "Your British accent is definitely ready for tourist central."

A wave of exhilaration swept through me, since this was only the beginning of the *best* first date I'd ever been on.

I unbuckled my sandals, pulled them off and massaged my right foot. But I paused to look over my shoulder at Liam, sitting beside me. "Don't you dare say a word."

He spooned ice cream into his mouth, swallowed, and said, "We'll cab it to your place."

I nodded and went back to massaging my aching foot.

We'd settled into a spot on the cement bleachers in

Aquatic Park that faced the cove, a big, round section of water with a long, narrow strip of beach. The sun had long since set, but this also pretty touristy area just west of Fisherman's Wharf was still buzzing. There were several people, mostly couples, sitting and talking quietly in different spots on the bleachers. The path along the beach had a steady stream of people walking in both directions, with a few walking dogs. The salty air wasn't nearly as thick with cool humidity since it had been a warm day, but I had pulled on my light sweater. My sunburn had chilled me once it became dark.

I switched to my left foot.

"Want some of this?" he asked. In a British accent. Then he laughed. "I can't stop. After talking like that most of the day, I feel like I'm *from* England."

I scooted back until my legs were stretched out beside his; our feet dangling off the edge. "That was crazy fun, but I'm glad to be talking normal again."

He angled himself toward me, scooped out a fair amount of his mint chocolate chip ice cream and, with the spoon, drew lazy circles in front of my mouth. "It's really good," he practically purred. "I don't mind sharing."

Our eyes connected; the spoon so close to my lips I could taste the mint.

Ice cream...yummy him...ice cream...yummy him...

"Who are you?" came out. And I cringed when he broke our eye contact to pop the spoonful he'd *hotly* offered me into his mouth.

He set the cup down on his left side and, with a straight face, held out his right hand. "I'm Liam Christopher Langley. And you are?"

I rolled my eyes and pushed his hand down. "I'm being serious. We've known each other for three years, but I had no idea you were—"

"A complete dork?" He waggled his eyebrows. "Or charming? Irresistible? Devilish? Maybe all of the above?"

Yes. To the last option.

But I said, "I don't understand any of this." I picked at the concrete. "I guess what I'm trying to say is, why is this just now happening?" Which really meant where had our obvious chemistry been the last few years? There was also something else I still couldn't understand. "And why *me*?" But that really meant why was he willing to take a chance with me, out of all the girls he knew?

"I don't know. Timing? But why is it so hard for you to understand why I like you? Because of what happened in the spring?"

I shrugged. "Yeah."

He sighed. "Stop thinking about that. Your only mistake was choosing to hang out with Ella and Quinn." He paused, then said, "And Natalie has told everyone who brings it up that Ella talked you into doing that as a way to get back at *her*."

Oh. Okay. Wow. She was absolutely right, too. I'd just been too screwed up to see it. And all the terrible things I'd said to her in the hallway, while crying and sounding like a jealous psycho with kids *watching*, filled my head. "I can't believe she doesn't hate me."

"Maddie, Natalie isn't who you think she is, and I...think you'd really like her," he quietly said. "And *no one* hates you."

He'd basically said what Noah had about Natalie a couple weeks ago. And the "no one" he'd emphasized probably meant Shane. But I already knew he didn't hate me, because of that day after rehearsal he'd tried to talk to me about my grandpa. I'd been such a bitch to him, too.

I dug my thumb nail into a crack in the concrete.

I also sensed what Liam was really saying. If we were going to officially become an *us*, I'd have to make peace with them.

Apologize. And forgive myself for my bad choices. But how would I even begin such a path? Especially with them?

"All that bullshit aside," he continued, "you were amazing in April."

I frowned and peeked at him.

He gave me his piercing gaze. "You didn't have a small part. But went out on the stage and were *Marty* during the rest of rehearsals and for each show."

I tried to smile. "Thank you. Really." Though I still wasn't sure how I'd gotten through playing cutesy Marty Maraschino and singing "Freddy My Love."

"You're doing the same thing with *Arsenic and Old Lace*. And that's why I think you're amazing, Aunt Abby." He grinned. "Well, those aren't the *only* reasons."

The warmth from earlier, after he'd told me he'd thought I'd needed him in March, swelled inside me. But this time the warmth caught my breath a second. Then my heart pummeled my chest as we continued staring at each other.

Inhale to count four...exhale to count eight...

"And I know I said last Saturday I didn't think it was a good idea for me to get close to anyone," he admitted. "I'm still not sure this is smart, either."

My eyes fell to the small space between us.

He was enlisting in the Marines for the right reasons and would make his family proud. Still, the part of me who didn't understand wanted to scream are you *freaking* crazy?

"But I don't want to be that guy anymore. I mean, it seemed like a good idea. I guess." He reached out, clasped my right hand and laced his fingers with mine. "But today has been fucking awesome." We shared a quick laugh. "And I... really like being with you. Like this." He shrugged. "I really like being around *you*."

I shivered and tingled and squeezed his hand. I then angled

myself toward him. "The feeling's totally mutual, Teddy Brewster. Even though you're a 'complete dork'," I added.

His face brightened. "I've always wanted to hear a girl say those things to me."

I giggled.

That left only one more thing that needed to be said. And done. "Maybe we should...kiss again?" I focused on our joined hands. "To make sure the first one wasn't once in a lifetime?"

He stayed silent, and for so long I wanted the concrete to open beneath me. But after everything he'd just said, how he could not—

He gently pulled me toward him.

I raised my head.

He gave me his illegal smile before our mouths fused. And the world around us melted.

Chapter Twenty-Five

I strolled into school Monday morning and caught Noah about to head upstairs.

"Hey!" I called out.

He stopped, and when I reached him I bounced in place. "How was your weekend?"

His head moved up and down with me as he said, "Fine. Why are you bouncing?"

I stopped and sang, "*Because I have the best news everrr.*" I laughed. "But we need to find Heather so I can tell you guys at the same time." Not that I wouldn't love sharing my Liam news over and over to anyone who would listen. In fact, I'd announce it over the school's PA system if I could. Wouldn't that be a super awesome way to start our first week together as a couple. Especially after the awesomeness of Saturday.

My face became as warm as my sunburned shoulders when I remembered our *long,* yummy goodbye standing outside my door. He'd insisted on walking me all the way upstairs.

Noah eyed me. "You're red. And singing and bouncing. On a Monday. Morning."

I grabbed his forearm. "We need to find Heather. Come on."

A minute later we did find her, talking with her neighbor at her locker.

She faced us, paused, then made a big show of shielding her eyes as she squinted at me. "Whoa. You're brighter than the sun right now." She lowered her hand. "I think there's a song in there somewhere, but" —she shook her head— "what's up with you?"

I took a deep breath and opened my mouth.

"Did Nicolas *finally* talk you into going on a date with him?" she hissed.

I frowned.

Noah rolled his eyes. "Heather, what is the deal with you and Nicolas Costello?"

I nodded. "Yeah. You really should ask him out."

Her face became cherry red. "So I think he's hot. Doesn't mean I want to date him."

Heather was clearly in denial about her crush on Nicolas. But it's not like I could challenge her since I'd tried to suppress my feelings for Liam. Thinking of him made me look left, toward the stairs, but I didn't see him. And his locker was along this stretch of hallway, but on the left side of the building.

"Are you going to tell us what the hell's up with you?" Noah angled his head right. "Because I have to go to my locker, too."

I told them about Monday and Saturday. Except our *whoa* kissing. But I'd tell Heather about that when Noah wasn't around. And I finished with another blinding smile, followed by bouncing in place. Then waited for them to respond as they stared at me.

I slowly stopped my bouncing.

Okay. Not exactly the response I'd been expecting. At the same time, my best news ever was probably surprising since our acting had been positively *brilliant* last week.

Noah faced Heather. "You owe me twenty bucks."

I froze for a few seconds before my mouth drifted open.

"I can't believe I didn't see it." She stuck her tongue out at him, then said, "Can I give it to you tomorrow? My neighbor's paying me today after I walk her dogs."

What the freak was happening here?

I vigorously shook my head. "You knew. *And* had a bet going?"

Noah subjected me to a you-have-got-to-be-kidding-me look. "Maddie, it was obvious Liam liked you. Well, not until you started your project whatever." He paused, then added, "And I really started paying attention."

"Yeah," Heather muttered. "Paying way more attention than I was."

Hearing Heather admit to her cluelessness made me feel a tad better. But still. Even Noah had figured it out. And did Liam know this?

I crossed my arms. "So when did all this become 'obvious'?" I couldn't be that dumb.

Noah shrugged. "He sat with us less and less at lunch after you started that project."

Right. But I'd assumed he'd wanted to hang out with Shane and all of them.

"And the way he reacted to your non-date with Nicolas?" he continued. "Then walking you home when you were sick? *And* carrying your backpack? Without you asking." He leaned toward us. "I'll tell you a secret. Guys don't do that stuff for girls unless they Like. Them."

I narrowed my eyes, then glanced at Heather, also glaring at him.

"You two were smiling at each other so much during rehearsals last week," he added, "that I went up to Shane on Thursday and asked him if Liam had finally made a move. He tried playing dumb, but I wouldn't leave him alone. And he let it slip that Liam was with *you* the night of Heather's party." He laughed. "Which explains you giving up your project. And now that I know what happened on Monday after rehearsal, all the smiling makes sense."

Hmm. Maybe our acting hadn't been award-winning after all. And Shane's slip had only confirmed everything Noah had suspected.

Heather held up her hand. "Wait a minute. Liam was with *you* the night of my party?"

I tried to smile as I nodded and shrugged.

She lowered her hand. "Why didn't you tell me that?" Her face fell. "I even told you he'd bailed. And the whole time he was with you." She released a sad laugh. "That's why Shane was being so vague. But why was it such a big secret?"

I cringed at the hurt dripping from her voice. "We just didn't want to hurt your feelings." Well, that had been part of the secrecy. "Liam stopped by to drop off homemade chicken noodle soup. And I was feeling really down about missing your party." Among other things. "So he stayed to keep me company." And because he'd wanted to be with me. It's not like I'd known that at the time, though. "I'm sorry. It all happened so fast and was unexpected. But I did want him to stay, since I realized I...liked him last week. I just didn't want to say anything." Her eyes fell to the floor, and I grasped her hand. "I didn't know then Liam liked me, too."

Noah groaned. "Him bringing you soup and staying with you on the night of a party are two more things guys don't do unless they *really* like a girl."

I leaned forward. "You can stop being Mr. Know-It-All any time now."

Heather looked at Noah. "You sneaky ass," she said through gritted teeth. "I just figured out you cheated! We made the bet on Wednesday. If I had known about Liam being with Maddie the night of my party, I never would've made that bet with you." She growled at him as his eyes widened in fake innocence. She glanced at me and her expression softened. "Knowing the truth wouldn't have hurt my feelings. Because I love you both."

I squeezed her hand. "I promise I'll never keep anything from you again."

She smiled, then sighed. "Now that I *know*, and after hearing Noah list all the other things, I have to admit he's right about Liam being pretty obvious he liked you." She shot Noah a dirty look. "But you can forget the twenty bucks."

He returned her dirty look.

Heather put her arms around me and we hugged. "I'm a little surprised by all this, but I still think it's fabulous. Really." She released me. "And it's so cool Shane doesn't care." She frowned. "But do you think you and Liam being together will get awkward at some point?"

I laughed. More like barked. "Why would it? Shane and Natalie are obviously over the moon for each other." And I now absolutely understood what that phrase meant.

Heather and Noah went back to staring at me.

I straightened. "Why are you looking at me like that?"

Heather's eyes widened. "You said Natalie's name. For the first time since April."

Oh. Wow. I had just said her name out loud. Without thinking about it, either.

"What has Liam done to you?" She gave me a sappy smile. "I love it, though."

"Yeah," Noah said, nodding, "it's Pretty. Cool."

Yes. Definite and necessary progress. And not only because I wanted to be with Liam.

I still had to find a way of making peace with Shane and Natalie. And forgiving myself. But after what Liam had told me Saturday, maybe that wouldn't be so difficult.

Chapter Twenty-Six

Shane delivered Mortimer's funny lines with so much commitment, my mind went blank.

I looked at Kassidy, standing near me behind Abby and Martha's dining-room table. She had the next line, but when our eyes met we dissolved into giggles.

He winced. "Was that too much?"

"No," I said. "That was perfect."

He angled his head back as his eyes filled with surprise. Because that was the nicest thing I'd said to him in forever. And guilt wound its way through me, slowly taking away my humor. Especially as it truly hit me how much I'd missed having him as a friend. A *good* friend who'd always been able to make me laugh, on and off the stage.

"Thanks."

I gave him a soft smile and nodded.

Baby steps were better than no steps.

"Mr. Peters," Kassidy said, facing him, "I don't know how on earth I'm going to keep it together during the shows. Between Shane and Liam and even Noah—" She laughed.

As did me, Mr. Peters, and everyone else.

201

Mr. Peters stood. "We still have over a month of rehearsals. By the time the show runs in November, all of you may no longer see this play, or each other, as funny."

He did have a point. But I couldn't imagine that, since we were having so much fun.

"And on that note," he continued, "I'm calling it a day, even though it's early. I'm meeting with Mr. Lowry and Mrs. Chaplin about our set. Which I'm sure you've noticed has barely begun."

We had noticed that. Mr. Lowry and his crew of community service volunteers had started painting the walls of the Brewster home; the large pieces lining the back of the stage. But that was it. And nothing had actually been constructed.

"The reason being," he added, "the upcoming choir concert."

Oh. Okay. Well that made sense. The risers took up almost the entire stage. And our concerts always had choreography.

"So we're meeting about how much can get done on the set without taking up too much space." He went for the stage right stairs. "See all of you tomorrow."

Kassidy pounced on me before I could follow Mr. Peters. And sprint toward Liam, who I'd hardly talked to or seen today.

"You and Liam are so stinkin' cute," she said, her eyes bright. "The way you two have been smiling at each other this afternoon? Like no one's watching you. Which they are."

My face became a tad warm at her last statement as we headed for the stairs.

"I have to admit," she quietly added, "I was a little surprised when I heard."

That was the second time I'd heard that today. And Taryn had been shocked to the point she'd been distant during show choir. Which had made me wonder if, maybe, she did like Liam. But my conscience was clear on that one, since I'd never said a word to her about dating Liam during my brief match-making phase.

"But I think it's great," she finished.

Liam walked up when we cleared the steps and was, of course, wearing his illegal smile.

I wanted to hook my arms behind his neck and kiss him a bazillion times. Just like Saturday night as he tried to leave. Though I hadn't been the *only* one delaying our goodbye.

Kassidy threw her arms around me. "We'll have to go on a double date," she whispered. "And soon." She released me, shot Liam a devious grin, then darted to *her* boyfriend. Who was watching us, and with the same grin his girlfriend had given Liam.

"What was that all about?" Liam stood so close I could hook my arms behind his neck.

If we weren't standing in the auditorium with a nosy audience.

I leaned forward and whispered, "We're suddenly very popular."

He also leaned forward, making our heads side-by-side. "You've noticed that, too, huh?" he whispered, close to my ear.

Goosebumps invaded my skin, even though I still wore my sweater.

We needed to leave so we could pick up where we left off Saturday night.

"You're a complete phony. And a liar."

Liam and I straightened, and turned to find Barrett standing near us, his face hard with anger and hurt and... Shoot, shoot, shoot.

I'd completely forgotten about Barrett.

"You told me only three weeks ago you *'weren't interested in anything serious'.*"

Every part of me became hot. From his accusatory stare, tone, and the fact he was right.

Liam's eyes narrowed and he faced him. "What the hell's your problem? You've been a dick ever since—"

"Your *girlfriend* is my problem! Who obviously asked me out as a way to get to you."

He'd spoken so loudly I saw, from the corners of my eyes, our castmates' heads whip in our direction.

Oh...my...God.

"What the hell are you talking about?" Liam asked, but in a low, steady voice.

Barrett threw his hand toward us. "What, it was a coincidence you suddenly wanted to pair up with her for a duet the Monday after our *so-called* date?"

I stared at Barrett, blinking like a total moron.

How could he still be upset about that?

I shoved my shock and embarrassment aside, and softly said, "Barrett, it wasn't like that at all." Well, not really. Liam had suggested us pairing up to save me from turning Barrett down. But I now knew the real reason behind his actions. I sighed. "I'm so sorry if I hurt your feelings. But at the time I really was telling you the truth."

"Save it, Maddie." He shook his head. "You used me, and I fell for it. Because I liked you." His eyes hardened. "Did you know I liked you? Is *that* why you were practically all over me when you asked me out?"

I lowered my head.

"Barrett, you need to back off."

I wanted to appreciate Liam's nasty tone and him defending me. But what Barrett said was the truth. I had been practically all over him when I asked him out. For my project. In fact, the only thing Barrett had wrong was me using him to get to Liam.

Guilt gripped my conscience and I mentally moaned.

How would I ever make this right with him? Was that even possible?

At that moment, Shane, Noah, and Heather surrounded us.

Shane gave Barrett a hard stare. "Everyone can hear *you.* "

Barrett's mouth tightened.

"He's right," Heather said in her calm, stage-manager way. "If you don't settle down *or* walk away, I'll have to get Mr. Peters."

Barrett glared at all of us for several seconds before taking a step back. "Unless we're on the stage," he said to me and Liam, "stay the fuck away from me."

I felt everyone's eyes on us as Barrett marched away.

Embarrassment joined my guilt at the silence that followed him, and I went back to staring at the floor. Then my guilty weight multiplied, lowering my shoulders, when it struck me this had to be exactly what Natalie had felt after I'd done this to her.

* * *

"Liam, he has every right to be mad at me."

Our closest friends had been super supportive after Barrett left, asking if we were okay. But their support hadn't eased my embarrassment and guilt. And something else Barrett said had started gnawing on my soul.

"No he doesn't. You went on one date. If you can even call it that," he muttered.

Silence fell as we approached my building.

Recalling Barrett's hurt and fury, I sent a quick thank you upward at the fact no one had heard about my *date* with Tyler. He must've chosen to forget all about me the second he walked away from our ridiculous argument. Another dating fiasco because I'd needed to prove...what? And I remembered Liam's question from the day he'd walked me home when I was sick.

What is this project, with all your rules, really about?

Now it seemed Project Dating Spree had been about something much bigger than proving I wasn't clingy. Though the word still stung, I couldn't shake the feeling Liam had been on to something. And had I proven anything with my project? That had caused a huge, unnecessary divide with a boy we'd considered a friend. A boy who, like Tyler, had called me a phony.

"Maddie, it's not your fault Barrett liked you as more than a friend."

We stopped at the stoop, and he grasped my hands and pulled me close. But because of our backpacks, we couldn't hug. So he rested his hands on my waist as I snuggled his shoulder.

"He'll get over it."

I hesitated, then asked, "Am I a phony? Tyler called me that, too."

He released an agitated sigh. "No." He leaned back to see me. "Tyler's an ass and doesn't even know you. And I think what Barrett's *really* pissed about is that he didn't get the girl."

"I did use him, though. And Tyler." I focused on his shoulder. "I also now know exactly how Natalie felt after what I did to her." I forced myself to look at him, expecting to see agreement, but all I saw was frustration. "I have to apologize to her. And Shane."

His eyes and face relaxed. "Forget about Barrett and Tyler, okay? And Shane and Natalie just want to be friends with you. Because you're" —he cleared his throat— "positively *brilliant*," he said in his British accent.

I laughed. And hope with what he'd said about Shane and Natalie replaced some guilt.

"Laughter. Good. But I have another, even better idea on how to cheer you up."

I smiled as he lowered his head and slid my arms behind

his neck. And I sank into him. Our kiss. Followed by another. And another. Then we had to come up for air.

"I feel better." He caught my eyes. "How you *doin'*?" he said in a deep, New York accent.

I shook my head to clear the haze and lowered my arms. "That's a new one."

"It's new to you," he clarified. "That one was actually the first one I perfected." He gave me his exaggerated, smoldering grin. "Let's go upstairs."

I giggled as he took my hand. "Liam, Ruth's up there. And don't you have to go home? Do your homework?"

He shrugged. "Right now my homework is keeping a smile on your face. And I promise I'll do my best at behaving myself." He waggled his eyebrows.

Yep. Too illegally adorable for his own good. And he was *all* mine.

As we headed up the stairs toward my place, he said, "So I need to talk to you about something. But first, I think we should go hiking on Saturday. Get out of this city. The weather will be really nice, too."

I nodded. "I would absolutely love that." It would also give us a chance to be more alone than anything else we did in the city. Especially with the craziness of Fleet Week. But what did he want to talk to me about?

Before I could question him, he said, "We should talk about the dance, too." We walked into the condo. "The theme is epic couples, which is so cool because we can dress up. Finally."

Ruth emerged from my grandpa's room and gently closed the door behind her. But when she saw us, she halted. And something about her grave expression caused me to freeze. Then my mom walked out of her bedroom. What was she doing home so early?

She was on the phone, and said, "Keith, Maddie's home

early. I'll see you in a bit." She tapped her phone, raised her head, and that's when I noticed her flushed face and puffy eyes.

I looked at Ruth, somber, and standing outside my grandpa's—we never closed his door. Not even when he was sleeping. Because we always had to keep an eye on him. To make sure he was okay. And didn't need us for something.

I tore my eyes from his closed door and they went back to my mom, standing outside her room. Her expression matched Ruth's, but also radiated clear...grief.

I started shaking and tightened my hands into fists. "No. He was fine this morning." I swung my head to Ruth. "He was up and eating when I left."

Mom walked toward us and stopped when she reached me. "Sweetie, after he and Ruth returned from their afternoon walk, she put him to bed, he fell asleep and—"

"No! He was *fine.*" My voice cracked, and Liam put his hands on my shoulders.

I leaned against him. But something deep and dark inside me snapped. My vision blurred. And my mouth watered from nausea so strong, I went around my mom, sprinted into the bathroom, slammed the door behind me, and went right for the toilet.

Chapter Twenty-Seven

Liam placed his right hand over my left and squeezed. My grip on the couch cushion beneath us eased a fraction.

I could just hear Mom's voice drifting into the living room from the kitchen where she was on the phone. Keith was in there with her, too. Holding her hand? She needed someone holding her hand more than I did. But it'd probably be really difficult for her to talk on the phone while holding his hand since she was right handed and—a laugh escaped.

I stiffened. And my body burned hot enough to melt.

Liam's hand tightened on mine.

I turned my head slightly left, and his concerned, piercing eyes caught mine. But I whipped my head forward. "Would you *please* stop looking at me like that? I'm fine."

He stayed silent.

I focused on the burnt wick of a candle sitting on the coffee table.

"Would you please stop telling me you're fine?" he replied, barely above a whisper.

"What do you want me to say?" I removed my hand from

underneath his and started playing with the hem of my sweater. "You don't have to stay. I know you have a ton of homework."

"And I'm not leaving you until I absolutely have to."

I heard the hurt in his voice. He was definitely being the sweet, strong, supportive boyfriend. But I didn't need him to stay.

Mom walked into the living room. Her bleary eyes rested on Liam and she gave him a warm, but weak smile. Communicating something with him. Gratitude? For staying with me while she made all the important phone calls? Keeping me from—I gritted my teeth.

I didn't need him.

"I just got off the phone with Aunt Elise," Mom quietly said. "She's going to help us with a very small gathering here on Saturday, since all your grandpa wanted was to have his ashes scattered where we scattered..." Her voice wavered.

I went back to playing with my sweater's hem.

"Aunt Elise is my dad's youngest sister and only living sibling," she explained to Liam. "And you're more than welcome to be here on Saturday, too."

I raised my head. "Mom, Liam has better things to do than—"

"No, I don't. I'll be here." He found my hand once more.

Mom focused on me, and I wanted to scream, *Stop looking at me like I'll break in half.*

"I couldn't get through to your brother," she continued, "but I did leave a message."

"Big surprise there," I muttered.

A heavy silence followed.

Liam gave my fingers a quick, gentle squeeze.

"I also left messages for Mr. Hathaway and Mr. Peters—"

"Why?" I freed my hand from Liam's and crossed my arms. "I can't miss school. Rehearsals. You know that."

Liam faced me. "Mr. Peters will understand you having to miss a couple days."

"Sweetie, he's right." Mom stepped forward. "And I really don't think it's a good idea for you to be at school, since you're clearly in shock."

"No. I'm fine." I stood, as did Liam. "I'm going to school tomorrow. And have homework." I eyed Liam. "So do you."

His eyes filled with the hurt I'd heard in his voice, and his shoulders wilted.

A flick of guilt on my soul tried to linger. But I absolutely didn't need him.

I headed for the front door, and he followed me.

He picked up his backpack. "Maddie, you don't have to go to school tomorrow."

I shrugged. "Well, I am. So I'll see you then."

He slowly nodded and tried to catch my eyes. "I'll call you later."

I shook my head. "I only want you to call me if that's what you want to do. Not because you think you have to check up on me. I'm *fine*."

He paused for a breath, then, "I'll call you later." He placed a long, soft kiss on my forehead, opened the door, and left.

I clenched my hands so tight my nails dug into my palms. But I had to do something to stop myself from chasing him down and begging him not to leave me. Because I could handle this all by myself. I also had to be strong for Mom, and help her and Aunt Elise.

I closed the door and went straight for my bathroom. Where I'd left my backpack.

Homework. That's what needed my attention. And Keith was here for Mom right now. Maybe I wouldn't have as much homework tomorrow night and could start helping her get ready for Saturday when I got home from rehearsal.

Right. Okay then. That would work. I could do this since I was fine.

* * *

I marched into school with my head held high. My only defense after shielding last night's sympathy and you-shouldn't-come-to-school-today comments from not only Liam, but also Heather *and* Noah. And now I'd have to face their worry and confusion. Along with everyone else's, specifically my castmates. Because I had no doubt all of them knew by now.

I lifted my chin a bit higher as I, side-stepping fellow students, made my way to my locker. But when I rounded the corner, I stopped.

Liam was leaning against my locker. Our eyes met, and he gave me a quick smile.

A tiny, sappy smile tugged the corners of my mouth, especially when I remembered him calling me as I got ready for bed. I'd loved hearing his soothing voice full of affection. But I'd also heard way too much concern. And that emotion was probably the main reason behind him being here first thing this morning. So I had to make it clear I didn't need this. Him.

I would absolutely not cling to him. To anyone.

I pressed my lips together to shed the sappy smile and finished the walk to my locker.

He straightened. "Hey."

The somewhat tense greeting forced my memory back to a week ago. When he'd surprised me here with "Ciao, *Bella*" in his hot Italian accent. Then given me his note. That I'd pinned to my bulletin board.

The Liam standing in front of me now in no way resembled the Liam from this same time only a week earlier. And I hated it and the way he was looking at me.

"Hi. What are you doing here?" I asked, opening my locker.

I felt his eyes as he answered, "Waiting for you. I wanted to see you."

"Why?" I opened my backpack. "You weren't waiting for me yesterday morning." I dug through my bag and yanked out my math book. But then remembered I had that class this morning and shoved it back inside.

"Only because Taryn caught me when I got here to talk about finishing our project."

I stared at everything inside my backpack, then realized I needed all of it this morning.

"I know exactly what you're doing right now."

I reached into my locker for a notebook I didn't need. "You don't know me as well as you think you do."

"Yes, I do. And what you're doing isn't going to work." He grasped the notebook and gently tugged it from my hand.

I closed my eyes.

Inhale to count four...exhale to count eight...

I tilted my head right to meet that piercing gaze of his. "I need that."

"And I need you to look at me." He stepped closer. "Maddie, there's *nothing* you can say or do that'll stop me from being here for you."

Until I cross the clingy line.

"Thanks. Really." I squared my shoulders. "But I don't need you." There. I'd said it. With surprising strength, too. Because it *was* the truth.

His gaze stayed in place as my words dangled between us. Then he handed over my notebook. "Let's have lunch alone today. On the rooftop since it's so nice outside?"

Darn him and his stubborn persistence.

But he seemed so incredibly genuine, so Liam, and I wanted to throw myself into his warm, strong, safe arms. And not let go until a teacher forced us apart with threats of detention.

No. I had to stay strong.

"I can't." I put the notebook into my backpack and zipped it up. "I have to finish some homework."

"Okay. Lunch in the library."

Why couldn't he let me handle this on my own?

Heather and Noah appeared beside us. Of course they were looking at me with—I mentally growled at them. And my locker feeling like Grand Central Station.

I slammed the door shut. "Before you two ask, I'm fine!"

They drew back, and I leaned toward Liam. "I don't need a babysitter at lunch. So feel free to sit with your best friend and his girlfriend."

I spun from their shock and *concern,* and marched away. With my head held high.

Chapter Twenty-Eight

"Maddie?"

The soft voice from close beside me penetrated my mind, and I blinked twice.

I lifted my eyes from the table to find J.R. staring at me. Followed by Noah. Followed by Kassidy, who'd said my name.

"It's your line," she quietly added.

My line. Yes. Rehearsal.

"I'm sorry, where are we?" And, darn it, I was Abby Brewster. The lead. I needed to concentrate. Because a real leading lady would never let her personal life interfere with her role.

"Actually," Mr. Peters said from where he stood right in front of the stage, his eyes trained on me, "why don't we all take a five-minute break."

I gritted my teeth before saying, "No. I'm fine. And no one else needs a break." I glanced at Kassidy, Noah, J.R., and Liam, standing back and off to the right of us—that's when I remembered what scene we were rehearsing. "I know where we're at now, okay?"

All I received were stares. Of *concern*. From them. And Shane, sitting cross-legged at stage left while holding his play-

215

book. And Heather, sitting beside him and holding her playbook.

That dark place deep inside me I'd put back and held together after yesterday's snap cracked just shy of shattering. "All of you need to stop looking at me like you are right now, because I'm beyond sick of it."

They kept their irritating gazes locked on me, though. Liam even took two steps forward, but I stood, which stopped him.

"Don't. Because I'm *fine.*" My voice hitched on the word, but I crossed my arms.

"Maddie, we're just worried about you," Kassidy murmured.

I narrowed my eyes into slits. "Well, you don't have to be. None of you have to be. So stop giving me that look I hate so much," I added through my teeth. I then whirled toward the house and walked to the stage's edge. And the second I saw Barrett in the front row between Taryn and Michael, I said, "Especially you. Who made your feelings about me yesterday —in front of everyone in here!—crystal clear."

Mr. Peters glanced sharply at Barrett, who'd lowered his head.

I smirked.

Mr. Peters faced me. "I don't know what that was all about, but if you need a moment to look over the scene—"

"None of you need to give me special treatment because my grandpa *died*!"

His eyes became round as that horrible word I'd shouted hung over us. Everyone. And echoed inside my brain. Then the word stole the oxygen from the auditorium.

He was really gone.

I struggled to take a breath. The walls of stage right and left closed in and started to crumble. Like an earthquake. "Mr. Peters, I..." I sucked in some air and darted for the stage right stairs. "I need a minute." I raced down the steps and toward the nearest aisle.

"Of course. But I think someone should go with you."

I sprinted toward the auditorium doors.

No more reading my grandpa the classics.

I burst into the lobby and tried to pull air into my lungs.

No more talking to my grandpa while he slept.

I fought for a good breath because of my heart hammering my chest.

No more smiles. No more laughter. No more hugs.

I hadn't seen or heard or had any of those in such a long time. But I had hoped I would. Just one more time. That's all I'd wanted.

And for him to look at me and know I was his Miss Maddie Renée.

The lobby's four sides surrounded me and slowly broke apart.

Inhale to count...to four?

Warm hands clasped my shoulders and eased me left.

My eyes locked with Liam's and I whispered, "I can't breathe."

"Maddie, keep looking at me and listen to my voice."

I managed to nod at his deeply, steadily spoken words.

"Take a slow, deep breath through your nose," he calmly said, staring into my eyes.

Right. I'd spent my entire summer learning to breathe like that.

Inhale to count four...exhale to count eight...

"Good. Take another one."

I did as he said.

No more reading to my grandpa. But we hadn't finished *To Kill a Mockingbird.*

"Keep breathing."

I inhaled to count four. But as I exhaled to count eight,

the darkness inside shifted into something...different...and spread to every inch of me. Then stung my eyes.

I trembled as Liam put his arms around me.

I rested my forehead on his shoulder. And shattered.

* * *

I wiped my wet cheeks with Buddy's fuzzy head as Mom walked into my room.

She sat beside me on my bed, then scooted until her back was against my headboard. She put her left arm around my shoulders and hugged me to her side.

"Mr. Peters wanted me to assure you you're not in trouble for what happened earlier."

I sniffed and hugged Buddy tighter when I remembered the awfulness I'd shouted at my favorite teacher. And in front of the entire cast.

"He also told me he'll be taking over the role of Aunt Abby until you're back at school. Then added," she slowly continued, "you'll be very missed."

The corner of my mouth lifted in a smile, and love shimmied through me, replacing some of my sorrow. At least my nasty behavior and total, public meltdown hadn't cost me the play. Or Mr. Peters's respect. Or my friendships, based on all the texts I'd received. Or Liam who'd, after I'd sort of calmed down, gone back into the auditorium to grab our backpacks and tell Mr. Peters he was taking me home.

A couple tears slid down my cheeks and landed on Buddy's head. "I was so awful to Liam today." The most incredible boy who was officially *my* boyfriend. "And Heather and Noah." The two most incredible best friends I'd ever had. "I owe them huge apologies." The same huge apologies I still owed Natalie and Shane.

"Sweetie, Heather and Noah are your closest friends and

understand. And Liam" —she gave me a quick hug— "was decidedly more concerned about you than himself when you two walked in the door. And before he left. Grudgingly," she added around a soft laugh.

I smiled through a few more tears as my hazy mind recalled him leaving me with Mom. But not before giving me a long, tight hug and saying he'd call later. Or even come back over. All I had to do was ask and he'd "drop whatever he was doing." Between that and everything he'd done and said since we'd walked into horrible reality yesterday afternoon, meant he really *did* want to be here for me. And maybe I needed to let go of the word clingy and let him. For myself and us. Especially since he'd been through this with his own grandparents.

"I really like Liam," Mom continued. "And the way he looks at you."

I lifted my head and caught her eyes filled with tenderness.

"Like you're the only person in the room." She smiled. "It's the look a mother wants to see a boy give her daughter." Her smile became a bit wistful. "It's also how your grandpa looked at your grandma."

I hadn't realized Liam looked at me that way. Under different circumstances, I would've burst into a sappy love song and started dancing. And imagining my grandpa gazing at my grandma he'd adored made me squeeze Buddy so hard his head became smooshed between my chin and arms folded against his neck.

"Your grandparents would have liked Liam, too." She laughed. "Your grandma would have called his dimples 'delightful' and been tickled by the fact he has an identical twin brother. And your grandpa would have admired his family, and him for wanting to join the Marines." She glanced at me. "That reminds me, Liam's mom called this morning. She must have gotten my number from the school's family directory. She expressed their condolences and asked if it was okay to send flowers here since we're not having a funeral."

His mom reaching out made me say, "Liam's grandparents passed away from Alzheimer's a few years ago. His dad's parents."

Compassion settled onto her face. "*Two* parents? I couldn't imagine..." She cleared her throat. "She seems like a lovely woman. And also asked about food." She rested her head against the headboard. "She insisted Liam wouldn't be coming here Saturday, empty handed."

That made me giggle. My first one since standing outside my building yesterday with Liam. And a tad more sorrow left me. "She makes miraculous chicken noodle soup."

"So you've said. And it's why I didn't protest *too* much her wanting to make something."

I sat up. She removed her arm, and I adjusted until my back was against the headboard, which made us stretched out, side-by-side. But I continued hugging Buddy.

"I also heard from your brother today."

I began swiftly lifting Buddy's legs, one at a time. "How nice of him to call back."

And only because it was a call the rat bastard couldn't avoid returning.

She turned toward me. "He looked into last-minute flights from Vancouver to here, but they're quite expensive right now. I'm guessing it's because of Fleet Week." She paused, then added, "So he and Autumn are going to drive here."

I stopped lifting Buddy's legs and glanced sharply at her. "*What?*" I screeched, which made her flinch. I faced her and my jaw hardened. But I managed to say, "He's actually coming back to San Francisco?" And the thought of him being here after everything he'd missed the last five years, especially with *my* grandpa, caused me to clutch Buddy's legs. "No. He doesn't have a right to be here and we don't need him." Those last four words clung to my brain. They'd been my mantra since yesterday afternoon. Specifically when it came to Liam. A boy who'd *wanted* to stay by my side as much as he could yesterday and today. Despite my trying to push him away. And as much as I loved Buddy, it was Liam I wanted to have my arms around at this moment. Minus the stranglehold.

"Maddie, I know this is hard for you to believe, but he does love your grandpa. Loves us." Her eyes found mine. "He just has too much Russell in him." Moisture consumed her eyes.

My grip on Buddy's legs tightened. But I imagined my death grip on Bradley *effing* Harrington's neck.

He could've made the choice not to be anything like that worthless man.

"They'll be here at some point Saturday, and we'll have to take it one minute at a time." She sighed. "I'm not sure how I feel about the thought of him being here."

Because he might as well be a stranger coming to visit. Who I'd have to acknowledge. And his girlfriend, another stranger. But it didn't mean I'd have to be nice to *him*.

"Just so you know," she softly added, then sniffed, "Keith will be here more than usual, through Saturday."

Right. One thing at a time.

I rested my head on her shoulder. "I figured. I think that's great of him." And I remembered Keith, standing in my bedroom doorway beside Mom last night. They'd come to check on me, but his warm *gaze* had never left her as she tried, extremely hard, to talk to me.

It's how your grandpa looked at your grandma.

How many times had I caught Liam's piercing gazes the last few weeks?

My eyes widened.

Oh. Okay then. And I'd deal with that stupidity later.

"You said the way Liam looks at me reminds you of how

grandpa looked at grandma." I felt her nod and added, "Did you know Keith looks at *you* like that?"

Silence followed. Until she sniffed twice.

"No. I didn't."

I smiled. "Well, now you do." She also deserved warm gazes more than anyone else on this planet.

She kissed the top of my head.

No. We absolutely didn't need Bradley Harrington showing up after five years. But I had the rest of the week to prepare myself for everything Saturday would bring.

I'd also have Liam by my side, right where I wanted and needed him.

Chapter Twenty-Nine

I stared at my reflection in the full-length mirror attached to the inside of my closet door.

Wide, black headband. Black, slim-fit sleeveless dress. Black sandals.

I squared my shoulders as voices, coming from the direction of our foyer, found me in my room. None of them sounded like Bradley. But I wasn't certain I'd even recognize his voice.

I needed to get out there and help Mom and Keith, and Aunt Elise. She'd been the first to arrive with her husband. Their kids and families, my cousins, were probably the ones who'd just walked into the condo.

I eyed the inside of my closet, the urge to shut myself in there with headphones and my phone so strong my body eased left. But then someone knocked twice.

"It's me. Can I come in?"

I smiled at hearing Liam's voice and relaxed my shoulders. "Yeah."

Thank God he was already here. And would be until we "kicked him out."

As I turned, he slid into my room and closed the door behind him.

Our eyes met, and he gave me his piercing gaze.

My pulse skipped. Especially as his mouth inched into an affectionate smile.

"Hi."

I paused, then said, "Hi."

Silence, outside of the numerous voices from down the hall, settled between us. Which was a little weird since I'd seen him every day this week but yesterday, despite the fact I hadn't been at school. We'd also talked quite a bit on the phone. And texted at least a million times.

He walked toward me, and that's when I noticed how handsome he looked. Even though he was dressed kind of similar to how I normally saw him. Khaki pants, but he wore a navy-blue polo shirt instead of the school's white one. And no sweater hiding his perfect arms.

He stopped when we were almost toe-to-toe.

I inhaled and recognized the yummy cologne he'd worn on our unforgettable first date. That had been, unbelievably, a week ago today.

How could life change so much in one week?

"Would it be weird to tell you how amazing you look?"

I buried those thoughts and smiled. "No. And thank you. So do you."

I lifted my arms to slip them around his waist, but then he reached into his right pocket and withdrew a small, white, square box tied with a pink ribbon.

"This is for you," he said, while turning the color of the ribbon.

My heart accelerated as I took the box. "You bought me a present? What is it?" Although the size of the box and thin ribbon clearly said jewelry.

"I think you're supposed to open presents to find out what they are."

I wrinkled my nose at him before untying the ribbon, which he took. I lifted the lid off the box that held a black velvet one. I raised my eyes to his. "Liam Langley, what did you do?"

"Just open it," he mumbled.

I took out the velvet box and handed him everything else. I then paused to take a slow breath, carefully opened what was clearly holding a piece of jewelry and—I froze. At the sight of a necklace with two shiny gold hearts, about the size of my thumbnail, linked.

My eyes grew as I stared at the most extraordinary gift a boy had ever given me.

I looked at him and giggled, since his face had turned hot pink. "It's beautiful." I hesitated, then asked, "Are they supposed to be...*our* hearts?" And if my assumption was correct, I wasn't the only one with a "sappy, romantic side."

He raised his eyebrows. "Um...that's actually a pretty cool idea, but...no." He ran a hand though his stylishly messy hair. "They're supposed to be your grandparents' hearts. Because of what you told me that Saturday night when you were sick? About how much they loved each other?" He shrugged. "It reminded me of my grandparents, and I thought...I don't know...you might need something like this. To get through today and tomorrow and...every day."

My assumption hadn't been right. But he definitely had a romantic side.

My heart and soul absorbed his words. *His* amazingness. And I searched my mind for something to say. Because "thank you" wouldn't even be close to good enough.

"But I like your idea, too," he added.

I continued gaping at my necklace. And the main lyrics from

"Somethin' Stupid" drifted through my head. In that moment, I completely understood that part of our song *he'd* chosen. But somethin' about this moment with him, combined with his gift, told me if I said I loved him, I wouldn't be spoiling a thing. Because I felt pretty confident his feelings for me were the same.

The urge to grab his hand and run far, *far* away from here replaced the urge to shut myself inside my closet. I'd never imagined the moment I realized I loved a boy would fall on such an...emotional day. It was no one's fault. But that didn't make it fair, either.

"Do you want me to help you put it on?"

I just had to get through today. And then I could lose myself in him. Us.

Love and piercing gazes.

"Maddie, do you actually not like the necklace and are afraid to tell me?"

I placed my left hand on his neck, brought his head down to mine, and pressed my lips to his. Which surprised him. For a second. But we kept our kiss innocent.

"I love it," I whispered against his lips. "I wish I could really show you how much I love it." *And you.* We also hadn't shared a *real* kiss since Monday afternoon.

"Yeah," he whispered back. "I'm right there with you." He placed the gift box and ribbon on my dresser, then grasped the velvet one I held and took out my necklace.

I gave him my back and, within seconds, I was gently rubbing the two linked hearts. I wasn't sure I'd ever take this necklace off, either.

Three loud raps on my door caused us to step apart.

"We're coming in," Noah announced.

I mentally scrambled to get my head back on straight.

"We met up at school and walked here together," Liam said as my door opened.

Noah walked in, followed by Heather, followed by—I did a double take.

Shane gave me a warm smile. "Hey."

Oh, my God. He'd come here with them? For me?

The buzzer screeched for the third time in the last half hour.

"And we picked up this really annoying, ugly stray on the way here," Liam added.

Heather and Noah laughed as Shane's eyes rolled upward.

Okay then. Maybe a renewed friendship with him had happened without me knowing, and I smiled as warmly at him. And at the thought.

Understanding, with a hint of relief, settled into his eyes.

"Couldn't stop him from following us here," Noah threw in.

"Very true." Heather squinted at Shane. "But you're more annoying than ugly."

"This is *loads* of funny," Shane said, focusing on me, "but your mom sent us for you."

Right. Reality was waiting outside my room. And the recent buzz might mean Bradley and his girlfriend had arrived.

Inhale to count four...exhale to count eight...

Heather walked up to me. "How are you doing?"

We wrapped our arms around each other and squeezed.

"I'm okay." I paused, then added, "Because all of you are here." And I meant every word.

She gave me another big hug and withdrew.

Liam reached out, my fingers melded with his, and strength rushed through me.

We followed Heather, Noah, and Shane into the hallway. But when my eyes landed on the young couple, specifically the guy, standing in the foyer with Mom and Keith, I halted.

Bradley had the same light-brown hair as me. His shaggy

style matched his scruff. We also shared Mom's big brown eyes. He'd filled out, too, but in a lifting-weights sort of way.

He'd looked like a boy when he left. And now here he was, a twenty-three-year-old man, standing steps away from me with his—my eyes felt like they might pop out of my skull when I registered the cute little blonde beside him was *pregnant*.

Oh...my...God.

"Is that him?" Liam whispered.

Mom turned toward us, her eyes as round as mine felt. In that second, I remembered her saying something about him "having some news." And then my eyes locked with *his*. That lit up.

"Look at you." He laughed. "My baby sister grew up."

Rage the temperature of hell replaced my strength. I gripped Liam's hand.

The rat bastard, who hadn't bothered to tell our mom about his *pregnant* girlfriend, did not just call me his "baby sister."

Bradley *effing* Harrington and his girlfriend walked toward us.

Heather, Noah. and Shane stepped out of their way.

When they reached us, she smiled at me. "Maddie, the little sister." She giggled. "You're not at all who I was picturing. The way he's talked about you, I was expecting a girl in braids. But you're a young woman. And so *beautiful*."

I didn't know whether to be flattered or offended by the way she stressed that word. Or what to think of the fact he'd actually taken some of his precious time to talk about me.

"I'm Autumn." She rolled her blue eyes. "If I'd been born two months earlier, my parents would've named me Summer." She turned her smile on Liam, then eyed our tightly joined hands.

I finally found my voice and managed to nicely say, "This is my boyfriend, Liam."

Bradley laughed again. "*Boyfriend*? Man, this is so surreal."

Thank God Liam was holding my hand, since that was the only thing stopping me from punching the smile off Bradley's face.

"Because the last time I saw you—"

"Was over five years ago," I stated. "When I was twelve. And in braids." I pursed my lips and tapped my chin with my left index finger. "Hmm. That would make me" —I snapped my fingers— "seventeen. Almost eighteen because my birthday's in January."

A dark silence followed my nasty sarcasm as I glared at my so-called brother.

"Bradley? Autumn?" Mom quietly said. "Why don't you two come with us? Aunt Elise and everyone are excited to see you. And will be very surprised by your...good news."

Bradley broke our stare and gave Autumn a tense smile. "You'll love Aunt Elise. She's our grandpa's youngest sister."

Our grandpa.

The rage I'd barely been controlling went to my head and I leaned forward. But Liam tugged me back, slipped his arm around my waist, and hugged me to him.

Autumn sent us a wary smile and followed my worthless brother. The father of her *baby*.

I was going to be an aunt? And Mom was going to be a grandparent?

"You're amazing," Liam murmured. "And you can grip my hand all day if you need to."

His soothing voice made my anger go from boiling to simmer.

Okay. I could handle this. I'd just ignore him. The way he'd basically ignored us for years. Though I couldn't include Autumn in this. She seemed nice, was pregnant with my…niece or nephew…and had done nothing but choose the wrong guy. And between Liam, my friends, and real family being here for *my* grandpa, ignoring my brother wouldn't be a hard thing to do.

Chapter Thirty

Bradley's laughter reached me in the kitchen, and I jerked the fridge door open. I swiped a bottle of water off the shelf and slammed the door shut. I then closed my eyes.

Inhale to count four...exhale to count eight...

"Hi. I thought I saw you come in here."

My eyes flew open. I turned right to find Autumn standing by the small island counter while caressing her tummy. And I really noticed she had the distinct, healthy glow of a pregnant woman. Who was head-over-feet in love, based on the *gazes* she gave my brother.

Even though he'd earlier admitted to everyone he "wasn't ready for marriage."

Another Bradley laugh drifted into the kitchen.

I gripped the water bottle for a few seconds before twisting off the top.

"Your friends are really nice. And funny." Autumn giggled. "Good job nabbing that cute boyfriend of yours. His dimples are super swoony."

I kept a sigh in check.

She was only trying to connect with me. But I still didn't want or need this woman I didn't know, talking to me as if we were suddenly besties. Or sisters.

"Thanks." I took a quick swallow of water, then said, "I think it's cool you're having a girl. And that she's due on Valentine's Day." Not a lie, though I still couldn't wrap my brain around the fact Bradley would be a dad, I'd be an aunt, and Mom would be a grandparent. But considering his distance the last five years, I didn't feel like a soon-to-be aunt. And I doubted Mom felt like a soon-to-be grandparent.

"She's feisty, too. A kicker." She continued rubbing her tummy. "Brad's hoping she'll be a soccer player."

Right. *Brad*. Apparently, he now preferred the shortened version of his name.

"But I think it'd be so much fun if she inherited the Harrington theater talent." She sent me a bright smile. "It must be such a rush to get on a stage, in front of an audience, and act, sing, and dance. Really well. I wish we lived here, so we could see your choir concert and show."

I tried to smile before taking another swig of water.

My theater and choir life had come up after *Brad* asked me how all of that was going. But Mom had been the one to really answer his question, since my reply had been, "Fine."

Autumn stepped toward me and her smile faded. "I know Brad hasn't been home in a while, and you seem pretty upset by that."

I gritted my teeth.

No. This woman I didn't know wasn't actually trying to have that conversation with me.

"But we drove a long way to be here for this," she added. "I'm sad I never got to meet your grandpa, either. Based on all the stories I've heard today, it sounds like he was a wonderful man. Before he got—"

"No," I stated through my teeth. "He was wonderful even then."

I started to grip my water bottle but remembered it was open.

Her face flushed. "I'm sorry. I didn't mean it that way."

"It's fine." I twisted the cap into place. "I should probably get back out there." In fact, I was little surprised Liam hadn't come to check on me. He'd been staying right by side. But then, a couple of my tween, third cousins had glued themselves to him, Noah, and Shane.

"Maddie, we're hoping our visit, me finally meeting all of you, and the baby, will mean seeing more of you." Her blue eyes filled with a hint of desperation. "I *have* convinced Brad we need to stay in Vancouver. And I almost have him convinced we should buy a house. You and your mom would love Vancouver. It's a beautiful city. Like San Francisco."

Hearing this pretty, pregnant woman's pleading words, combined with her adoration for her boyfriend who didn't deserve it, caused me to tremble.

My everything burned with fury and resentment that my brother had abandoned me just like Russell, our worthless "father." And now *we* were expected to happily jump on a plane and fly to Vancouver—I halted as the word abandoned reappeared with breathless force.

My big brother, who I'd adored, *abandoned me. Just like Russell.*

My grandpa had left me, too, though not intentionally. But when he'd started calling me Molly back in April, the hurt had seized my heart and soul with the same strength the moment I realized as a kid I'd never have a dad like my friends did. And I'd experienced the same powerful hurt when Bradley resorted to sending postcards with never a hint he'd come back here.

My grandpa forgetting who I was, combined with Bradley and Russell...Oh. Wow.

Maybe that's why I'd hung on to Shane so tightly. Our break-up had been mutual and beyond necessary. But I'd turned him into another guy who didn't want me. And *clung* to him.

My eyes widened as I recalled Liam's Project Dating Spree question from that day I was sick and he walked me home.

What is this project, with all your rules, really about?

Right. Okay then.

I'd taken my abandonment issues out on two boys, four including Liam and Shane. Because I'd been *sick* of being left behind. Forgotten. So I'd changed the rules. None of them had deserved any of that, either. Even Tyler. And especially Liam. Who hadn't left me.

I reached up with my left hand and clasped the linked hearts.

But I had lost a friend because of my awful choices. I'd been really close to forever losing Shane's friendship, too. And all because of two Harringtons who weren't even worth it.

Oh...my...God.

I refocused on Autumn, staring hard at me. Probably because I'd been silent for so long. "You seem like a nice person. And I want to be excited for you and about being an aunt." I set my water bottle down on the counter. "But visiting you guys in Vancouver isn't in my future. Because my brother is a young version of Russell. Our *father*?" She barely nodded. "And you and your baby deserve way better. I'm sorry."

I avoided her eyes as I walked around her, then stalked into the living room. And headed for Bradley *effing* Harrington, still on the couch with Aunt Elise and looking at a photo album.

When I reached him, he and Aunt Elise glanced up, but I said directly to him, "You really are a selfish rat bastard!"

The room became so silent a bird chirping in a nearby tree filtered through our open windows. But I kept my hard stare locked on my brother who'd become immobile.

"She looks at you the way grandpa looked at grandma. The way Keith looks at Mom. The way Liam looks at me." I leaned forward. "Do you look at the *mother* of your baby that way?"

He frowned and slowly handed the photo album to Aunt Elise.

"I'm guessing by that look you have no idea what I'm talking about. So I'll spell it out for you. Autumn adores you. Just like I did," I enunciated. "Until you left us. Just like Russell."

Shock hit his eyes and face, then he stood.

Mom appeared at my right side. "*Madeline*, this isn't the time."

But my eyes never left his as he said, "Maddie, I'm...sorry." He frowned. "But why are you so angry? I needed to go do my own thing. What's wrong with that?" His frown deepened. "And it's not like I didn't stay in touch."

My hands tightened into fists. Liam wasn't right beside me to stop me from punching him, either.

Bradley pointed at me. "You're graduating this year. And you're going to go off and do *your* own thing."

I leaned toward him. "My own thing is staying here to go to college. Not leaving my family without a backward glance! And *normal* brothers and sons return calls, e-mails, and come back to visit," I finished, followed by a sneer. "They *don't* send four stupid postcards a year."

He drew back.

"And you're right, Mom. This isn't the time. But since we have no idea when or if we'll see him again, he's not leaving without hearing the truth." I narrowed my eyes. "You have no right to be here, *Brad.*" Remembering watching and experiencing my grandpa's mental decline, I added, "You weren't here for grandpa. For any of this. You didn't see him forget—" My voice cracked and I cleared my throat. "Forget who you are. Or see his confusion. Or discomfort. Or watch him refuse to eat. Or read to him every night because it made him calm."

He lowered his head.

Maybe he did have a soul. Unlike Russell.

"Then you show up with a girl who's five months pregnant? Something pretty important you failed to mention to Mom," I muttered. "And act like you haven't been gone for *five years?*"

He sighed, and Mom put her arm around me, but I stepped left.

"No. Not cool, *Brad.* And if I could kick you out, I would!" I crossed my arms. "Because as far as I'm concerned, you're another Russell."

His jaw tightened.

Perfect.

"And, just like him," I continued, "I don't need or want you in my life."

He swallowed, and something resembling hurt flickered in his eyes. And I couldn't work up an ounce of anything beyond cold satisfaction.

I backed up and right into a solid someone.

"Let's go for a walk," Liam softly said.

I shook my head and said to Mom, "I'll be in my room until he leaves."

Hurt flashed through her eyes, too, but mingled with some understanding. Still, tears blurred my vision at seeing her looking at me that way. Especially since she'd counted on my help today. But I couldn't handle *him,* his pregnant girlfriend, or being reminded of Russell. And I wanted my grandpa so badly the ache squeezed my soul.

I'd make this up to Mom. Somehow.

I spun from her, Liam, everyone, and sprinted into my bedroom. Where I grabbed Buddy, hugged him to me, went for my closet, and shut myself inside the darkness.

My tears then exploded from my eyes and I sank to the floor. Sorrow...frustration...anger...resentment...guilt...and all the other yuck came out of me and fell on Buddy's head. To the point I fought to catch my breath between waves of tears.

"Maddie," came Liam's soothing voice through the door, "you don't have to sit in there by yourself. It's just us in here. And we closed your bedroom door."

I inhaled and said, "I just...need a few...minutes. I'm—" I moaned. Because I was so obviously far from the word *fine*. "Please...give me...a little bit."

"Okay," came Heather's calm, stage-manager voice. "You stay in there as long as you need, and we'll stay right outside the door. So we can talk to you. Or maybe we should focus on something else. Like a game. Twenty questions? We play it on family road trips."

I smiled through my tears and sniffed. "Sure." But it came out as more of a gurgle.

I wiped my cheeks using Buddy's right arm, since his head was now damp.

"We're sitting down," Heather said, "and I'll go first. We'll only pick stuff in your room, but you can't pick anything in your closet. Because none of us have x-ray vision."

"That's a *big* assumption you just made," Liam said, using his gruff, old-man voice.

I laughed with them, which caused my eyes to become only damp.

The most incredible boyfriend and friends ever.

"I have my object, too, so Maddie you go first."

I scrambled to remember the twenty-questions strategy,

because I hadn't played this game in forever. "Can you...hold it in one hand?"

"Yes. Great question, too. Liam?"

A pause, then, "Is it heavy?"

"No. And that was good, too. Shane?"

Another pause, then, "Can you sleep with it?"

Something about his question, and the almost wicked way he'd asked, caught my hazy attention as I sniffed twice.

"Hmm," Heather replied. "Yeah. I guess. So yes. Noah?"

"Is it hard?' he asked, and I heard the smile in his voice.

I straightened and looked over my right shoulder. As if I could see Noah through the door.

The boys couldn't be talking about what it *sounded* like.

"No," she answered. "Well, sometimes. But mostly no— what's so damn funny?"

The boys burst into laughter as I covered my mouth with Buddy's head and giggled.

"Oh. Ick." Heather growled. "You three are *disgusting* and so inappropriate."

"You're playing twenty questions with three guys," Noah countered.

"That's no excuse. And if you aren't going to take this game seriously—"

"Heather, we needed a good laugh. Right, Maddie?" Noah called out.

I smiled as moisture returned to my eyes. But these were the kind of tears that hit when a girl realized she was safe. And surrounded by unconditional love.

"Yeah," I called back. "That was pretty funny."

"See? So lighten up, H. And I think you picked a book. I saw you look at her bookcase."

A long pause, before, "I did. Which means you can go next."

"How you *doin'* in there?" Liam asked in his deep, New York accent.

Which reminded me of the last time we'd really kissed. Maybe he'd asked his question that way on purpose?

I leaned against the door. Based on the closeness of their voices, I knew he and Heather were right on the other side. As close as they could possibly be to me.

A couple tears slid from my eyes, and I said, "Better. But I'm not...ready. So keep playing the game. And making me laugh."

"We can do that," Noah said. "Who's got the first question?"

I kept an arm around Buddy and reached up with my free hand to hold my gold hearts.

Chapter Thirty-One

My eyes popped open and I lifted my head. Then groaned from the kink in my neck.

I looked around as my eyes adjusted to the darkness.

Oh. Right. My closet. I also still had my left arm around Buddy.

I leaned forward, and that's when I noticed I didn't hear my friends on the other side.

I shifted to my knees, grasped the handle, and inched the door open. And saw Liam, stretched out with his back against the wall, his eyes closed and head tilted left.

I smiled, opened the door farther, and scooted until I was about halfway out of the closet. We were alone, but my bedroom door was open. I didn't hear anything but his steady breathing.

How long had I—we—been asleep?

I glanced at my window to see early evening sunlight streaming through the blinds.

His head suddenly came up. His eyes drifted open and found me.

"There's Sleeping Beauty," he murmured with a sleepy grin oozing so much cuteness my heart tingled. He rolled onto his right side. "How was your nap? We lost you during round five of twenty questions, but didn't want to open the door and have you fall out." He yawned. "And we couldn't believe you slept through what had to be the Blue Angels' show."

Wow. I had been out cold. This place rattled from the force of their planes shooting over the city. "I didn't mean to fall asleep."

His grin slipped. "Emotional exhaustion will do that." He picked up *Pride and Prejudice*, laying in his lap. "And me, either. But reading sometimes puts me to sleep." He put my book aside, sat up, and his gaze became piercing. "Shane, Heather, and Noah stayed as long as they could." He paused, then added, "And everyone else is gone, too. Well, except Keith."

My shoulders slumped from relief. Until guilt wound its way through me when I remembered Mom's hurt expression. "Is my mom mad at me? You can bc honest."

"Maddie, there's only one person who probably isn't too happy with you right now." He frowned. "But he deserved everything you said to him."

I picked at the bottom of my dress. "Yeah, but I didn't need to go off on him in front of *everyone*." I winced. "And my mom looked so hurt—" My voice broke on the word.

He reached out and grasped my busy hand. "I think she's more worried than mad, okay?"

I nodded, though I wouldn't know that for sure until I saw her.

"We should go for that walk now. Maybe to the park?" He cleared his throat. "*What d'ya say?*" he said in his thick, Australian accent.

I giggled.

I'd never get tired of his accents and impersonations.

"That sounds perfect. I just need to change my clothes."

He stood, then helped me up. And immediately wrapped me in his arms.

I nestled my head against his shoulder and breathed him into my soul.

"I really want to kiss you, but I think I need some gum first."

I hugged him tighter. "Me, too. To both."

I'd needed to have Buddy close to me earlier. But he had nothing on Liam Langley.

"Oh! You two are up."

We sprang apart at the sound of Mom's voice from my doorway. And she gave us her aren't-you-two-cute smile.

My guilt eased at not only her smile, but the relief settling into her eyes. Thank God. But I'd still have to figure out a way to make today up to her.

"Are you hungry?" she asked, walking toward me. "There's *plenty* of food."

"Actually," I began, glancing at Liam, whose face had turned candy-apple red, "we're going to go for that walk. If that's okay?"

Her smile deepened. "I think it's a lovely idea. Keith and I were talking about getting out of here for a bit, too."

Liam eyed me. "I'll wait for you in the living room." He shot Mom a quick grin and headed swiftly out of my room.

She laughed. "He was a hit today. As were all your friends. Especially with your little cousins. And I was shocked speechless when Shane walked in with them." She focused on me. "You two must be friends again? Because you and Liam are together?"

I shrugged and nodded. "That's part of it. But I also want us to be friends again." I also wanted to be friends with Natalie. But first I had to apologize. To both of them.

"Wonderful. I've always thought he was a good kid."

Silence followed, and I looked at the floor. Because I had to make amends with *her*. Though I'd never admit to my abandonment epiphany. She didn't need to know everything.

"Mom, I'm so sorry for what I did and leaving you to handle everything today."

She put her arms around me, and I returned her hug.

"Sweetie, I had Keith and Aunt Elise to help. And what happened with your brother..." She released me to lean back and catch my eyes. "The timing wasn't superb. But I'm also not surprised by what you did or said." Her mouth hardened. "And it's obvious what his *news* was."

I nodded.

"Autumn is pregnant." She placed her hands on her face and huffed. "I'm having such a hard time grasping that reality." She laughed, but without humor. "And that I'm going to be a grandmother in four months." Her eyes became damp as she lowered her hands. "Did *not* see that one coming."

My back turned rigid.

Because Bradley effing *Harrington really was a rat bastard.*

"The fact he doesn't want to marry Autumn," she continued with an edge in her voice, "and didn't feel it necessary to share their news with us when they found out, tells me he is nowhere near ready to settle down and be a dad." She paused, then added, "And might be in denial about the baby and how their lives will change the second she's born."

Yep. Just another Russell Harrington.

"But he privately told me he intentionally didn't tell us about the baby when I talked to him on Tuesday, because he wanted to 'surprise everyone'."

I rolled my eyes.

She tucked a lock of hair behind my left ear. "But what you said to him made an impact."

I straightened.

"He was extremely quiet the rest of the time he and Autumn were here."

I guess that was something. But I still couldn't work up anything but satisfaction.

"I'll be spending the day with them tomorrow. We have a lot to talk about," she added under her breath. "I'm also hoping I'll be able to get him to rethink marrying Autumn."

"Good luck with that," I muttered.

"I know, I know. But it's worth a try." She refocused on me. "They're staying with Aunt Elise and Uncle Hayden for a few days. There are no inexpensive hotel rooms right now."

Good. He'd be across the Bay in Berkeley. Far from me.

"Would you like me to tell you how it goes tomorrow?"

I vehemently shook my head. "Mom, I meant what I said to him. Maybe someday I'll feel differently. When we're both older." *If he ever grows up and becomes a* real *man*. "I know this is going to sound harsh, especially with Autumn being pregnant." I shrugged. "But as of today I'm done with him."

Sadness filled her eyes. But after liberating my anger and resentment with him, the heaviness inside me had almost disappeared. I still had to work through forgiving myself for my series of bad choices. Though that day seemed much closer than it had only yesterday.

"Okay. You're almost eighteen, and I'll respect your decision."

She came forward. We shared another long, tight squeeze.

And she deserved so much better than having a son like Bradley.

"I'm sorry you have so much schoolwork," she said, releasing me. "I think it'd be good for you to get out of here for a while. Spend tomorrow doing something fun with Liam? Especially since the weather's so nice."

Right. My endless list of homework from missing three days of school. I was also still learning Abby's lines.

"If you want to take Monday off, just to have a little fun tomorrow, I'm okay with that."

Wow. That sounded beyond tempting. But I said, "I'd really love that, but I can't because of the play." I'd already missed three-and-a-half rehearsals, which was unheard of during musical and play times. I'd probably set a P.A. Theater record for absences.

She cracked a grin. "I had a feeling you'd say that. So I'm ordering you to go have some fun tonight, young lady."

As soon as she left and closed the door behind her, I turned and fully opened my closet. I then bent forward to grab Buddy, smiling up at me from the floor.

I carried him to my bed where I paused to give him a bear hug. Like the ones my grandpa had given me. And I sighed before placing Buddy against my pillows.

Okay. Maybe now I could concentrate on love and piercing gazes.

Chapter Thirty-Two

I stared at the clear sky transitioning to sapphire as the sun set behind us. The evening's warmth reminded me of our date a week ago, but with my T-shirt and jeans, I didn't need my sweatshirt I'd balled up and placed under my head.

We were stretched out on a blanket. Bursts of laughter and loud conversations and dogs barking in their nearby play area occasionally reached our spot on the vast, open grassy area.

If not for the fact I didn't want to miss a second with him, I probably would've fallen asleep again. Although we hadn't said much since leaving my place. But our silence was soothing. Like his voice had been so many times this week. Especially when he'd talked me down from my panic attack Tuesday afternoon.

He'd been so right when he said I'd needed him back in the spring. He'd also said the same thing, without saying it, at school on Tuesday. When I'd been awful to him. Again.

I rolled my head left to find him also staring at the sky. "I'm so sorry about how I acted on Tuesday. And Monday before you left." I hadn't been too nice then, either.

He rolled his head right. "Maddie, you were in shock and hurting. So don't think about any of that." He squeezed my hand. "It never happened, okay?"

I gave him what had to be a sappy, lovesick smile. "Thanks. For being so *amazing*."

His mouth inched into his illegal smile. "Thanks. For noticing." I laughed, and he released my hand to roll onto his right side. He then propped himself up on his elbow. "I know today, and this week, was really tough. But that's why we should talk about the dance."

Oh. Yeah. Our first dance of the year with the epic couples theme. The first year since we'd been at P.A. the activities committee advisor had approved a Halloween-type dance.

"It's a week from today, and I think we should go. It'd be good for you."

I rolled left to better see him, but kept my head on my makeshift pillow. "I don't know, Liam. I'm not feeling up to finding costumes and getting all dressed up for a few hours. When would we even have time this week to find costumes?"

"Okay. Fair enough. But" —he waggled his eyebrows— "I know who our epic couple should be. I figured it out earlier while I was reading your book."

I smiled. "Elizabeth and Mr. Darcy?"

"Yeah." He laughed. "Perfect, right?"

Actually, his idea was pretty perfect. Still, I said, "We'd *really* need costumes."

"Why?" He shrugged. "We could be a present day Elizabeth and Darcy. I mean, it's not like it hasn't been done a million times with that story."

He had a point. But then a thought occurred to me. "Nobody would know who we were."

He stared at me. "And I'll bet nobody would know who we were *with* the right clothes." He unleashed his smile, followed by gazing at me through pleading, puppy-dog eyes.

I wrinkled my nose. "I'll bet that look got you and your brother out of so much trouble."

"Not often," he admitted. "But it did get me my second bike. And a few other things."

I struggled to keep a straight face as I said, "It won't work on me."

"Maddie, come on." He lowered himself so we were eye-to-eye. "You know you need this, and it'll be fun. I'll wear a suit. Be all uptight. And you have to have something in that huge closet of yours you can wear."

"It's not that big." But I did have a dress buried behind other clothes and still in its black garment bag that could work. "I do have something. It's just..." I tore my eyes from his to look at the blanket. "If I wear the dress to this dance, I won't be able to wear it to prom."

Of course he became silent at my kind of embarrassing confession.

"You already have a prom dress?" He paused, then said, "Or did you buy it last school year to go to prom with—"

"No!" I buried my face behind my right arm, because shoot, shoot, *shoot*. And I had no choice but to clear up his confusion. "I've had it since the end of sophomore year. Mom and I saw it on sale after prom season. It was love at first sight and, okay, I did plan to wear it last year, but—" I covered my head with my arms.

Oh, my God, oh, my God. Now would've been a spectacular time for the world to end.

He pulled my arms away from my head, but I kept my eyes shut.

"Why are you so embarrassed?" he asked around a laugh. "I think that's cute." He released my arms. "*You're* cute."

I slowly opened my eyes. To find him giving me a sappy, lovesick grin.

My heart sighed. Or maybe my soul did.

"Maddie, wear the dress and be my Elizabeth. Please?"

Oh. Wow. Illegal smile and pleading eyes with a "Please" to match.

Charming, devilish, and definitely irresistible.

"You win. *This time*," I added with a pretend glare. "But we're going to look like we're dressed for prom."

He grasped my right hand and placed my fingers against his lips. "Who cares?" He gave them a quick kiss. "We can say we're dressed for that scene at the ball. Where they dance?"

I nodded once. "Deal. Kiss on it?"

"You're a mind reader."

He scooted closer, and our mouths came together. For our first real kiss in almost a week.

Love burned inside me. And when we paused for a breath, I whispered, "Liam, I love you, and I know you love me, too."

He blinked several times, as if trying to clear not only his eyes, but also his head.

Right. I'd kind of blurted out my feelings. But at least they were out there. Now he needed to agree with me. So I waited, and the silence, except for dogs barking, surrounded us. Until a combination of embarrassment and frustration plowed through me, and I sat up. Then crossed my arms. "In case you were wondering, it's your turn to say something."

He also sat up. "Sorry." He shook his head. "You caught me off guard."

I groaned. "Is that really all you have to say?" I leaned forward. "And don't you dare sit there, scrambling for a denial. Between this incredible necklace you gave me, and how amazing you've been, and how you look at me, and our duet song you chose, I know—"

He kissed me and said, "I wasn't scrambling for a denial. But you weren't supposed to tell me I loved you." The corner of his mouth lifted in a lazy grin. "I'm pretty sure I was supposed to say that to you."

Oh. Well. I guess I *might've* stolen the moment from him.

"So Madeline Harrington" —he pressed his forehead to mine— "I love you, too." He laughed. "Whoa. That felt so awesome to say to you. And to hear."

I threw my arms around his neck. And sighed. Pretty loudly, too. Then the lyrics from "Somethin' Stupid" drifted through my mind. "Is that the real reason you chose our song?"

He squeezed me before leaning back just enough to give me his piercing gaze. "Yeah."

His eyes wandered away from mine. "It was the day you *auditioned* for show choir."

I gaped at him.

I wasn't sure why his confession was surprising me. But that day had been a month ago. Which felt like a year ago. And everything he'd done since that day made even more sense. Though at the time he'd been saying the opposite of what he felt. For reasons I now understood.

"Something about you up there and the song you were singing...I don't know." He shrugged. "I just knew."

I recalled the way he'd been looking at me, with a half-smile, that hadn't been because of sympathy. It had been the first of his many piercing gazes. "I'll make my stupidity up to you."

He frowned. "You're not stupid, so forget about all the project stuff." He pulled me to him. "And it's not like I was acting great during all of that."

I smiled into the spot where his shoulder curved into his yummy neck. But as we sat there, holding each other, a reality that had been far from my mind crept into my thoughts.

My smile dipped and I hugged him tighter.

How was I *ever* going to let him go when he left to become a Marine?

Chapter Thirty-Three

I found Natalie and Shane exactly where Liam said I would—at Natalie's locker. And not too far from where her locker had been last year.

I slowly approached them and kept my eyes off the place that represented such a dark time. A darker, despicable version of myself.

They were talking while smiling and gazing at each other. And I grinned.

I'd hated seeing them looking at each other like that in the spring, after they became a couple. But not for the reasons I'd told her *that* day. The jealousy had really come from the fact I'd been an emotional mess and never experienced a boy gazing at me with clear love. And vice versa. Until now.

My second unforgettable Saturday night with Liam, combined with Shane's unexpected support that day, fueled me with even more strength to finish weaving my way toward them.

The hallway was filled with kids talking and laughing while at their lockers, or heading to class. The noise level seemed a bit louder than usual, too. But that may have been because I'd been gone for three days.

Natalie saw me and she froze as her dark eyes widened. Then Shane turned and he froze.

When I reached them, I said, "Hi."

Natalie didn't move, but Shane faced me.

"Hey. How are you doing? Liam told me you didn't wake up until almost five."

I nodded. "Thanks for being there on Saturday. And for being such a good friend."

He smiled. "Yeah. Of course."

I glanced at Natalie, her eyes still wide. I gave her a friendly smile. "He must've told you I fell asleep in the closet?" Of course, I had no idea if he'd told her *why* I was in the closet. But even if he had, I suspected, based on all the nice things I'd been told about her, she wouldn't say a word to anyone, either.

Her shoulders relaxed. Probably because it was clear I wasn't here to continue the war.

"Yeah," she softly replied. She hesitated, then said, "I'm so sorry about your grandpa. About everything he went through. And you." Her eyes became shiny. "I'm really close to my grandpa. My grandparents. And can't picture them..." She bit her lower lip and shared a long, for-them-only look with Shane.

"Thanks." Okay. It was time. "I should've done this a while ago." I took a shaky breath and said, "Natalie, *I'm* so sorry for what I did to you in April. And all the horrible things I said." I flinched when I remembered a couple of really nasty accusations I'd thrown in her face. "I wasn't myself back then."

A burst of laughter behind us caused me to jump as Natalie stepped toward me.

"Maddie, I don't blame you. Or hate you." Her eyes hardened. "I blame that crazy bitch, Ella Walker." She rolled her eyes. "And her blind follower, Quinn." Her face eased into warmth. "I'm just glad you got away from them. Because I *know* how evil they are."

Evil. Totally the truth.

"But thanks for the apology."

An immense load of guilt tethered to my heart and soul loosened from her warmth. To the point of near weightlessness, and only because I had one more apology.

She gave me a tentative smile. "Is it okay to tell you I think you and Liam are going to be so fucking cute together?"

I laughed. More like barked. But still, she was right. And Liam and Noah had been right about her being pretty freakin' cool. "Yes. You can definitely say that." I looked at Shane, fighting a smile, probably at his girlfriend's bluntness. And, maybe, at all of this finally happening. "I'm really sorry for *everything*." The guilt became untethered and left me in a quiet breath. I then added, "And for being so clingy. Because I never wanted to get back together."

His face flushed. "Maddie, I never should've said that about you." He and Natalie shared another, for-them-only glance. "I had a lot going on then, too. I was unloading on Liam and the word...slipped out. I swear I didn't mean it." He frowned. "But I didn't expect the asshole to repeat it, either."

Actually, Liam repeating that was the best thing that could've happened to me. But that was between me, myself, and I. So I said with a tiny smile, "I think he still feels bad about it."

"Yeah. And mostly because of that project you—"

Natalie elbowed him. And he looked like he'd swallowed a golf ball. Just like his best friend had after he'd blurted out what Shane said about me. Apparently, Natalie and Shane shared everything, too. But Liam...That *stinker*.

I closed my eyes.

Inhale to count four...exhale to count eight...

Better. Still, the next time I was alone with Liam Langley, I'd kiss him. Then kill him.

I opened my eyes. "I can't believe he told you about that. He was sworn to secrecy." And he and I clearly needed to have a long chat about his big mouth.

"He was pissed about you and Nicolas and it—"

"Slipped out?" I gave them my Barbie smile. "I need to go wring someone's neck."

Natalie giggled. "I thought your project sounded pretty cool."

Shane shot her an exaggerated scowl, which she returned.

"But speaking of Nicolas," she continued, dragging her eyes from Shane, "do you think you and Liam—"

"You're back." Kassidy appeared at my left side and we hugged. "The Brewster house missed you like crazy last week. And I love Mr. Peters, but he's obviously no Aunt Abby."

My smile stayed huge, but was genuine, as we released each other.

Her eyes wandered to Natalie and Shane, then back to me. And I saw understanding flash across her face, followed by a soft grin.

"How are you?" she asked.

"I'm okay. And thanks for all your texts last week. Especially Tuesday," I quietly added.

"Maddie, we're friends." She grasped my left hand long enough to squeeze my fingers. "What happened on Tuesday was totally understandable."

The same feelings from Saturday, as I sat in my closet while my incredible boyfriend and friends made me laugh after the "inappropriate" turn the game had taken, shrouded me.

Safety and unconditional love.

"So I was about to ask," Natalie began, watching me

closely, "if you and Liam might...want to sit with all of us today. At lunch?"

I halted.

Wow. Okay then. I'd kind of wanted him all to myself, but I needed this. Needed them.

"That's a *fantastic* idea." Kassidy laughed. "Especially since Liam's talking to Nicolas again."

I laughed with Natalie and Shane. And I sighed at the fact Liam had made amends with him. They then focused on me, their eyes wide with an unspoken "So?"

I smiled at each of them. "I'd love that." Their smiles grew, and I remembered my best friends. And the fact one of them had an enormous crush on Nicolas. "Is there room for Heather and Noah?" *Specifically an empty spot beside Nicolas.*

"We'll make room," Natalie assured me.

"Thank you," I said, directly to her. "For being so cool."

She nodded.

Peace consumed me as I headed for Liam's locker. And I couldn't stop my huge, goofy grin at the thought of seeing him. Or at the thought of our lunch plans. With *our* friends.

Chapter Thirty-Four

"I can't believe Mrs. Chaplin is making us perform our duet in front of everyone," I grumbled to Liam as we approached the choir room. "And knowing we haven't had a chance to rehearse." I stopped us outside the room. "We're going to suck."

She'd surprised me by expressing her condolences on Monday. But she'd followed up her rare act of kindness by saying Liam and I were the only ones she hadn't seen. And that we were "required" to be as prepared as possible by Wednesday. Though she knew we had rehearsals.

"It won't be that bad," Liam replied. "At least we can use our papers with the lyrics. But we won't really be able to do our dance routine," he added, and I heard the smile in his voice.

I looked up and narrowed my eyes. "Which is fine, since I'm still mad at you for telling Shane about Project Dating Spree."

He released a dramatic sigh. "Based on the way *we* said goodbye Monday and yesterday, I'm going to seriously enjoy watching your nose grow, Pinocchio." He squinted at me. "Which should be any second now."

I wrinkled my nose at him, but then Barrett heading toward us caught my attention.

He lowered his head before walking between us and into the room. Still without a word.

My eyes locked with Liam's, and he said, "Maddie, he'll get over it. And he's now acting more embarrassed than pissed."

I nodded and shrugged. But I still couldn't wrap my brain around how he could've liked me that much to be so hurt. He hardly knew me.

"C'mon, Sheila," Liam said in his Australian accent. "Let's go *wreck* this duet."

I fought a smile. "You're liking that one right now. But what happened to Italian Liam?"

He gave me his exaggerated, smoldering grin. "That one is for when we're alone."

Between his grin and lowered voice, my head became cloudy. But as he grasped my hand, the same question from Saturday while we held each other floated through my mind. And lasted through Mrs. Chaplin's typical ten-minute voice exercises. Then it was time for our duet.

I forced myself to remember the movement we'd rehearsed *once*, almost two weeks ago. I also wanted to lose myself in this special song with him. But I trembled as we stood several inches apart, angled slightly away from each other, while holding our papers with the lyrics.

Mrs. Chaplin tapped a key on her computer, and the familiar opening notes of "Somethin' Stupid" filled the choir room through her speakers.

I inhaled, tightened my diaphragm, and we started singing.

Our voices melded as we eyed each other playfully over our shoulders and inched closer together during the first verse. But

I lost the choreography for the second verse and started sweating underneath my shirt when I ended up two steps behind him. And the music.

His eyes grew with humor as he fought to keep his flirty expression. Which made me giggle through the beginning of the third verse, until we went back to playfully eyeing each other. Then he laughed through the end of that verse. We awkwardly stepped together for our dance routine during the instrumental break. But we couldn't really dance because of our papers. And that made us laugh, as well as our classmates. So when the break ended, we could barely sing. Until the end, when we sang those three amazing words five times. While gazing at each other.

The music ended, and our classmates burst into applause we didn't even deserve as we fully released our laughter.

"Well, thank you, Maddie and Liam," Mrs. Chaplin said, but with, surprisingly, a touch of amusement in her voice. "I'm sure that will be quite charming. After several *more* rehearsals?"

My humor disappeared as I glanced at Liam, who'd also pulled on a straight face.

"I want to see this again in a week," she added, without humor. "Lyrics memorized."

We nodded and stepped off the mini-stage.

"My place after school on Friday?" he mumbled.

"Yep," I answered before he went to his seat in the back of the tenor section.

And after rehearsing, we could go on our second date. Somewhere on the private side where he could be Italian Liam.

* * *

He smoothly pulled me toward him, dipped me—and my back popped.

"Ooh, that felt good," I said around our laughter.

He brought me up while clapping from his bedroom doorway mingled with our song.

I turned to find Lucas leaning against the doorframe, and wearing the Langley brother smile. But with a hint of devil.

Lucas signed to his brother, his smile deepening, and Liam rolled his eyes.

"What did he say?" And it occurred to me Liam needed to teach me some sign language.

"That you're a better dancer than me."

I gave Lucas a bright smile. "Thanks!" I replied. More like chirped.

Liam walked toward Lucas as I went to go stop the music.

"What do you want?" he asked his brother.

When I reached his desk, I used his wireless mouse to pause the song. Then my eyes landed on a short stack of United States Marine Corps materials laying to the left of his laptop.

I frowned, glanced at Liam, who was glaring at Lucas.

"Would you get the hell out of here?" His signing matched his tone.

Lucas laughed, sent me a quick wave, and left.

"If I could close my door, I would." He sauntered toward me. "But since we're now *together*, we can't be in here with the door closed anymore." He waggled eyebrows. "But only when someone's home."

I tried to smile, but my eyes wandered back to the USMC materials. I shouldn't have been surprised to see all of that sitting on his desk, but dread slithered up my spine, tightening my neck and shoulders. Especially when I thought about Saturday night. "Been doing other kinds of homework?" I pointed at the stack before dragging my eyes to him.

His face brightened with recognition. And excitement. "Oh. Yeah." He stopped when he was right beside me. "I've been meaning to tell you I enlisted last Friday."

His statement hung between us as I stared at him. And everything around me turned foggy. Frigid. To the point I shuddered.

"But this week's been crazy."

No. He didn't just say what I thought I heard.

"It's what I wanted to talk to you about last Monday. But then..." His voice, that sounded as if he were at the end of a miles long tunnel, trailed into silence.

That's right. He had wanted to talk to me about something before we walked into tragedy.

"I thought it'd be cool to enlist during Fleet Week. Because the Marines work so closely with the Navy. And no one else but my family knows. Not even Shane." He smiled, a bit shyly. "I wanted to tell you first."

The fog reached my eyes. I blinked several times, then squinted at him.

Under different circumstances, I would've drowned in love and flattery at his words. But my heart began thumping inside my chest. I sharply inhaled through my mouth. And I suddenly remembered him saying on Thursday he couldn't come over after school Friday, because he had "something to do with his family." I hadn't given it much thought, either, being so caught up in everything happening in *my* life.

I ripped my eyes from his to focus on the floor and pressed my lips together.

Inhale to count four...exhale to count eight...

"And I swear I wasn't trying to hide it from you or anything. But I couldn't tell you a week ago because...last week and weekend wasn't about me. You're not pissed, are you?"

I struggled to keep deep breathing through my nose. To

stop his bedroom walls from closing in and crumbling around me.

"Maddie, you haven't said a word. What's wrong?"

I released a loud exhale and raised my head. He was giving me his piercing gaze, but I said, "You told me you weren't enlisting until *after* we graduated. Which is in May."

He raised his eyebrows. "I never said that."

My mind frantically rewound to those conversations. Then I mentally groaned since he was right. All he'd ever said was that he was enlisting. Still, dealing with this reality wasn't supposed to be happening in early *October*. "Fine," I grumbled. "So what does all this mean?"

He paused before saying, "Well, I have a few steps to go through, between now and graduation, that include some tests. But as long as I pass those and high school" —he laughed — "I'll get my shipping orders. For boot camp?"

Tests...shipping orders...boot camp...and did he really just laugh?

"Where and how long is boot camp?"

"In San Diego. For thirteen weeks," he quietly added.

From the sounds of it, almost as soon as we graduated, he'd leave. For three months and one week. "Then what?"

"Graduation. Ten-day leave. Three weeks of special training, and I...get my assignment."

Which meant we really only had this school year.

My heart and soul gasped as that realization took over my brain. And air supply.

Inhale to count four...exhale to count eight...

He pulled me into his arms. "I know how all this sounds, but it won't be—"

"I don't want you to do this," I blurted into his shoulder.

He froze, but I couldn't feel bad. Because all I'd said was the truth.

He slowly released me, turned, and headed for his door,

which he closed. He then faced me. "Okay. I surprised you. And you've always been a little sensitive about this."

"Only because I don't want *you* to join the Marines." Wow. More honesty. And based on his deep frown, he didn't appreciate it, but I couldn't stop now. "Liam, I love you, and I'm not just saying that as your girlfriend." I stepped toward him. "I'm saying that as your *friend*. I can't stand the thought of something happening—" No. I couldn't even go there. Or I'd break apart. "You can't do this." I folded and rubbed my arms. "You can't leave me, too."

Now my words hung between us as he narrowed his eyes.

Okay. I hadn't meant for clingy, abandoned Maddie to emerge. But everything I'd said before my last...needy statement...had come from a place of love.

My heart continued its painful thumping as he slipped his hands into his pockets.

"Maddie, I'm not leaving you, my family, and friends, because I'm a selfish asshole who has to go find himself. Or some shit like that."

I flinched, though I deserved that. But, darn it, I didn't want him to leave *us* so soon after graduation. What was wrong with feeling that way?

"And I love and appreciate your concern. But you're really getting ahead of yourself."

I lifted my chin and shrugged. "Am I? You don't know where in the world they'll send you when you're done with boot camp and the special training."

He sighed. "You're right. But you know becoming a Marine is who I am."

I walked toward him and stopped when we were toe-to-toe. "A part of me understands why you want to do this." I tried on a smile that I hoped didn't reflect my desperation. "But I'm not the only one in this room who can act, sing and dance. You're also funny. And adorable. Everyone loves you. I can't be the one person in your life who thinks this is crazy."

Hurt engulfed his eyes and face. He stepped away from me.

I closed my eyes.

Shoot, shoot, *shoot.*

"I'm so sorry." I opened my eyes. To find him almost glaring at me. Which I deserved. Especially since I'd not only insulted him, but also his parents. "I didn't mean it that way."

"Actually, it sounds like you're being pretty honest right now." He crossed his arms. "Anything else you'd like to tell me while we're on this subject?"

My shoulders fell. "You don't have to get nasty. I said I was sorry."

"And I expected you to be...I don't know...proud of me. Because you're my girlfriend and friend." He leaned forward. "Be proud of me like my family. And other friends. Who all know I want to be a Marine."

I stepped away from him.

Wow. I guess my feelings made me the worst girlfriend ever. But how could he expect me to bounce with joy at the possibility of never seeing him again once they sent him away?

"I *knew* this wasn't a good idea." He ran his hands through his hair. "And it's why I never wanted a girlfriend."

I gaped at him as his muttered words filled my already full head. "Liam, I didn't mean to call you crazy. Because I am proud of you. But that doesn't mean I have to like any of this."

"Okay. Fair enough. But you also want me to change my mind, and I won't." He looked at the floor. "So maybe we should...rethink this. Us."

Panic flared within me, and I straightened. "No. You did *not* just say that." And I shook my head to get rid of his words. Because he couldn't have meant what he said.

"It's going to be hard enough to leave next summer," he

mumbled. "Three months is a long time. And it's not like we'll be able to text or talk on the phone while I'm at boot camp." He lifted his shoulders. "And I *don't* know where they'll send me." He shoved his hands back into his pockets. "It's probably better this way. For both of us."

My head and vision blurred. His room again turned frigid, and I hugged my arms to me.

He couldn't really be doing this. Not after everything that had happened between us. And everything it took for us to get where we *were* minutes ago.

I looked at the spot in front of his bed where we'd been rehearsing our song.

"This is supposed to be *o-pen*," Liam's mom loudly said, followed by two hard knocks.

He cleared his throat and ripped the door open. And there she stood, her left eyebrow arched in irritation.

Hysterical laughter bubbled inside me at her incredibly wrong assumption, but I swallowed it. And the sickness that had settled inside my throat.

"Sorry," he muttered. "We were talking."

And you were demolishing my heart.

My lower lip quivered as I turned and picked up my backpack I'd dropped beside his desk. "I'm also leaving," I managed to say while swinging my bag onto my shoulder.

I avoided looking at him, side-stepped his mom, and darted down the hallway and out of the condo. Where I paused outside the closed door. Then shattered for the third time in not even two weeks.

Chapter Thirty-Five

My phone buzzed and dinged over my ambient music.

I swiped my phone off the floor and—my body sagged.

Heather had texted, *Hey. Can you pry yourself away from Liam long enough to text me back?* followed by the emoji sticking out its tongue.

I stopped the music, threw my phone on my bed, and hugged my knees to my chest.

All she wanted was to know if coming over at six to help me with my fancy updo for the stupid *dance* tomorrow night would be early enough.

My tears returned with a vengeance as my mind, for the millionth time, sifted through all things Liam I'd been trying to suppress by meditating for the first time in forever.

His illegal smile. Puppy-dog eyes. Soothing voice. Accents. His *Italian* accent. His exaggerated, smoldering grin. His piercing gazes. Addictive kisses. Him telling me he loved me.

His stony expression as he broke up with me.

I wiped my cheeks.

Okay. I hadn't handled his news well. At all. And my big mouth had let a terrible, insulting word slip out. But he'd caught *me* off guard. I guess I could understand his excitement in following his path to becoming a Marine. But why enlist now? The Marine Corps wasn't going anywhere. He could've waited. Enlisted during the summer. To give us a chance to really be together before he left. And it was my fault I'd assumed he'd wait until after graduation.

But even if he had waited, having the conversation in June wouldn't be any easier.

You also want me to change my mind, and I won't.

Actually, that had never crossed my mind until today. During my embarrassing moment of desperation. And remaining clinginess. But shock had taken over my brain and mouth. Though my heart and soul didn't want him to leave to become a Marine, it was totally selfish thinking. Especially since it sounded like he'd made his decision long before we knew each other. He'd called me on my selfishness, too. Which made me the big, dumb jerk.

My phone buzzed and dinged again, and I moaned. Because I knew it wasn't him.

I glanced at my bed. My phone had landed near Buddy's big feet. And I sniffed my tears away as I stood. I then headed out of my room.

Thank God Mom was still at work, getting caught up, so I could be alone for this.

When I reached his still closed bedroom door, I paused. I hadn't been in his room since the Sunday night before—I inhaled through my nose and slowly opened the door.

At her insistence, Ruth had straightened up his room before leaving us for good a week ago. She'd wanted to come over on Saturday, but she'd already had plans with her daughter's family, visiting from out of state for Fleet Week.

Fleet Week. One reason Liam had decided to enlist early.

I took another deep breath and stepped into my grandpa's room.

The warm, evening breeze coming through the partially open window made the curtains billow. She'd also made his bed. And straightened and wiped down the table he always ate at.

Also known as the last place I'd seen him.

I tore my hazy eyes from there and they landed on his nightstand, now holding only two things; the lamp and *To Kill a Mockingbird*. She'd positioned the book near the edge and angled it toward his bed. As if in a kind of tribute?

A couple tears fell from my eyes. I forced myself to walk toward the reading chair.

I stared at it as I remembered all the time I'd spent there since he came to live with us. I'd read him so many books the last several months, I'd lost track of the number after five.

I sat, pulled my legs up to my chest, and gently rubbed the hearts on my necklace.

Mom had picked up the urn with his ashes, but had placed him on the living room window seat, surrounded by the flowers we'd received. But at this moment I wanted him to be right here, once more, before we scattered his ashes near the Farallon Islands. To be with my grandma. At the same time, it didn't feel right to move him from such a cozy, warm spot. So I imagined he was with me and listening. Because this had been *my* spot with him since March.

"I...fell for that boy. Who's going to become a Marine. And I" —my voice wavered— "don't want to let him go." I hesitated, then added, "I don't *want* him to go. Because of that he...broke up with me." I swiped my wet cheeks with my free hand. "He thinks it would be best for us." I continued to gently rub the hearts and added, "But that can't be the end of our story."

* * *

Heather picked up after a few rings and said, "What the hell happened to you yesterday? Was your mouth too busy with Liam's all night?"

I cracked a smile, despite her assumption being so cold it belonged in Antarctica. "No. And sorry about that." But because of my newest project I'd concocted after talking to my grandpa, I had to tell her the truth. "Coming over at six is perfect. I have to tell you something, though." Then I unloaded everything that happened yesterday afternoon with Liam. When I finished, I added, "You can't tell *anyone* he enlisted a week ago. I mean it, Heather."

"Maddie, I promise I won't say a word. That's huge news, and it's not mine to share. But I'm glad you told me. And I'm sorry he..." Her voice trailed into a sigh. "But I'll be honest. I was wondering if his decision might be kind've...hard on both of you."

I curled into my pillows against my headboard. "Yeah. But I love him. And I have to be supportive." The not-so brilliant epiphany I'd had last night. Even though letting him go would surely kill me. But his path wasn't about me. Or us. "So I came up with a new project." *Epiphany two.* "It's why I still need you to help me with my hair."

After I told her my plan, which made her giggle, we hung up, and I stared at my phone.

Now I had to make sure Liam showed up at the dance.

Inhale to count four...exhale to count eight...

I went back into my phone and chose his name. But of course I got his voicemail.

"Hi," I breathlessly said, "it's me." I cringed. "I'm really sorry about yesterday and would love a do-over. So I came up with a new project. Which means Elizabeth will be at the dance tonight at eight. Her Mr. Darcy better be there, too, or I'll never speak to you again. And that'll make rehearsing and performing our duet pretty difficult," I swiftly added.

I hung up and squeezed my eyes shut.

This had *to work*.

Chapter Thirty-Six

I glared at my reflection in the bathroom mirror.

"Maddie, I don't do this for a living," Heather grumbled as she curled a thin lock of my hair, copying the girl in the YouTube video now paused on my laptop, sitting on the counter.

"It's not you. You're doing a great job." I picked at my thumbnail. "I'm still upset Mom and I couldn't find the biggest part of my project." That I'd planned on wearing over my dress. But only long enough to get the desired reaction from Liam.

Who hadn't called or even texted me back. The main reason for my edginess.

"Tell me again he'll be there."

She released my hair and a perfect tendril hung on the right side of my face. "He'll be there. And all you told him was to be at the dance or else. You didn't say to call or text you back. He could also be busy—"

"Doing what? What could be more important than us?"

"*I don't know.*" She moved to the left side of my head.

I reached up to gently rub my hearts. "Sorry. I'm not

trying to be neurotic. I just really want to see him. Make things right."

He'd better be there tonight, too. Or I'd march to his building and plant myself on the front stoop until he showed his cute face. That I would try *not* to punch if it came to that.

"And you will. Because he'll be at the dance tonight."

My edginess subsided as she patiently curled my hair. "Thanks for doing this. And for being such an awesome friend."

Our eyes met in the mirror, and she smiled. But there was sadness behind it.

I frowned. "I know you don't want to admit you're upset Nicolas already moved on."

To the captain of the girl's lacrosse team.

She released my hair and another perfect tendril hung on the left side of my face. "No. You and Noah were right. I'd love to have his yumminess all to myself." She stared at the floor. "But all Nicolas does is barely give me quick smiles and nods, even though he went to *my* birthday party. I don't exist," she muttered.

I mentally snarled at him, and turned in my chair to pull her down and into my arms. "Heather, you're stunning. Nicolas isn't good enough for *you*." And I'd meant every word of that last sentence I'd practically snarled.

She huffed and pulled away. "Thanks. But not like you. Or his date tonight." She moaned. "Vicci Cervantes looks more like she belongs on the cover of *Seventeen* than a jock. I'm sure she'll look incredible tonight as his Morticia Addams." She pointed at herself. "And I might as well be an overgrown, ten-year-old girl dressed like this."

I smiled at her and her bright red, Thing 1 T-shirt and jeans. She'd also spray dyed her long, dark hair turquoise pulled into a tight ponytail on top of her head. And Noah, being awesome friend number two, would be the other half of the "epic couple" as Thing 2.

"Heather, you and Noah are going to look so freakin' fantastic." I laughed. "Seriously. It was such a good idea. For going as friends?"

She shrugged. "Yeah. I guess. But it would be nice to feel like a girl for a night." She lifted her chin. "A woman. Like you'll look tonight. And Vicci. And probably every other girl going to this dance with a boyfriend."

My smile faded. "This is only the first dance of the year. And you *will* have a real date—no offense to Noah—by Snowflake Formal." I'd just have to sharpen my matchmaking skills.

She barely nodded. "You're right." She turned off the curling iron and set it on the counter. "But enough about me, Miss Elizabeth. How'd I do?"

I tore my eyes from her to focus on my reflection. And I smiled, since my hair looked kinda similar to Keira Knightley's updo in the ball scene of that movie version of *Pride and Prejudice*. "It's perfect. I love you."

Heather clapped quietly. "So, time for the dress?"

I stood. "Definitely that time."

Several minutes later Mom was zipping me into my tight, silver, shimmery dress with spaghetti straps and modest V-neckline. And Heather was fluffing out the full skirt that would swish around me while dancing; the main reason I'd fallen in love with the dress. It reminded me of the elegant gowns the actresses wore during big dance numbers in some of those old musicals.

When they were done, all of us stared at me in my full-length mirror.

Mom's eyes glistened, and I said, "It's just the fall dance."

She lifted her shoulders. "I know, I know. But it is your last fall dance." She laughed. "I'm really happy you talked me into buying you this dress since you look exquisite. I also love the necklace Liam bought you." She shook her head. "I'm starting to think he might be perfect."

Not perfect when I thought of *his* stubborn side. But he was pretty close to the word.

I grinned as my cheeks became a tad on the rosy side. "Thanks."

"And if your grandparents were here, they'd agree with me." Her smile dipped. "As a matter a fact, your grandpa probably would've strongly questioned me letting you leave this condo looking so beautiful."

Now my eyes glistened. Because I could hear my grandpa's voice and that conversation in my head. But I blinked until my vision cleared. I could not ruin my makeup. Any of this.

"*You're* stunning," Heather murmured. "But you look more like Cinderella going to her ball than a modern-day Elizabeth Bennet going to a dance." Her green eyes filled with humor. "You might knock Mr. Darcy sideways, than out cold."

If he showed up.

"So I'm still not clear as to why Liam isn't picking you up?" Mom asked. "He's been quite the young gentleman the last couple weeks."

Very true. But I'd hatched a convincing lie for Mom. And anyone else who happened to ask why he and I hadn't come to the dance together. If they even noticed. Hopefully my message from this morning stopped him from telling anyone about yesterday. Namely his best friend.

Heather and I glanced at each other, and I said, "Well, with Heather coming over to help me get ready, and her date being Noah, we just decided all of us should meet up at the gym."

Mom frowned.

"It's fine. Really." I gave myself a final once over. "I think I'm ready."

And I once again begged the universe he'd be there. Waiting by the entrance for me?

Oh, please, please, please.

* * *

I tapped my high-heeled foot. "What time is it?"

Heather took a breath as she, for the third time, pulled her phone from her back jeans pocket. She, Noah, and I were right inside the gym's main entrance and exit. The high-energy dance music coming from behind the closed doors to the actual gym filled the enormous space.

And I hadn't wanted to leave my phone at home. But it's not like I had pockets, and a crossbody phone case did *not* go with this dress.

"It's ten after eight, and you need to relax."

Not possible. Because Liam Langley, future Marine, was never late.

"I still don't get why you two didn't come here together," Noah said, standing beside Heather. "There's something you and Thing 1 aren't telling me. And it's Not. Cool."

He looked pretty cute in his bright red, Thing 2 T-shirt and jeans. He'd also fixed his now turquoise hair so it stood straight up.

"Fine," I mumbled. But I wouldn't tell him everything like I had with Heather. "Liam and I had a bit of a...misunderstanding after school yesterday. Not a big deal." But my hope was beginning to deteriorate as he continued to not be here—*no.*

He loved me, and I'd apologized. Three times. And I'd never known him to hold grudges. Well, except with Nicolas. But those two, based on how much Liam had been making

Nicolas laugh this whole week during lunch, really were back to a-okay.

"So you two had a big fight," Noah stated.

I glared at him.

Heather slapped his chest with the back of her hand. "She said *misunderstanding*."

He groaned. "And that's code for fighting." He focused on me. "Do you want me to text him? I'll keep it cool. We were all supposed to hang out at this thing tonight."

I tried to smile at him. "I appreciate that, but no. I told him to be here or else. And he'll see right through your message."

"But maybe something happened," Noah continued. "And he doesn't know you don't have your phone." He pulled his phone from his pocket. "Let me text him."

He did have a point. But then I remembered my vow if, for some reason, my Mr. Darcy didn't show up. And maybe something had happened. But still. He was just as stubborn as me.

"No." I stepped back. "He and I are not over. I'm going to his place."

"Maddie," Heather protested, "you're dressed for an actual ball. Not a nighttime march to Liam's building."

"I don't care." I turned from them. "I'm going to get my Mr. Darcy."

I jerked open the closest door and almost collided with a couple dressed as Raggedy Ann and Andy. "Sorry," I muttered, going around them.

I stepped into the warm, night air, and marched toward the sidewalk. At that moment, Liam—Mr. Darcy—quickly rounded the corner while fighting with his tie.

And when our eyes locked we stopped.

Chapter Thirty-Seven

His eyes became round, and his mouth inched open as he slowly looked me down and up.

My body tingled and became hot.

"*Holy* Elizabeth Bennet. You look—"

"You're over *ten minutes* late. You're never late. And it's why I was coming to get you."

He gave his head a quick shake before he walked toward me. "I know. I'm sorry. But it's not my fault." He stopped until he was close enough to hug. And kiss a million times.

I breathed in his familiar cologne that also made him good enough to eat.

He cringed. "Well, it's not all my fault." He reached up to again roughly adjust his black tie. "This dumbass thing is already driving me crazy. And I was in such a hurry, I couldn't get it right. So my dad had to help me." His face turned hot pink, reminding me of when he'd given me my necklace. "I guess that makes me a dumbass."

I batted his hands away and gently straightened his tie into perfect. That's when I noticed his costume. A sharp, black, three-piece suit with matching dress shoes. He'd also combed his thick hair straight back and into "uptight." And the style made his puppy-dog eyes stand out.

Hel-lo Mr. Darcy.

"Thanks," he said, while giving me his piercing gaze. "You really look—" He laughed again. "I can't think of the right word. You made my brain short circuit."

I giggled, and looked him up and down. "*You* look perfect. That suit looks brand new."

His smile faded. "It is new. Because my mom insisted a modern-day Mr. Darcy wouldn't be *caught dead* in anything but this." He gestured at himself. "So she made me go shopping with her today." He rolled his eyes. "And of course Lucas and Willow *had* to go, too."

I smiled. "So they spent the day torturing you."

"Pretty much." His eyes wandered back to mine. "But I deserved it after yesterday." He sighed. "I mean, I was confused and hurt. But I shouldn't have said what I did and... let you leave like that. Especially after everything you've been through. It was a dick move," he quietly added.

"No. I did hurt you." I paused, then said, "And I didn't mean to make you sound *anything* like my brother." *Or Russell.* He nodded as I leaned forward. "Because what you're doing is heroic. Not crazy. Or selfish." I straightened. "I guess you're not the only one with a big mouth."

The corner of his mouth lifted in a smile.

"And though I don't understand your rush, I am proud of you, Liam."

He grasped my hands. "I love hearing that from you. And I've been waiting to enlist since I was a kid and didn't want to wait anymore. But I get that I caught you off guard."

I gave him a bright smile since this was the perfect moment to say, "I promise I'm over my surprise. And now need to tell you about my newest project."

He grinned. "Right. You mentioned that in your message.

I wasn't avoiding you this morning, either. I actually planned on calling *you* after I got back from my long run with Lucas and Shane. And the only reason I didn't call you back," he quickly continued, "is because I wanted to surprise you." He leaned back. "But I guess I should've since it seems you really thought I wouldn't show up. Because you said you were coming to get me?"

I shrugged, squeezed his hands, and his grin grew.

"Oh, and I told Shane about enlisting. And he and Lucas decided they're going to be my drill sergeants until...Well, you know."

"Yes," I strongly said. "I think that's awesome of them. And while they're doing that—do you have your phone? I obviously had to leave mine at home."

His grin became smoldering as he reached into his inside jacket pocket to retrieve his phone. Like a modern-day Mr. Darcy would, and whoa was *that* hot. The grin helped, too.

"About your dress." He handed me his phone. "Why can't you wear it to prom, too?" He waggled his eyebrows. "Because it'll give me something to look forward to."

The heat from his slow once over returned. "I'll think about it. What's your password?"

He rattled off the four-digit number, and I went onto the Internet.

"What are you doing?"

"*You'll see,*" I sang as I brought up a picture of what would soon be the newest edition to my wardrobe. And I bounced in place as I showed him the white T-shirt with a huge red heart on the front. Which contained three special words.

His eyes widened as he stared at the image. "A Marine's girlfriend." He lifted his eyes from his phone and unleashed his illegal smile.

"Mom and I spent the day trying to find this shirt, so I could wear it for you tonight. Well, not all night. But we ended up having to order it from this site. It should be here next week." I handed over his phone. "And the T-shirt inspired *Project* A Marine's Girlfriend."

He laughed as he slipped his phone back into his jacket pocket.

A thought occurred to me, so I asked, "But can I even wear it when it gets here?"

He pulled me into his arms. "Technically, no. Not until I graduate. But I love you for it. And the shirt will definitely look hot on you." He nuzzled my neck, which made my insides zing. "So I won't stop you from modeling it for me so I can take a picture."

I giggled. "I love you, too. And the main part of my project is I promise I'll be nothing but supportive and proud and excited about you becoming a Marine." We hugged. "But your family and our friends will have to pry me off of you the day you leave for boot camp."

He leaned away from me, his expression now serious. "The feeling is totally mutual."

We held our piercing gaze for a few seconds. Then I said, "We need to seal this with a—"

He released me, cupped my face, and our mouths melded. *Yummy*.

We broke apart, and he cleared his throat.

"*Ciao, Bella*," he practically purred.

I released a dramatic sigh. "Finally."

Our arms went back around each other.

"I told you that one's for when we're alone."

"And how much longer will that be?"

"Until you say the word."

I nuzzled *his* neck. "We might be out here all night."

"Yeah," he said on a breath. "I'm right there with you."

Author's Note

I hope you enjoyed Book Three in the Pacifica Academy Drama Series that will continue with Heather's story, the Christmas novella *Silver Bells for Me and (Saint) Nicolas*. Each book can stand alone, but it's recommended they're read in series order for maximum enjoyment.

And if you have a moment, please feel free to leave a rating and brief review at wherever you purchased the book. Authors always appreciate and need honest, reader reviews.

Christine Miles is a full-time writer living in Albuquerque, New Mexico.

An avid reader and writer since elementary school, her passion for literature inspired her to pursue a BA in English and an MA in Creative Writing. She writes YA and Adult Contemporary Romances with sassy, independent heroines and swoony heroes who love them for their strength.

When not writing romances, she loves traveling, binge-watching shows on streaming apps, reading mysteries and thrillers, listening to music, and spending quality time with her family, friends, and dog.

You can find her on Facebook and Instagram. Sign up for her newsletter to get ARC's and updates at www.christine-milesauthor.com.

www.ingramcontent.com/pod-product-compliance
Lightning Source LLC
Chambersburg PA
CBHW061613190726
48288CB00007B/2303